# Winter's End

## Seasons of Faith

## Book Two

# Rebekah Lyn

# Other books by Rebekah Lyn

## Seasons of Faith

*Summer Storms*

*Winter's End*

*Spring Dawn*

*Christmas Vows*

## Coastal Chronicles

*Julianne*

## Jessie Cole Trilogy

*Undaunted (*previously sold a*s Jessie)*

*Destiny's Call*

# CHAPTER ONE

Bodies jostled and bumped to the music of *Tangled Web* all around Amanda, making her cringe with disgust. Pulling her arms in closer to her body, she pushed her way to the back of the crowded club. The sound of the band dimmed slightly as she entered the restroom. She moved toward the sink, her feet sticking to the dark concrete floor. In the mirror, she examined her porcelain skin and frowned at the smudged mascara around her eyes. She pulled a tissue from her purse and blotted her face, disgusted that she was perspiring. Amanda Barnes didn't perspire.

The door opened and three women came tripping into the restroom, laughing raucously.

As she disappeared into a stall, a woman wearing a tiny mini skirt exclaimed, "This band is amazing!"

"I know, hurry up. I don't want to miss their next song." A tall woman in skinny jeans that accentuated her long legs peered over Amanda's head into the mirror and pulled her hair into a messy ponytail. The third woman, in a low cut sweater that barely contained her ample bosoms, chugged the remainder of her beer and dropped the plastic cup on the floor.

"The drummer is hot," gushed the mini skirted woman as she emerged from the stall and washed her hands.

"He is way out of your league, Alex," retorted the tall woman.

"And you think you're more his type?" Alex sneered. "I doubt he likes Amazon women."

"I don't know, a lot of guys like the long legs." The tall woman gave a sly smile as she pointedly glanced at the petite girl.

"Come on, you two, they are starting again."

The women filed out of the restroom, leaving Amanda alone once again. She sighed and took a last look in the mirror before returning to the boisterous crowd. Dancing near the stage, she found her coworkers,

Tiffani, an anorexic looking blonde with bony shoulders peeking out of her cap sleeved t-shirt, and Wendy, whose thick brown hair whipped around her long face as she banged her head in time with the music.

"I can't believe I let you guys talk me into this," Amanda shouted over the music.

"Oh come on, this is Michelle's big break, and they really are great," Wendy replied. "Besides, she comes to all of our events. Least we can do is show her some support."

Amanda shrugged. "I'm going home. I'll see you guys tomorrow."

"Don't go." Tiffani grabbed for Amanda's arm. "We're going for drinks when the band finishes."

"No, I'm not in the mood." Amanda removed Tiffani's hand and stepped back.

"You want us to walk you to your car?" Wendy asked.

Amanda shook her head, knowing Wendy was afraid of even the thought of a dark parking garage. Turning on her heel, she threaded her way to the door. A blast of cold air hit her face as she stepped out onto the sidewalk. Shrugging on her short pea coat, she fastened the four buttons and flipped up the collar against the brisk wind.

"Oh you have to be kidding me," she mumbled. "I must've left my keys at the office."

Amanda turned right up Orange Avenue, her strides long and hurried as she made her way back to the block of towering office buildings. In five minutes, she stood before a wall of glass windows and doors, fumbling through her purse for her ID card. She swiped the card, the lock disengaging immediately.

She crossed the empty lobby, her high heels echoing on the marble floor. When she reached the bank of elevators, one stood open as if expecting her. In less than a minute, she exited onto the sixth floor, lit only by a few emergency lights. Not bothering to search for a light switch, she weaved through a maze of cubicles until she reached her desk.

"Thank heavens," Amanda whispered at the sight of her keys lying next to the computer.

She looped a finger through the keychain, then froze at the sound of a loud thud down the hall. Peering around the edge of her cubicle, she saw a shadow moving across the hallway toward another row of cubicles. When she heard the squeak of a wheel, she relaxed her tensed muscles, laughing at herself for being afraid of the janitor. Leaving her desk, she walked back towards the elevator. Just before pressing the elevator button, she decided to stop in the restroom. It was a thirty-minute drive to her apartment in Altamonte Springs and suddenly her bladder felt fuller than a ten-year-old's water balloon.

Motion-activated lights flicked on when she entered. Tottering past the sinks, barely able to walk without crossing her legs now, she entered the first stall only to find there was no toilet paper. Every ounce of her being was crying out for relief as she turned to the next stall.

The bathroom door opened and a man wearing a black hooded sweatshirt, dark jeans, and sneakers barreled towards her.

Amanda stepped aside seconds before the man reached her, causing him to crash into the closed stall door. Unfazed, the man grabbed her arm as she tried to run past him. He twisted her arm above her head and pinned her body against the wall. Without thinking, Amanda swung her free arm, fingers clawing at air, trying to scratch his face.

She connected, leaving three long gashes down his right cheek. He roared with anger and slapped her, making her ears ring. She pushed with a strength she didn't know she had and the man temporarily lost his balance.

Amanda wrenched her arm free and made for the door. She was almost to the door when she felt her hair being pulled, her head arching backward. An arm wrapped around her waist, pulling her closer, then with one hand, he slammed her face against the counter. There was a loud crack and Amanda felt her nose break. Blood flowed down her face, into her mouth.

While she was still stunned, the man used one of his feet to sweep her legs out from under her and she fell to the floor. He crouched over her and she felt him clawing at the buttons of her jacket as she struggled to orient herself. With a fierce yank, he ripped the jacket open, buttons flying across the small room. She looked in his eyes and saw craven lust. She tried to scream, but he pulled a rag from his pocket and shoved it into her mouth as soon as she opened it.

The man now straddled her, unbuttoning his jeans. Amanda brought her knee up and hit him in the groin, causing him to double over in pain. She tried to free herself, but he had sunk onto her legs and weighed more than she had anticipated. He howled with rage and reached for her hair again. He pulled her face up close to his and she could smell alcohol on his breath.

"You should have just let me buy you a drink," he growled, then smashed the back of her head against the cold tile floor. He raised her head again and smashed it over and over, until her world went dark.

# CHAPTER TWO

The clock read two fifteen when Michelle finally sank onto her bed and pulled off her boots. After *Tangled Web's* successful debut at The Social, she was still too excited to sleep, so she slipped into a pair of sweatpants and a baggy shirt and turned on the TV. She flipped past several infomercials before wandering into the kitchen and thumbing through a cookbook that was lying open on the counter.

Her interest was piqued when she came across a recipe for chai mousse. She skimmed the list of ingredients and checked her pantry, surprised to find she had everything called for, including half a pint of heavy whipping cream. She neatly organized several bowls on the counter and started measuring out ingredients.

She watched the beaters of the blender spin, whipping the cream into stiff peaks, and felt some of the anger that had shadowed the evening dissipate. If Amanda wasn't going to stay for the whole show, why did she bother coming at all?

Michelle gently folded the whipped cream into a mixture of chai concentrate and vanilla pudding mix, then scooped the fluffy mouse into colorful ramekins. With the ramekins lined up in the refrigerator to chill, Michelle turned back to the cookbook where she found one of her favorite recipes for cranberry scones. She pre-heated the oven to 375 degrees and mixed up a double batch.

By four-thirty, she had two-dozen scones packed up in a cake carrier, and decided to go to work early. Casual Friday had never felt so good as she stepped out of the shower into a pair of soft blue jeans and a cashmere argyle sweater.

The parking garage was empty when Michelle pulled in. She felt a shiver of fear tickling her neck as she stepped out of the car, her footsteps echoing on the concrete. She emerged from the garage onto Orange Avenue and crossed the empty street. Her eyes darted back and forth, searching for any threats awaiting her along the short block to the towering office building. When she reached the glass doors, she swiped her ID card. A metallic click sounded as the lock disengaged and she tugged on the handle.

While her computer powered up she went to the break room to make a pot of coffee and arrange the scones for when her coworkers arrived. As usual, the room was littered with debris from yesterday's lunch and dishes were stacked in the sink. Ignoring the dishes, she wiped down the table and gathered the empty chip bags while she waited for the coffee to brew. The rich aroma coming from the pot reminded her she hadn't eaten since before the concert and her stomach began to rumble. She took a scone and her coffee back to her desk where she found the computer still booting up.

"One of the biggest investment firms in the country and our computers are five years out of date," she muttered, shaking her head. Her eyes, strained from the smoke in the club, started watering, and she glanced in the mirror hanging above the computer. Standing up, she decided to go the restroom and flush them out.

She pushed the door open and waited expectantly for the automatic lights to come on, but she was only greeted by darkness. Thinking she hadn't activated the sensors, she stepped into the room and waited another five seconds, but still no light. In exasperation, she reached for the trashcan sitting next to the door and tried to prop the door open to allow light to come in from the hall, but the door fell closed, pushing the plastic can aside.

Michelle stood in the dark, puzzled. Tilting her head to one side, she took a couple of short breaths and noticed a smell she couldn't quite identify. She pulled the door open again, holding it with one foot as she peered into the alcove where the sinks were, less than three feet away. She recoiled when she saw a body lying in a dark pool on the once black and white tiles. She looked away quickly, her stomach roiling, but she couldn't keep from taking a second look. That's when she recognized the badly beaten face of Amanda. Michelle stumbled back, grabbed for the wastebasket, and vomited.

Back in the hall, she leaned against the wall and slid down to the floor, arms wrapped protectively around the garbage can, ready to hurl again at any second. She sat for several minutes until her breathing slowed and her stomach seemed to settle down. She desperately wanted to wash her face and blow her nose, but didn't dare enter the bathroom again. She pushed herself up onto unsteady feet and hugged the wall back to the break room where she pulled half a dozen sheets off the roll of paper towels by the small sink. She blew her nose and splashed her face with cold water.

Slowly her legs stopped shaking and Michelle was able to return to her desk where she picked up the phone to dial 9-1-1. As she began to dial, flashes of every police drama she had ever watched on TV flashed into her mind. The police always suspected the person who found the body, and she hadn't had the best relationship with Amanda. What if the police thought she had done it?

The dial tone of the phone changed to the fast busy of being open too long. She returned the receiver to its cradle and stared at it. You have to make the call, she told herself. Won't it look worse if you just leave her lying there until someone else comes in? That might be hours. She picked up the phone again and dialed.

"9-1-1 what's your emergency?" a deep male voice answered almost immediately.

"Hi, um, there's a body in the bathroom," Michelle stammered.

"What is your name?" the man asked. Michelle marveled at how calm he sounded.

"Michelle, Michelle Burton. I went to the restroom and she was just lying there."

"All right Michelle. The police are on the way. I have your address, but can you tell me where exactly you are?"

Michelle hesitated. "I'm at my desk, on the sixth floor. My office number is 6130."

"Okay, can you stay right there until the police arrive?"

"Yes." Michelle could hear sirens already.

"I'm going to stay on the line with you until the police arrive. Is anyone else there with you?"

"No, I couldn't sleep so I came in early. Most people won't be here until after eight."

"Do you know who the victim is?"

"Yes, she's one of my coworkers. Her name is Amanda Barnes." Michelle felt a sudden pressure in her temples and she rubbed at them with her free hand. She heard the dispatcher speaking but couldn't understand his words.

Michelle felt a hand on her shoulder and turned, fear coursing through her. A short, round woman in a police uniform looked down at her with kind eyes. Michelle dropped the phone and fell into the officer's arms.

"Michelle, I'm Officer Bauer. Can you tell me what happened?" Her honey-like voice seemed to pour over Michelle. Her sobs slowed and she looked up at the officer.

"I went into the restroom, but the lights didn't come on. I tried to...and then the door wouldn't...and there she was..." Michelle couldn't complete a thought.

"Can you show me where she is?" Officer Bauer asked.

Michelle nodded and led her down the hall. She saw several other officers already at the bathroom, their flashlight beams bouncing from the open door.

"Detective, this is Michelle Burton; she's the one who called it in." Officer Bauer gave Michelle a sympathetic smile and stepped over to speak to one of the officers in the doorway.

"Michelle, I'm Detective Mike Emerson. Can you tell me what happened?" The detective was a tall man with nearly completely gray hair and brown eyes that reminded Michelle of a Bassett Hound.

Michelle took a deep breath and tried to tell him everything she had done that morning. It took nearly ten minutes for her to get the whole story out in between new bursts of tears. Detective Emerson took notes and asked questions to clarify some of the points.

"The scones I made are in the break room over there," Michelle said, pointing to an opening several yards down the hall. "Would you like some for your team?" Shock was setting in and Michelle's eyes seemed to glaze over.

"Not right now, Ms. Burton. Can you tell me if you touched anything? Moved the body at all?" Emerson asked.

Michelle shook her head. "I only touched the door, oh and the garbage can. I don't know where that is now. I had to throw up in it."

The medical examiner, a robust woman with auburn hair who exuded a surprising amount of energy for the early hour, arrived alongside a gurney wheeled by a young man and a woman whose faces seemed frozen in perpetual scowls. The bathroom lights were still off; only the beams of five or six flashlights illuminated the scene for the medical examiner.

"This won't do. We need more light in here," she said.

"We're working on it, Dr. Robinson. Seems the perp took out or broke all of the light bulbs. Some work lights should be here in five minutes. I can fill you in on the details we have so far while we wait," said Detective Emerson.

"All right Mike, what have we got?" Robinson asked, giving Michelle a cursory glance before turning her full attention to Emerson.

Emerson turned to introduce the medical examiner to Michelle, but she was walking toward the break room. He shrugged and gave Robinson the run down of all he knew. As he was finishing up, two officers appeared at the end of the hall with a pair of halogen work lights and extension cords. In another two minutes, the lights were plugged in and the gruesome scene was bathed in harsh yellow light.

# CHAPTER THREE

Dr. Robinson pulled on a pair of latex gloves and Emerson followed her into the bathroom. There was blood spatter on the mirror, the countertop, and the bottom of the stall doors. Amanda's face was bruised and caked with blood; her coat was open, displaying a white sweater stippled with blood. Her black skirt was bunched up around her thighs. The doctor walked around the body, taking it all in before kneeling beside her and inserting a thermometer into the liver.

"Preliminary time of death was between eleven last night and two this morning," Dr. Robinson announced after several minutes. Emerson wrote this in his notebook.

"I'm guessing cause of death was blunt force trauma," Emerson commented.

"Most likely. We'll know for sure when we get her on the table." Robinson removed her gloves and looked around for a garbage can. Not finding one, she handed them to her assistant, a young man no one had noticed before. She instructed the crime scene techs to take photos of some marks on Amanda's neck and thighs, then left the increasingly crowded room.

Dr. Robinson glanced back at the body and shook her head. "At least she put up a fight. Be sure to bag her hands before transporting her. Maybe she got some of the killer's skin under her nails."

Emerson glanced up the hall and saw Michelle emerge from the break room carrying a plate of scones. She approached the officers who were milling around.

"Would anyone like a scone? I made a pot of coffee as well," she offered in a detached tone.

Surprised by her change in demeanor, Emerson glanced at Officer Bauer, who simply shrugged. He knew people grieved in different ways, but in his experience, those who were the calmest in these types of situations were usually trying to cover up the fact that they had something to hide.

A couple of the officers looked at Emerson as if seeking his approval to accept the offer. He gave a nod. After all, many of them were coming to the end of their shifts and were probably famished. They smiled and followed Michelle to the break room. The scent of freshly brewed coffee wafted down the hall to Emerson and he felt his own stomach grumble.

Emerson watched as the crime scene guys photographed the scene, gathered the buttons that had flown from Amanda's coat, and dusted for fingerprints. It was painstaking work, but Emerson knew he had a good team. He glanced behind him and saw Dr. Robinson approaching, a scone in one hand and a Styrofoam cup of coffee in the other.

"You really should try one. They are remarkable. Not many crime scenes offer refreshments." She winked at Emerson.

"Maybe on the way out. I want to make sure we don't miss anything here."

Robinson shrugged and the pair watched in silence as evidence was gathered. Nearly an hour later, the techs started packing up their equipment and Dr. Robinson stepped forward to oversee the transport of Amanda's body.

Emerson strode into the break room where he found Michelle laughing with three of his officers around a small table. Pouring himself a cup of coffee and taking one of the remaining scones, he approached the table.

Officer Davidson, a rookie, jumped up and offered the detective his seat. The other officers excused themselves as well, leaving Emerson alone with Michelle. He took a bite of the scone and chewed slowly, extending the silence at the table. He wanted to see if Michelle would break the silence first, but she busied herself with wiping crumbs from the table and gathering the empty coffee cups.

"We're going to need you to come down to the station; give us your fingerprints so we can identify anything you may have touched." Emerson said in a casual tone.

Michelle didn't respond.

"We'll need to go over your statement again as well." Emerson took a sip of the coffee as Michelle turned to look at him.

Emerson held her gaze. Her eyes were still red from crying, but otherwise it was nearly impossible to tell that she had been a hysterical mess less than an hour ago. He heard voices coming from the elevator lobby and stalked off to see who had been allowed up. Two women stood just outside the still open elevator, their path blocked by three officers.

"I'm sorry, ladies, this area is off limits," one of the officers was saying as Emerson approached.

"Off limits? What are you talking about? This is our office," asked one of the women, a defiant air about her.

Emerson noticed the second woman had taken a step back into the elevator, her head tucked down against her chest.

"What's going on?" the defiant woman demanded.

Emerson stepped forward, in between two of the officers. "There's been a murder," he replied bluntly, his eyes trained on the women, studying their reaction. The defiant one barely flinched, but the other woman's head shot up and she let out a loud gasp.

The defiant woman's gaze moved past Emerson and he turned to see what she was looking at. Michelle was leaving the break room.

"Michelle," the defiant one called out.

Michelle stopped, waved at her friend, then turned and disappeared around the corner.

Emerson turned back to the women. "Did either of you ladies know Amanda Barnes?"

"Of course we know her," the defiant one said, then paused. "Wait, is Amanda dead?"

"Were you friends with Ms. Barnes?" Emerson asked.

"Friends? I wouldn't go that far. We worked together and occasionally she would tag along when we went out, but she always thought she was better than us." Some of the defiance had left her, but Emerson recognized there was no great sense of loss at the news of Amanda's death. He filed that away for later.

"Were you with her last night by any chance?"

The timid woman stepped forward. "Michelle's band had a show last night," she said quietly. "Amanda came but she didn't stay long."

Emerson pulled out his notepad and scratched this information down. "I'm going to need to talk to both of you. I'll need your contact information?"

Both women opened their purses and pulled out business cards. Emerson exchanged his card for theirs, shoving them into a pocket of his notepad.

"Now I'm afraid you are going to have to go back downstairs. The office will be closed for the rest of the day."

Emerson watched until the elevator door closed. Turning to the officers, he glared and bellowed, "Call downstairs and make sure they don't let anyone else up to this floor."

Without waiting for a response, he went in search of Michelle. He found her at her desk, thumbing through a drawer. She pulled a file and fanned through the pages, seemingly oblivious to Emerson's presence.

"Ms. Burton," Emerson cleared his throat as he spoke, "I need you to come to the station now."

Michelle looked up, surprise in her eyes. "I can't leave right now. I have a report due in two hours and a conference call at one."

"Ms. Burton," Emerson was growing impatient, "your office is going to be closed today. Now if you don't mind I'd like to get you to the station so we can get your statement while it's still fresh."

"My statement? Statement about what?"

"About Amanda Barnes' murder." Emerson could feel his blood pressure rising. Why was this woman acting like she didn't know what had happened.

"Amanda's dead?" Michelle's eyes grew wide and she fell back in her chair as if she'd been kicked.

Emerson shook his head in disbelief. Either she was a great actress or she had already blocked everything out of her memory. This wasn't going to be easy.

Emerson heard movement behind him and turned to find Officer Bauer. She gave him a slight jerk of her head, indicating he should step aside. He looked back at Michelle, who was rearranging the pages on her desk, then he allowed Officer Bauer to replace him in the cubicle.

"Michelle, do you remember me? Officer Bauer?" the officer asked and laid a hand on Michelle's shoulder.

Michelle looked up at Officer Bauer and Emerson thought he saw her eyes moisten. Slowly, Michelle nodded.

"Good. I know you've had a rough morning, but we are here to help you." Bauer spoke like a mother to a scared child. "If you go with Detective Emerson, he will write down everything that's happened this morning and then you can go home."

Emerson quirked an eyebrow at Bauer, offering her a silent salute.

Michelle rose reluctantly and followed Emerson down the hall. As they waited for the elevator, Emerson studied her: average height, with straight brown hair that fell just below her shoulders. Her brown eyes were downcast as if the toes of her brown leather boots held some intricate secret. She wore jeans and a thin sweater that suggested soft curves. Emerson appreciated that she wasn't one of those pencil-thin girls that always looked like they needed a good meal. She wasn't a great beauty, but he did find her attractive; maybe it was how vulnerable she seemed at this moment.

They emerged from the building and were greeted by two dozen news reporters, cameramen, and ancillary staff; all shouting questions, shining bright lights in their eyes, and shoving microphones in their faces. Michelle tucked her head down, allowing her hair to curtain her face. Emerson put a protective arm around her shoulders and guided her to the waiting car.

# CHAPTER FOUR

"I can't believe Lizzie left me in charge. I've only been doing this a couple of months. What was she thinking, leaving me with all of these VIPs checking in?" Stephen waved a stick of biscotti as he spoke, bringing an amused smile to Chef Gustave Flambert's usually stoic face.

"Do not forget the fundraising dinner for Eli's Hope," the chef reminded him, stoking Stephen's anxiety.

Stephen bit into the crisp biscotti and dropped into a chair. His brown hair was disarrayed from where he had been pulling on it for the past fifteen minutes. It had only been three months since Elizabeth Reynolds had taken him under her wing as her newest concierge protégé at Hotel Lago, and now he was in charge of the whole team while she took a week long vacation. Granted, the whole team was only Elizabeth, Stephen, Jessica, and Ben, but Stephen had never been in charge of anything in his life. He had begged Lizzie to leave one of the others in charge — they had been with the hotel longer anyway— but she assured him that he was ready for this and she had faith that he would do an excellent job.

"You have an affinity for this work, Stephen," Lizzie had told him before she left. "You have the ability to make people feel comfortable within minutes of meeting you. Jessica and Ben are great at their jobs; they take care of the details, but they don't build relationships like you do, and this job depends on relationships. I know with you in charge, the guests will feel welcomed and the rest of the team will make sure nothing falls through the cracks. It's only five days. I'll be back before you know it." Lizzie smiled and gave him a hug.

That had been three days ago. Now Lizzie was hundreds of miles away at a ski resort in Vermont and Stephen was facing the biggest day of his career at Hotel Lago. Silken Pleasures, a luxury cosmetics company, had chosen a boutique resort over a high-end chain for its annual executive retreat. Quite a coup for Hotel Lago. Ten high profile company executives were scheduled to arrive that afternoon and their list of requests had been meticulous, down to the 700 thread count Egyptian cotton sheets they wanted on their beds.

Stephen shook his head, gazing out the chef's office window into the kitchen where cooks and dishwashers were cleaning up after the breakfast rush. "I can't worry about the dinner until tomorrow." He paused and looked the chef in the eye. "Wait, the dinner is your problem, not mine."

Chef Gustave laughed. "I had to try to pass it off to you."

Stephen remembered how scared he was of the chef only a few months ago and now here he was confiding in him. Maybe Lizzie was right about his ability to build relationships.

"You will have to play host to the big donors and the foundation president," Chef Gustave commented in a more serious tone.

Stephen nodded. "Tomorrow, I'll worry about that tomorrow. If I make it through today." With a sigh, he stood and tossed the half-eaten biscotti in the trash. "I should go see if housekeeping has the rooms ready yet."

"Good luck." The chef stood from his seat behind the desk and gave Stephen an encouraging pat on the back as he left the office.

"Morning, boss," Ben greeted Stephen when he entered the front office. Ben sat at a desk piled with glossy folders, stacks of various letters, brochures, and itineraries lay on an adjacent table. He paused from stuffing the folders.

"Oh good, you started on the welcome packets." Stephen offered his colleague a relieved smile.

"Of course, boss." Ben didn't make eye contact and returned to collating the papers before placing them in the next folder.

"Please don't call me boss," Stephen sighed, taking in Ben's downcast eyes. "I'm just doing the best I can while Lizzie is away."

"Whatever you say. Ouch!" Ben dropped the papers and sucked on his index finger. "I must have a dozen paper cuts," he said, glancing down at the finger.

"Let me help." Stephen stepped closer to the table to acquaint himself with the literature, licked one of his fingers, and started to collect the papers.

"I'm sure you have more important things to do," Ben said, a hint of sarcasm in his tone.

"It's all important with this group," Stephen replied. "If the slightest thing goes wrong, it could hurt the reputation of the hotel."

"Why do we want more of these groups?" Ben asked. "They seem like more of a pain than they are worth."

Stephen thought a moment before answering. He had asked Lizzie the same thing when she was briefing him. Groups or even individual guests with the level of expectations this group had were difficult to impress and they weren't forgiving of even a minor mistake. While they might bring a lot of money into the hotel, they also had the potential to destroy the name that the employees of Hotel Lago had worked long and hard to build.

Hotel Lago had steadily risen as a boutique hotel catering to both executives and families in the heart of downtown Orlando. Visitors came for the spacious rooms, outstanding food, and detailed service despite its distance from the city's attractions. Two years ago, the resort had been featured in *Travel & Leisure* magazine as an up and coming vacation resort. The owner was working to purchase one of the neighboring buildings; an apartment complex built in 1960, to expand the resort, particularly the spa area.

"These are very powerful women and their opinions matter in the corporate world. With Mr. Kingsley looking to expand the resort, we need more of these groups." Stephen paused and caught Ben's eye. "Plus I hear they tip pretty well."

Ben smiled and started collating for the next folder. "What time is Jessica coming in?"

"She'll be here at noon. The corporate jet arrives at one and the guests should be here by one-thirty. I was hoping the rooms would all be cleaned by now." Stephen looked at the clock on the wall; it was nearly ten. "When we get these done, I will check with housekeeping again." The men worked in silence for several minutes.

A side door leading to the front desk area opened and Angela, a young woman with a freckled face and golden hair cascading down her back, appeared in the office.

"Stephen, there is a florist looking for you," Angela announced.

"Great!" Stephen finished stuffing the last folder and dropped it on the desk. "I'll be right out."

Angela nodded and returned to her station. Stephen pulled a list of floral arrangement requests from a file in his desk drawer and went to meet the delivery.

In the lobby, he found the florist with a cart loaded with vases full of roses, irises, carnations, asters, and brown-eyed Susans. Stephen stopped in his tracks as he took in the arrangements, feeling something was wrong. He scanned the list in his hand and his heart dropped.

"Would you mind setting each of the vases on the table over there?" Stephen gestured toward a large coffee table in the center of the lobby. The florist complied and Stephen looked at each arrangement individually.

"This isn't right." Stephen felt his chest tighten. Eight of the arrangements met the specifications he had sent to the florist, but two of them, those for the president and vice president were both wrong, horribly wrong.

"This one absolutely cannot have carnations. It is supposed to be hydrangea, spray roses, and eucalyptus." Stephen held the vase intended for the president, which currently held yellow roses, white carnations, and more baby's breath than Stephen had ever seen.

"Sorry, man, I don't know anything about that." The deliveryman held out a clipboard for Stephen to sign.

"I'm not signing for this. It's your job to get the order right; to find the flowers that are requested."

"I don't know what to tell you. I just make the deliveries." He held out the clipboard again.

"Wait here. I need to make a phone call." Stephen put the flowers on the table and returned to the office.

"This is not going to be a good day," he muttered as he picked up the phone and dialed the number for Amy's Floral Designs.

"It's a lovely day at Amy's. How can I help you?" A bright voice answered on the third ring.

"This is Stephen at Hotel Lago. I need to talk to Amy about a delivery." Stephen's voice was surprisingly calm, considering his whole body was shaking with anger.

"I'm sorry; Amy is not in right now. Can I help you?"

"Unless you can correct the two orders your delivery man brought over in the next five minutes, I don't think you can. How can I reach Amy?"

"Let me pull the order." The girl put Stephen on hold and he paced in front of his desk listening to a sappy love song. "Okay, which arrangement is the problem?" she asked.

"There are two," Stephen replied and looked at his list. "I faxed over a list, do you have that?"

"Yes, I'm looking at it now."

"The first two are completely wrong." There was a brief silence and Stephen paced impatiently, the few steps the short phone cord would allow.

"Yeah, I see a note on here." The girl snapped a piece of gum. "We didn't have any of the peonies, hydrangea, or chrysanthemums in stock."

"I sent this list more than two weeks ago. Wasn't that enough time for you to find the right flowers?" Stephen's voice rose as he started to lose his cool. No one seemed to care that this could make or break him.

"Hey, don't yell at me. You're right; you need to talk to Amy. I'll tell her to call you. What's the best number to reach you?"

Stephen gave the girl his cell phone number. "I need the correct arrangements by noon."

"I'll let her know." The girl hung up before Stephen could say anything else.

He slammed the phone down and dropped into his chair. For a moment, he sat there, his hand shaking with anger, then he took a long, deep breath and reached for a Rolodex. He'd made fun of Lizzie for keeping a Rolodex when it was so much easier to keep contacts on the computer, but at this moment, he appreciated her system. Rather than filing contacts alphabetically by name, Lizzie filed them based on the service they provided, and to get into Lizzie's files you had to be good. Flipping to "'F," he found more than a dozen cards for florists.

Stephen lined the cards up on the desk and scanned them to see if he recognized any of the names. One card jumped out at him: Jackson Compton. Stephen remembered meeting Jackson a few weeks ago at the Orlando Science Center. Lizzie had introduced the two men and raved about the work Jackson had done for a wedding at the hotel the year before. Stephen picked up the card and dialed.

"Fields of Bloom, this is Cindy, how can I help you?" The woman who answered the phone was professional, but sounded in a rush.

"Cindy, this is Stephen at Hotel Lago. I have a situation and I was hoping Jackson might be able to help me out." Stephen's palms were sweating. He cradled the phone between his shoulder and ear to wipe them on his pants.

"Mr. Compton is with a client right now. I would be happy to help you."

"I have some VIPs arriving in a few hours and the floral arrangements we received from another vendor are a mess. Apparently what we are looking for is hard to find this time of year." Stephen tried to sound confident and in control.

"What are you looking for?"

Stephen read off the list of flowers requested by the president and vice president. He thought he heard Cindy choke back a laugh when he finished the list.

"You weren't kidding. The peonies are going to be the hardest, but there are some hybrid roses we can substitute if necessary. Mr. Compton happens to have the largest selection of flowers in the city and I think we might have everything else. Can I call you back in five minutes?"

"Really? That would be great." Stephen's heart slowed from the marathon it had been pounding out in his chest.

"Talk to you soon."

Stephen opened his Outlook and skimmed the emails that had arrived in the past hour, relieved there were no last minute changes to the plans for the afternoon. There was an email from Lizzie, though. He opened it, expecting there to be some last minute words of advice. Instead, it was an electronic postcard with a photo of a ski lodge, pristine white mountains in the background.

*Wanted to wish you luck today. I know you will be great, that's why I am hitting the slopes all afternoon. See you in a few days! Lizzie*

Stephen shook his head. He found it hard to believe she wasn't going to spend the whole day obsessing about how things were going, considering what a perfectionist she was, but he had to admit she'd been less concerned about work since she and Ian had gotten serious about each other. This ski trip was the first time the two families were meeting, so maybe she was keeping busy and not thinking about work. Stephen hoped so. She really deserved it after the summer she'd had.

Between bringing her house back from the verge of collapse, being attacked by her landlord's stepson, and weathering four hurricanes, Stephen had watched a new confidence emerge in her. Things had been stop and go with Ian for a while. Stephen didn't quite understand why — they were perfect together — but Lizzie had seemed conflicted about their relationship. Maybe it had something to do with how close she and Jeffrey had become. Stephen had noticed the two of them spending more time together a few weeks after the attack.

"Stephen, your phone's ringing." Ben's voice roused Stephen from his thoughts. He reached for the phone, pleased to see the number of Fields of Bloom on the caller id.

"Hotel Lago, this is Stephen."

"Hey, Stephen, it's Jackson. I hear you have an emergency."

"Jackson, thanks so much for calling me back. I hope Cindy didn't interrupt your meeting."

"Not at all. I was finishing up and she mentioned she was working on something for Hotel Lago. Why didn't you call me first man? You wouldn't have had this problem with me." Jackson's voice was joking, but Stephen suddenly knew how right he was.

"Lizzie told me to use Amy. You know how she likes to help new businesses, but I don't know if we will ever use her again after this fiasco. She didn't even call to tell me they couldn't get the flowers, just created an arrangement, and hoped to pass it off on me."

"Don't worry. I have two of my best employees working on this and we'll have them to you in a couple hours."

"Thanks, Jackson. I can't tell you how important these guests are to us."

"Anything for Lizzie. Give her my love."

"I will and thanks again." Stephen hung up the phone and returned to the lobby where the deliveryman was still waiting.

"Look, buddy are you going to sign for this or not?"

"I'll sign for eight of them, but you are going to have to take the other two back." Stephen pulled a pen from his coat pocket and made a notation on the invoice.

"I don't know," the deliveryman looked nervous. "I'm supposed to have you sign for all of them."

"Well, you'll just have to work that out with your boss. I've already called and told them I'm not accepting these arrangements." Stephen waved down a bellman and indicated he needed a cart. The deliveryman took the clipboard back and wheeled out of the lobby with the two offending arrangements.

"Will you please take these to the storage room until we are ready to deliver them?" Stephen asked the bellman.

"Sure thing. Give me a call when you're ready and I'll be happy to deliver them as well."

Stephen wanted to believe the bellman was just being helpful, but he knew the tip he would get for these deliveries was what drove him.

All of these big groups had gratuities for baggage and room deliveries included. One of the first things Lizzie had taught him was how important it was to make sure the deliveries were shared equally among the bellman. He'd learned how to plan a whole week's worth of deliveries so that no bellman had more earning opportunities than another. He made a mental note to add the floral deliveries to this bellman's account.

On the sixth floor, Stephen met the housekeeping manager, Lucian, a slender Jamaican man with a dazzling smile. The hotel had six suites, each named after lakes in Italy. Lucian held a pile of towels and was entering the Lake Trasimeno suite when he saw Stephen.

"Good mornin'!" Lucian greeted him. "We're almost done here, but two rooms be running behind. The front desk moved some guests last night because of a leak."

Stephen nodded. "I heard. Have they checked out yet?"

"I hear them moving around, maybe an hour ago."

A young Hispanic girl exited the suite and moved to the housekeeping cart. She didn't meet Stephen's gaze as she quietly collected the Crabtree & Evelyn toiletry bottles.

"Amelia, when you finish the bathroom, go check rooms 605 and 607," Lucian directed. Amelia nodded and returned to the suite. "Poor girl, shyer than a deer," Lucian said with a sympathetic shake of his head.

"Do you think all of the rooms will be ready by one o'clock?" Stephen felt the knot in his stomach returning. Nothing was going to be easy today.

Lucian smiled, displaying a row of large, slightly crooked teeth. "No worries, mon. I have them ready. You wanna walk through? Soon as Amelia gets the amenities in the bathroom, this room be done."

"Lead the way."

Entering the hotel suites never ceased to amaze Stephen. The colors in the Lake Trasimeno were breathtaking. Pale yellow walls exuded the warmth of the Tuscan sun onto the polished wood floor. Two walnut Louis XIV armchairs covered in olive green velvet flanked the large window overlooking Lake Eola, with a simple walnut desk in between. A comfortable empire-style settee covered in a Dijon mustard-colored fabric with whimsical brown curlicues faced a 32-inch flat screen television, one of the few modern touches in this antique-inspired room. He passed through an arched doorway to the bedroom, which held a queen-sized bed under a cream duvet, accented with olive and gold throw pillows, and a reading area furnished with a classic Erin chair, ottoman, and a pendant floor lamp.

Stephen spent the next fifteen minutes inspecting the suite, scrutinizing every corner and crevice. When he found dust or dirt, he cleaned it himself. In the bedroom, he noticed a small tear in the upholstery of the Erin chair and pulled a radio from his belt.

"Mark, I need to replace one of the chairs in the Lake Trasimeno suite. Do you have anything that will match the furniture in here?" Stephen asked.

"I'll have to look. We don't have much in storage. I might be able to swap it out with something from the lobby," Mark replied.

"See what you can do and let me know when it's taken care of."

"You got it."

When he was satisfied the suite was up to par except for the chair, Stephen returned to the hallway. Lucian had already moved on to the next suite. Stephen popped his head in and found Lucian, along with two other housekeepers, feverishly cleaning. The rooms had been unoccupied the night before and all of the linens already changed, so now the workers concentrated on scrubbing the floors and tile, making sure fresh drapes were hung, and every inch of the room gleamed.

# CHAPTER FIVE

Detective Emerson expertly whipped the midnight blue Crown Victoria into a parking spot and cut the engine. He pushed the car door open and pulled his tall frame from the uncomfortable seat. Michelle remained motionless. Emerson grumbled, slammed his door shut, and rounded the back of the car. At the passenger door, he lifted the handle, but found it locked. He slammed the roof and reached into his pocket for the keys.

"What's goin' on Mike?" a young, freckle-faced rookie called from the sidewalk.

"I got a difficult witness," Emerson snarled. He shoved the key into the lock and yanked the door open. He gripped Michelle's arm, pulling her from the car.

"You're hurting me," she cried, trying to shake him off. Emerson loosened his grip slightly, but didn't let go, afraid she would duck back into the car.

"Come on," he growled impatiently. His suspicions were growing with each of her changes in behavior. She'd been silent for the entire ride, stonewalling his attempts at neutral small talk. The sooner he got her in to see the department shrink, the better.

When they entered the police station, Emerson led Michelle to a conference room with a small, round table, four sleek black leather chairs, and a print of the Everglades hanging on one of the taupe-colored walls. There were no windows and only one door into the room. Emerson directed her to take a seat.

"I gotta report to the Captain. There'll be an officer right outside, so don't get any ideas about taking off." Emerson gave her a stern look, but Michelle's gaze was fixed on the Everglades scene. He shook his head and left her alone, hoping she'd realize this wasn't a game. He threaded his way through several corridors, tossing off a wave when he heard guys call him greetings. When he reached the Captain's office, he paused to straighten his jacket.

Emerson knocked on the door and waited for the Captain to acknowledge him. Judith Raley, a fifty-three-year-old veteran of the Orlando Police Department, wore a black tailored suit with a crisp, white blouse and thick, square, black glasses. Her hair was the color of ash, coiffed in a tight bun at the nape of her neck.

"Detective, come in. What have you got?" Captain Raley pointed at a seat across from her.

Emerson declined her offer. "I just wanted to let you know I have the woman who made the 9-1-1 call in one of the conference rooms. Not sure if she's a suspect or not, but I'd like to see if Doc Mendenhall could meet with her. She's been all over the place this morning." Emerson gave her a brief synopsis of Michelle's behavior. Captain Raley nodded when he finished.

"I'll give the doc a call and find out if he's free. Which room are you in?"

"Three fifteen," Emerson replied.

"All right. You go ahead and start your interview and I'll send someone down if the doctor isn't available." Raley dismissed Emerson and reached for her phone. On the way back to the conference room, Emerson ran into Abigael McDonald.

Promoted to detective six months ago, McDonald was always eager to please the senior detectives. Emerson couldn't help but return her cheerful smile when her brilliant green eyes met his.

"I hear you caught an odd one this morning," McDonald said with the slightest trace of an Irish accent.

"You can say that again. I don't know if she's faking or if she's really this messed up." Emerson paused and rubbed his chin. "How would you like to run a background on my witness? I need a rush on it."

McDonald straightened her shoulders and held her head higher. "Yes, sir." She hesitated, then asked, "You think she did this? I hear the crime scene was pretty brutal."

Emerson shrugged. "I've seen crazier things. Let me know if you find anything." Emerson stopped for a couple of glasses of water before returning to the conference room. He set one of the glasses in front of Michelle and then settled in a chair. Michelle continued staring at the picture, barely blinking.

Emerson studied her and noticed a small scar above her right eye. If he hadn't been watching every inch of her face, searching for a tell, a twitch, anything that would betray what was really going on inside her mind, he probably would have missed it. He wondered where it had come from, if she'd been involved in something violent before. There was a knock on the door.

"Come in," Emerson barked without moving. A short balding man, with deep brown eyes, and large ears stepped inside.

"Hey, doc," Emerson gestured toward the chairs. Dr. Mendenhall entered the room and approached Michelle. He offered her his hand, but she didn't take her eyes off the picture.

"She's been like this since we got here," Emerson advised. The doctor nodded and took the seat next to Michelle.

"Ms. Burton, I'm Dr. Charles Mendenhall. Do you know where you are?" He spoke softly. Michelle didn't answer, but Emerson saw her eyes flick to the doctor for just a second. Mendenhall looked to Emerson, who gave an encouraging nod. The doctor reached out and gently turned Michelle to face him.

"Michelle, I'm here to help you. Can you tell me where you are?" Mendenhall waited several seconds. When she made eye contact with him, he gave her a kind smile. Michelle stirred as if just waking, and looked around the small room. Emerson gave her a sarcastic wave from where he still stood by the door. She looked back at the doctor.

"I'm at the police station," Michelle finally replied.

"Do you know why are you are here?" the doctor asked.

"Amanda was killed." Michelle's eyes grew moist and the doctor pulled a handkerchief from his pocket, but she waved it off.

"That's right," Dr. Mendenhall confirmed. "Can you tell me what you saw this morning?"

Michelle looked at the floor, shifted her gaze to Detective Emerson, then settled again on the Everglades picture. Emerson wondered what it was about the print she found so interesting, or was it comforting? Several seconds passed and Michelle remained quiet.

"Michelle, I know it may be hard to talk about, but we really need your help, and so does Amanda," Mendenhall gently prodded. The men waited, but again there was no response.

"Detective, would you mind bringing us some more water?" the doctor asked, giving Emerson a look indicating he wanted to be left alone for a few minutes.

"Sure." Emerson collected his empty glass and slipped out the door.

When the door closed, Mendenhall decided to change tactics. "Why don't you tell me a little about yourself? What do you like to do in your free time?"

"Music. I'm in a band. We actually had a big show last night." Her words were distant, as if her mind was far from the police station.

"Really? What do you play?"

"In the band, I play bass, but I also play piano and saxophone." She spoke faster now, with enthusiasm for the new topic. "We opened for a band called *Wonderland* last night. It was amazing."

"Tell me about last night." The doctor leaned back in his chair and crossed his legs.

Michelle's face flushed and her eyes brightened. "It was our first time playing at The Social. I met the guys from *Wonderland* over the summer and they came to a few of our shows at another bar downtown. We were only an okay group at the time, but when we got Nadia to replace Tina, things really took off."

Michelle paused to give the doctor a conspiratorial smile. "I always knew Tina was holding us back. I don't know why she joined the band to start with. She never wanted to practice or play any original music."

The doctor smiled and nodded for Michelle to continue.

"The bar patrons started to take notice and soon we were filling the place. When Andy asked us to open for *Wonderland,* I was thrilled."

"We had a little over a month to get ready for the show, so I suggested we write a couple of our own songs. We couldn't open with just covers. Matt and I wrote three songs and added them to our regular shows. After the first gig, we knew they were a hit. People came up to us afterward wanting to know if they could buy the songs online." Michelle paused, eyes glazing over as if lost in thought.

"That sounds exciting," Mendenhall remarked.

Michelle flinched as if startled by his voice. Her gaze refocused on him and she smiled.

"You have no idea."

"What happened at the show last night?" Mendenhall tried to steer the conversation again.

"The club was full, the largest crowd we'd ever played for. I couldn't see faces, but I knew some of my friends from work were there and I was so proud to hear the audience singing our songs. The girls I work with heard them singing our songs."

"Was it important these women see you as successful?"

Michelle didn't reply.

"What did you do after the show? Did you celebrate?" Mendenhall hoped he could lessen the shock by drawing her through the hours preceding finding the body.

"A group of us went out to a few clubs, then went to Denny's." Michelle didn't elaborate.

"Who were you with?" Mendenhall asked. "Was it just you and the band?"

Michelle thought a moment. "No, Tiffani and Wendy from work were there, and a couple of guys who have supported us from the beginning, Marty and Elliot." Michelle smiled. "And of course, Andy and the other members of *Wonderland*. It was quite a party."

"What time did you get home?" Mendenhall asked.

"It was around three, I guess, but I wasn't tired."

"I imagine you had quite an adrenaline high. What did you do when you got home?"

"I tried to watch TV, but couldn't sit still, so I went to the kitchen and started baking." Michelle laughed. "Some rock star I'll make, baking when I can't sleep. I'll be the Martha Stewart of rock n' roll."

Mendenhall smiled. "Did you go to bed once you finished baking?"

Michelle shook her head. "It was already close to six, so I took a shower and went to work. I figured I could get some things done before everyone else came in."

"And what did you do when you got to the office?"

"I turned on my computer, went to the break room, and made some coffee. My eyes were bothering me and started watering." Michelle's speech slowed and Mendenhall feared he was about to lose her.

"I went to the bathroom to splash some water on my face, but the lights didn't come on." Michelle stopped. Her gaze had floated around the room throughout her narrative, but now they locked on Dr. Mendenhall.

"Did you see anything in the bathroom, Michelle?" Mendenhall was still reclined in his chair, hoping he was projecting a comforting air.

"Why wouldn't the lights come on?" Michelle asked.

"I'm not sure," Mendenhall replied. "Did you go inside even though the lights were out?"

Michelle closed her eyes and shook her head. "I don't remember."

"Try to remember," Mendenhall urged. He leaned forward and placed a hand on one of Michelle's. "You are safe here. Try to remember what you did next."

Michelle opened her eyes and looked at him. "The next thing I remember is the police at the office talking about Amanda being dead. How is that possible? She was at the show last night. I know she didn't want to be there, but she was, at least for a little while."

"Why didn't she want to be there?" Mendenhall asked.

"We aren't the best of friends. She only went because Tiffani and Wendy guilted her. We all went to some stupid dog show Amanda was in last year with her Lhasa Apso." Michelle giggled. "Princess Arial, that's her dog's name."

The conference room door opened, and Detective Emerson returned carrying a tray with two carafes of water and several glasses and mugs.

"I brought some tea and hot water as well. I thought maybe it would help you relax." Emerson smiled and placed the tray on the table. Michelle thanked him, took a tea bag, and poured the steaming water over it into a plain white mug. Her hands shook as she returned the carafe to the tray.

"Michelle, do you mind if I talk to Detective Emerson for a moment?" Dr. Mendenhall asked. Michelle shook her head and Mendenhall rose from his chair. The two men stepped into the hall.

"I don't think she is faking the memory loss. She's had a very emotional twenty-four hours and I believe she is repressing what she saw in order to preserve the memories of a success she had last night. She understands Amanda's dead, but only because she has heard the police talk about it all morning.

"She can't face the reality of discovering the body for a number of reasons, not the least being there seems to be some bad blood between the two of them."

"Really?" Emerson asked with a raise of his eyebrows.

"Yes. It may only be some competitiveness at work or simply a difference of personality, it's hard to say at this point, but she did tell me they weren't the best of friends. Did you know Michelle is in a band? Apparently they had a big show last night."

"Yeah, a couple of women at the office were saying something about a concert. I'll be bringing them in for questioning later." Emerson ran a hand through his thin gray hair. "What else did she tell you?"

"Well, she wasn't alone until about three this morning when she went home. She was out with a number of other people celebrating the show. How does that fit with your time of death?"

"Not great. Preliminary TOD was between eleven and two. Depending on what time she actually got home, she could have committed the crime at the tail end of that window."

"It takes someone pretty cold to commit a crime in their place of business, leave the body, and return hours later like nothing happened. I really don't think she is a viable suspect," Mendenhall offered.

"You're probably right. I'm going to need a list of the people she says she was out with though to corroborate her story." Emerson pulled his notebook from his pocket and reached for the door handle. Mendenhall stopped him.

"Tread softly. I'm hoping at some point she will be able to work through the memories of what happened this morning, but I am afraid if we push her too hard she will bury them even deeper. As it is she's going to need professional help to get through this." Mendenhall stepped aside and followed Emerson back into the room.

# CHAPTER SIX

At quarter to twelve, a valet alerted Stephen to the arrival of the new flowers. He flew from his desk, anxious to see them. Jackson Compton entered the lobby, carrying a tall arrangement of pure white hydrangeas, cream spray roses, and springs of fragrant eucalyptus, followed by one of his assistants who carried a silver bowl filled with white lisianthus and hydrangeas accented with half a dozen pink peonies.

"These are exquisite," Stephen exclaimed after a cursory look at the arrangements.

"I'm glad you like them," Jackson said with a smile.

"You have absolutely saved my life, but you didn't have to come out here yourself." Stephen reached for the larger of the two arrangements and turned the vase so he could see it from all sides. "I hope I didn't interrupt anything important you were working on."

"It's nice to do the deliveries every now and then. That's how I started out in this business, you know, doing deliveries when I was in high school."

"Really?" Stephen asked in a distracted tone as he waved over a bellman to collect the flowers.

"I know you're busy; I just wanted to make sure the flowers got here safely and met your approval. I'll get out of your hair. Be sure to call me next time you have one of these high maintenance types," Jackson said, giving Stephen a slap on the back.

"I don't mean to be rude." Stephen worried he'd offended the florist.

"You're not. I remember being where you are now. Take a deep breath and remind yourself it will all be over in a few hours." Jackson chuckled. "Well, in this case, a few days."

"Thanks." Stephen offered a halfhearted smile. "I hope I survive."

Stephen gave Jackson a final handshake and hurried off to find Lucian. He found the executive housekeeper in the last of the VIP rooms. The room was a disaster. The bed pillows had been shredded, feathers littered the floor, a large puddle filled the bathroom, and a putrid odor assailed him. He felt like he was going to be sick. It would take hours to clean this room and he only had forty-five minutes.

"It's not as bad as it looks, mon," Lucian said when he noticed Stephen's pale face. "I have Claire, Amelia, and Nolan working on it. We will have it ready in time."

"It looks like a wild animal was held in here." Stephen toured the entire suite in disbelief. "You'd think someone who received a comp upgrade because of a leak in their original room would have some respect."

"Engineering just finished unclogging the toilet." Lucian laughed. "They tried to flush a stuffed bear down it. They must have been high on something good."

Stephen shook his head. "Make me a list of everything that's damaged and we'll send them a bill."

This made Lucian laugh even more. "You think they gonna pay a bill? Mon, you be lucky if they gave you a real name or address."

"But…all this…who will?" Stephen turned in a circle overwhelmed by the destruction. The glass in the frame of a picture of Lake Giada, which had hung in the sitting room, was shattered, and Stephen heard it crunching under Amelia's feet as she walked toward the settee. There was no way this room would be habitable tonight. Stephen needed a back up plan. He tried to run through the hotel inventory Lizzie had insisted he memorize his first week, but he couldn't focus. These executives had such specific room requests, he couldn't think of anything else to meet their expectations.

"Keep working, but I'm going to see if there are any other rooms we can use. I'll radio you if I find something." Stephen hurried off.

Back at his desk, Stephen pulled up the hotel inventory on his computer and opened his trusty binder to the page of room requests. He scrolled through the computer looking for suitable alternatives. Fortunately, this one wasn't a suite, and was for the president's assistant rather than one of the executives, but the requests had been just as precise.

All of the rooms had to have views of Lake Eola, on the sixth floor, and they all had to have 700 thread count Egyptian cotton sheets to start with. The hotel only had fifteen rooms on the sixth floor with a lake view, and the group took up twelve of those rooms.

The only person allowed to have a corner room was the president, eliminating the remaining corner room. None of the rooms could have blue paint, except the chief financial officer's room, eliminating another room. His last room, located between the blue room and the forbidden corner room, would be separated from the rest of the group, which would also go against their request to have all of the rooms together and no other guests mixed in with them, but it was his only option.

Stephen decided to risk it and prepare the separate room for them, just in case Lucian wasn't able to pull off the miracle he promised. He radioed Lucian to let him know, then called Jessica and asked her to stop at Macy's on her way in to work to buy another set of Egyptian cotton sheets. When he hung up the phone, Stephen allowed himself to stop for a moment to catch his breath. Ben handed him the stack of completed welcome packets.

"Hang in there," Ben encouraged. "Once they get here, things will go smoother."

"Really? You think so, because I don't. Have you looked at their schedule?"

Ben's easy-going manner irritated Stephen. Nothing ever fazed him and his catch phrase for anything that came his way was "It's all good." Well, today, it wasn't all good. It was all bad, one disaster after another. Stephen could feel the beginnings of a migraine and reached into his desk drawer for a bottle of Excedrin. He popped a couple of pills without any water and pushed himself out of the chair.

"They were supposed to be shipping a box of gifts here. Go see if it arrived in this morning's deliveries. If so, start separating them according to this list." Stephen snapped open the rings of his binder and removed one of the plastic protected pages.

"What do you want me to do if they aren't here yet?" Ben asked, taking the list.

"Start writing up the bellman delivery cards. Make sure they are even. I know you gave Roger extra deliveries last time." Stephen narrowed his eyes with these last words.

Ben nodded sheepishly and left for the loading bay. Stephen noticed Jonathan was in his office, so he went to provide an update on the challenges of the day.

"Sounds like you have everything under control," Jonathan commented without looking up from the stack of reviews on his desk.

"Did you hear anything I said? One of our deluxe rooms was trashed," Stephen reiterated.

"I heard you. It happens sometimes. Lucian will take care of it," Jonathan replied, tapping the stack of paper together before inserting it into an electric stapler. With the distinctive bite of staple into paper, Stephen turned and walked away, stunned at Jonathan's lack of interest.

Sure, Jonathan had distanced himself from the day-to-day concierge and group operation since promoting Lizzie to Manager of Concierge Services three months ago, but this was an important day for the hotel all around. Feeling more alone than ever, Stephen returned to the Lake Trasimeno suite to make sure the floral arrangement had been delivered.

The flowers were stunning on the black marble table in the entryway. Stephen gave silent thanks for Jackson's outstanding work and willingness to help. The two floral arrangements had cost as much as all eight of the others combined, but they were well worth it. The radio on his belt crackled and he heard Lucian calling his name.

"Go ahead, Lucian," Stephen responded.

"I need you in room six-fifteen," Lucian advised.

"I'll be right there." Stephen's chest was tight. They couldn't possibly have cleaned the room already could they? A laundry cart sat in front of room six-thirteen, filled with the tattered remains of the pillows and towels the color of a pumpkin. The putrid odor he'd smelled when he'd first entered the room now emanated from the towels and he hurried past. When he entered the room, he looked around in amazement.

A new picture hung over the settee, not a single feather could be seen, the bathroom floor was pristine, and the whole room smelled of a fresh spring day. Even the windows had been scrubbed and shined like new. Claire, Amelia, and Nolan stood by the closet, their faces beaming with pride. Stephen couldn't find any words.

"I told you, no worries, mon," Lucian gave him a proud smile.

"I will never doubt you again," Stephen extended a grateful hand to Lucian. He turned to the housekeepers. "I don't know how to thank you. Your work today goes above and beyond the call of duty." They smiled and thanked him, then filed out of the room. Stephen called down to the bell stand to have the last vase of flowers delivered. When they arrived, he positioned them on the coffee table and stepped back to admire the room one more time. His cell phone rang and he answered it without checking the caller ID.

"This is Lex with Executive Limos; you asked me to call when I was leaving the airport."

Stephen checked his watch; it was already one-fifteen. The group would be there in less than fifteen minutes. "Thanks, Lex, I appreciate it. Catch every red light if you can." Stephen suggested.

Lex chuckled. "I'll see what I can do."

Stephen returned the phone to his pocket and ran down six flights of stairs to the lobby. He arrived, out of breath, with sweat beading on his forehead. He knew he must look awful after running around like a crazed person all morning. He made sure the bellmen and valets were ready for the arrival, gave the front desk a heads up and stationed Ben by the front door, then grabbed his extra suit from the back office and dashed into the bathroom. He quickly changed clothes and splashed a generous amount of cologne. He joined Ben at the front door just as the limos pulled up.

# CHAPTER SEVEN

Michelle followed Emerson through the winding halls of the police station until they emerged in the afternoon sun. Her stomach growled, reminding her it had been hours since the scone and coffee she'd had at the office. Only hours? It felt like a lifetime ago, she thought.

Emerson opened the car door for her and she slipped inside. When he had adjusted his utility belt and plunged the key into the ignition, he paused and turned to her.

"Thanks for getting me through the reporters back at the office," Michelle said.

"Part of the job," Emerson replied. "We don't want the killer to know any more about the case than absolutely necessary."

"Oh," Michelle's stomach suddenly tightened. "You don't think he will come after me do you?"

"I doubt it. All the news will report is you discovered the body. It's not like you saw him fleeing the scene and were able to give us a description."

Michelle found Emerson's detached and almost cavalier approach to all of this disconcerting. "Should I find a place to stay until you find him, just in case, you know?"

Emerson shrugged. "Are you sure you don't want me to take you home? You can pick up your car from the garage tomorrow."

Michelle could feel his scrutinizing gaze on her, but she turned her face to the window. "That's okay. I'd rather get it now and be able to stay home the rest of the weekend."

Emerson started the engine and maneuvered through the parking lot. When he turned onto Hughey, Michelle realized the parking lot was actually at the back of the police station, and the front of the building, overlooking Hughey, was now playing host to several news crews finishing their mid-day reports.

Michelle dug into her purse for her keys, her heartbeat increasing as they pulled into the parking garage. She directed Emerson to her car. He stopped directly behind it and turned to face her.

"Don't forget to let me know if you decide to stay someplace else the next few days, in case I have any more questions."

"I'm not sure what else I can tell you," Michelle replied, anxious to get to her car.

"I know it's been a tough morning, but you might be surprised what will come back to you after you've had some time to yourself. If it will make you feel better I'll see about putting a patrol officer in your neighborhood tonight."

This change in Emerson was unexpected. The warmth in his voice now didn't fit with the cold and terse treatment he had offered her all morning.

"I'd appreciate it," she replied.

"All right then. I'll be in touch." Just like that, he dismissed her.

Michelle's hands trembled as she tried to unlock her car. She glanced back to Emerson, still idling behind her. Taking a deep breath, she inserted the key and opened the door. She watched in her rearview mirror, but Emerson didn't move until she started the engine and shifted into reverse. He pulled forward with a wave, allowing her to back out. She moved slowly, her senses alert for anyone lurking in the shadows.

In a matter of minutes, she was on Interstate-4, unsure where she wanted to go. Part of her didn't want to be alone, but at the same time, she didn't want to have to relive the morning with any of her friends. Her foot slowly depressed the gas pedal and she slipped into the flow of traffic headed for the attractions area.

The parking lot of Downtown Disney thronged with vehicles stalking the aisles in search of a parking spot. Michelle crawled along behind a mother and three blonde-headed children. At least they aren't in strollers, she thought. Those take forever to get loaded into the car. The mother shot Michelle an annoyed look over her shoulder and corralled the children in front of her.

"I'm not going to run over your kids, lady," Michelle grumbled, becoming impatient with this little family. Four spaces ahead she saw the white back-up lights of a Mercedes illuminate. Quickly she put on her blinker and surged forward to fill his space.

Stepping out of her car, Michelle shouldered her purse, checked traffic, and crossed the parking lot to join the multitude of tourists wandering among the Disney shops. Passing through the doors of World of Disney, Michelle found herself swallowed up by a sea of people speaking at least three different languages. She moved through the rooms of men's apparel, women's apparel, children's apparel, toys, jewelry, and home goods.

"Excuse me, miss," an Asian man said after bumping into her near a case of watches.

"It's all right," she replied, but he was already gone. Overwhelmed by the pressing crowd, she made her way to one of the exits. The aroma of fresh popcorn wafting on the cool breeze made her stomach growl once again. Scanning the area to get her bearings, she turned right and weaved through the crowd to the Earl of Sandwich.

Inside, the line snaked back and forth, four times, filling the lobby of the fast food café. Michelle joined the line, studying the menu as she waited. Her cell phone rang and she recognized Tiffani's number. She considered sending the call to voicemail. On the fourth ring, she answered.

"Michelle, are you okay? I've been calling for hours." Tiffani's voice was panicked and Michelle felt bad she hadn't called her friend sooner.

"I'm fine. I guess you've heard everything." Michelle excused herself from the line, stepped outside to the patio, and found a corner table where she took a seat on the cold, wrought iron chair.

"No, the police wouldn't tell us anything, but the news said Amanda is dead."

"Did they mention who discovered the body?" Michelle asked cautiously.

"They just said a coworker found her, but I know it had to be you. Wendy and I managed to get past the police in the lobby and made it up to our floor, but a couple of other cops stopped us at the elevator. We saw you coming out of the break room."

Michelle was silent, debating how much she should tell her friend. She couldn't imagine Emerson would want her to say anything, especially since he'd mentioned needing to question them about the previous night. Plus, after telling her story to the police at least three different times, she wasn't ready to go through it again.

"I really don't want to talk about it right now," Michelle replied.

"Come on," Tiffani whined. "This is the biggest thing to ever happen to us."

"The police are going to want to talk to you about the concert last night," Michelle tried to deflect attention from herself.

"Oh yeah, we know. This old guy took our numbers. He was a real jerk about us getting into the office."

Michelle allowed herself to smile a little at the thought of Tiffani and Wendy trying to talk their way past Emerson. He'd mentioned his encounter with them during her interview. He was none too pleased with Wendy's brazen attitude.

"I was about to get some lunch. I haven't eaten in hours. You mind if I catch up with you guys later? Why don't you call me after you talk to the police?" Michelle stood, ready to get back in line.

Tiffani gave a loud sigh, and Michelle could imagine her friend's pouty face. She was lucky it was Tiffani who called and not Wendy. She knew Tiffani would relent when Wendy would have demanded a full debriefing.

"Okay," Tiffani said. "Do you have any idea when they might be calling? I have a pedicure scheduled tonight."

Anyone else might have found Tiffani's lack of concern over finding Amanda's killer callous, but Michelle knew Tiffani kind of lived in her own little world and things like this never really penetrated her mind.

"I don't know, but I would assume pretty soon since they are done with me and it's possible you guys were the last people to see her alive." Michelle worried this last bit might unnerve Tiffani the minute it was out of her mouth.

"Oh, good, I won't cancel anything yet, then. Talk to you later."

Michelle shook her head at her friend's innocence and rejoined the line. Fifteen minutes later, she left with a bag containing a Caprese sandwich, a bowl of potato salad, and three chocolate chip cookies. The smell made her mouth water and she considered finding a quiet table by the water to dig in right away, but the crowd seemed to have doubled while she was inside and now it was a struggle just to walk back to her car.

In the parking lot, it was her turn to be stalked for a parking spot, causing her to hurry to snap her seatbelt and back out. After several narrow escapes with other vehicles darting in front of her or backing without looking, she was thankful to catch a green light out of the parking lot and headed home.

# CHAPTER EIGHT

Lex drove under the porte-cochere and brought the first limo to a smooth stop. He tipped his hat to Stephen as he exited the vehicle. Stephen gave a subtle nod, then turned his attention to the back door. Lex opened it and assisted a tall, slender woman in her late fifties, with dark blonde hair styled in a short bob and tucked behind both ears. Stephen recognized her as the owner and president of Silken Pleasures and stepped forward to greet her.

"Mrs. Therriault, welcome to Hotel Lago, I'm Stephen." Stephen felt her look him over before accepting his offered hand. Then she reached up and fixed the collar of his shirt. He was mortified. Already she was correcting him and she hadn't even entered the building.

The next woman to emerge from the vehicle was the vice president, Heidi Pullerton. She stood two inches shorter than Mrs. Therriault, with silky black hair that fell to her waist, olive skin, and piercing blue eyes. Stephen knew her mother was Japanese and her father had been stationed at a military base in Okinawa when the two met.

"Ms. Pullerton, a pleasure to meet you." Stephen shook her hand as well, then stepped aside so Ben could greet the remaining executives.

Stephen escorted the two women inside, bypassing the front desk. He took them straight to their rooms and handed them their keys. Heidi went to the Lake Trasimeno suite with her boss and they made a tour of the three rooms together. Stephen remained in the entryway, waiting to see if there was anything he could do for them before returning to oversee the rest of the group's check-in.

"This will do," Mrs. Therriault finally said. "Go with Heidi and make sure she is comfortable, then have a bottle of champagne sent to my room."

Stephen assured her it would be there in minutes, then showed Heidi to her room. While he waited for her to scrutinize the room, he quietly called room service for a bottle of Perrier-Jouet champagne and a bottle of Brocard Chablis Grand Cru, for Ms. Pullerton's room.

"I don't see the bottled water I requested," Heidi complained when she completed her tour.

"We put it in the refrigerator for you." Stephen stepped into the sitting room where there was a wet bar and opened the small refrigerator to show her the twelve bottles of Evian lined up exactly as she had requested, with the labels at a ninety degree angle to the door. Heidi smiled and plucked one of the bottles from the shelf.

"Is there anything else I can do for you? A bottle of Chablis will be here in a few minutes."

She took a step closer and placed her palm on his cheek. Her skin was soft as silk and he felt his heartbeat quicken. Her smell was intoxicating and he couldn't take his eyes off hers. She gave his cheek a gentle pat and turned her back on him.

"I need to rest. You may go now." She walked into the bedroom, unzipping her dress as she walked. Stephen watched her gently swaying hips until she closed the bedroom door behind her.

Stephen returned to the desk, ripped off his suit coat, flicked on the desk fan Lizzie kept in her office, and held it up to his face.

"What's the matter?" Ben asked.

Stephen shook his head and then fluffed his shirt, trying to cool down. His heart raced, from both anxiety and attraction. He'd never met a woman as beautiful as Heidi.

"We should have a few minutes of peace while they settle into their rooms. Did you get everyone else checked in okay?" Stephen asked.

"Yeah. I can't believe there are only two guys on the entire executive board," Ben shrugged, "but then again, it is a make-up company. Not many guys I know who would want to deal with that crap."

"Not just cosmetics; fragrances, and lingerie as well," Stephen corrected.

"Well, the lingerie I wouldn't mind being an executive of," Ben replied with a wicked grin.

"Where's Jessica?"

"One of the women, Donna Katanis, I think it was, isn't she the assistant? Anyway, she wanted to have some of her things pressed. Jessica is waiting for her to unpack so she can deliver them herself." Ben rolled his eyes. "Who wants clothes ironed as soon as they arrive at a hotel?"

"Okay. I'm going to check with chef and make sure everything is going smoothly for their dinner." Stephen set the fan down and slipped his coat back on. "Oh no," he paused, "did anyone mention if they'd had lunch yet? It's not on their schedule, but I didn't even think to ask."

"They ate on the plane, had it catered before they left Islip," Ben replied.

"Oh, good, call if you need me."

"You're just going to the kitchen," Ben teased.

Stephen pushed the swinging door from the service corridor to the kitchen and was assailed with the smells of rosemary, basil, roasting chicken, and apple pie. He inhaled deeply and realized he hadn't eaten since six that morning. He'd have to see if he could grab a sandwich on his way out.

Chef Gustave stood behind a massive stove with eight gas burners. A pot of vegetable soup simmered on one burner, while three others were occupied with asparagus, boiling potatoes, and some kind of sauce Stephen didn't recognize.

"Did the big ladies arrive?" Chef Gustave asked without looking up.

"They did. Everything smells so good." Stephen had learned to flatter the chef before asking him for anything.

Gustave frowned and lifted a spoon of the sauce to his nose. "It's okay, not my best."

"What is that exactly?" Stephen asked with a bit of trepidation.

Gustave looked at him for a moment and laughed. "You've never had *béchamel*?"

"Becha what?" Stephen looked bewildered. He'd been studying French cooking the past month, trying to learn more about the chef's homeland, but he didn't recall reading about this.

"It's a basic French sauce that can accompany white meats like rabbit, pork, and chicken or it can be used as a filling in lasagna. It is quite simple really, just butter, flour, milk, nutmeg, salt, and pepper, but you can use this base to make a Sauce Moutarde by adding egg yolks, French mustard, parsley, and lemon juice. It's been a few years since I last made it, so I have been practicing. Something just isn't right, though."

The chef sighed and dumped the contents of the saucepan into a nearby garbage can.

"It sounds," Stephen paused searching for the right word as his stomach roiled, "delicious."

"Don't judge it before you try it. I will save you some for dinner tonight." Chef Gustave reached for a new pan and cut in two sticks of butter.

"Oh, you don't have to do that." Stephen tried to beg off, but the chef would not be deterred. "Okay, I will give it a shot later. How's everything looking for their dinner?"

"You know me. It will be beyond their wildest dreams." Chef Gustave puffed out his chest and gave Stephen a large smile.

"Just don't make it so good you can't meet their expectations for the rest of the week," Stephen chided. The chef looked abashed.

"Do you not know by now, every meal is better than the last with me?"

Stephen chuckled. "Yeah, yeah, I hear you. We'll just have to see if that stands true when these guests leave." On his way out, Stephen stopped near one of the line cooks.

"Anything left over from lunch?" Stephen asked out of the side of his mouth.

The cook gave him a sidelong look and then flicked his eyes across the room towards a walk-in cooler. Stephen made his way to the cooler and went inside. A minute later, the cook met him and pulled a covered plate from behind a giant jar of mayonnaise.

"I thought you might forget to eat today." The cook offered Stephen the plate with a shy smile.

"Thank you, Marco." Stephen took the plate, peeked under the foil, and found a grilled chicken sandwich with pesto, tomato, and lettuce on a focaccia bun, along with sliced fruit.

"Tell Ben and Jessica. I have one for each of them as well, if they haven't already eaten," the cook whispered. He was new to the kitchen staff and was always trying to please Lizzie and her team. Stephen wondered if he wouldn't rather be in the front office with them.

"I haven't even had time to ask. I'll send them down as soon as I can. Thanks again." Stephen threw a cloth napkin over the plate and slipped out of the kitchen.

He crossed the hall and turned right, then exited the back doors onto the loading dock. The sun was shining and the sky was crystal clear, the kind of sky Florida only saw in the winter when the weather was cold enough to keep the humidity down. He jogged past a few housekeepers loading laundry to be cleaned into a van and settled at a picnic bench. There was a light breeze and the temperature was in the fifties, but it felt good to Stephen. He placed the black cloth napkin on his lap and pulled back the foil from his plate. He said a quick prayer, then dove into the sandwich. It took him only five minutes to inhale the meal, then he scurried back to the office.

Jessica was sitting on the edge of Stephen's desk, laughing with Ben when Stephen returned to the office. She stood and sobered as soon as she saw him.

"I hear we don't need the extra sheets after all," she said.

"Maybe not, but it won't hurt to have them on hand in case something happens. Thanks for doing that." Stephen ran his fingers through his hair, trying to focus on what needed to be done next. "Marco has a plate for each of you in the kitchen. Have you had lunch yet?"

"I ate before I came in, figured we wouldn't have much time for a break this evening. Do you think he will hold it for me until later?" Jessica asked hopefully.

"I'm famished," Ben replied. "I'll see if he can tuck away a plate for you. Mind if I head down there now?" he asked Stephen.

"Sure, go ahead. No calls while I was away, right?"

"Not a peep. Maybe they are already sloshed and passed out." Ben laughed and headed for the door.

The thought horrified Stephen. "No! That would be awful. If they miss their dinner tonight, Chef will kill me. He's been planning this menu for three weeks. You know how much he hates people dictating to him and we've received close to a hundred emails about the food for this week."

Jessica rubbed gentle circles in the center of Stephen's back. "Don't worry. I'm sure they are catching up on emails and calls. These types don't ever leave the office. They'll be calling you soon enough." As if on cue, the phone rang. Stephen looked at the caller ID, Renee Therriault. He took a deep breath and answered.

"Good afternoon, Mrs. Therriault, this is Stephen, how can I help you?"

"Did all of our boxes arrive? I would like to make sure the deliveries for this evening are made by the time we return from dinner." Renee Therriault spoke with such an air of superiority it made Stephen shrink inside himself.

"We received twelve boxes this morning. Would you like to review them?" Stephen tried to keep his voice from shaking.

"No, I'll send Donna down to do that. She has the lists of who gets what. She'll be downstairs in ten minutes."

"Very good, I'll be waiting for her. Is there anything else?" He was afraid of the answer, but knew she expected him to make the offer. There was a moment of silence and he thought he might escape.

"There is one thing." Renee's voice dropped to just above a whisper. Stephen listened intently, his hand gripping the phone tighter with each word she spoke.

"Yes, I'll see what I can do and get back to you," he stammered. When she hung up, he held the phone a moment longer, surprised by her request.

# CHAPTER NINE

"What's wrong?" Jessica asked with concern.

Stephen dropped into his chair and loosened his tie, suddenly finding it hard to breathe. He looked up at Jessica and saw her lips moving, but didn't hear her. All he could hear was Renee Therriault's sultry voice asking him to arrange a private meeting with Mr. Kingsley, the hotel owner.

Darren Kingsley was one of the wealthiest men in the country. He owned thirty-five resorts and five restaurants. While his main residence was in the exclusive Isle Worth neighborhood of Orlando, he also had homes in Miami, New York, and Italy. The only person who ever knew where Mr. Kingsley was at any given time was his assistant, Lila Harding. Stephen had never spoken to or even seen Lila, much less Mr. Kingsley. How was he supposed to arrange a private meeting with him in less than four days? Fortunately, Renee hadn't made any specific demands on when the meeting should occur.

Jessica tapped him on the shoulder and Stephen jerked.

"What does she want you to do?" Jessica asked.

"I can't talk now. Donna is probably in the lobby already. We have to inventory the gift boxes. Grab your notebook and follow me." Stephen jumped to his feet and raced out of the office.

The elevator doors were opening as he rounded the corner. Donna Katanis stepped off wearing a pair of jeans, a pink button-down shirt neatly tucked in, and a pair of strappy silver sandals. Her chestnut hair was pulled back in a ponytail, adding to her youthful appearance. Stephen guessed she was in her late twenties and wondered how she had landed a job as the executive assistant to a CEO at such a young age.

"Good afternoon, Ms. Katanis, right this way," Stephen greeted her and led the way to the storage room where luggage was held until it could be delivered. One corner of the room was reserved for groups and held a tower of boxes marked with the cosmetics company's logo.

Donna opened the leather portfolio she carried and removed a spreadsheet.

"The deliveries for tonight are in," she moved closer to the stack and scanned the labels, "these two boxes. Would you open them, please?"

Stephen grabbed a pair of scissors from a nearby desk and cut through the packing tape. Inside the first box, he found fifteen plush white bathrobes. The second contained gift boxes with cards already attached to each one. Donna opened one of the gift boxes to reveal a diamond-studded watch and a pair of diamond earrings on a midnight blue velvet cushion. Jessica gasped.

Donna's cool smile quieted Jessica. One by one, she removed the boxes, checking each one and finding the same items inside. The last two boxes were for the male executives, and in place of the earrings were a pair of diamond cuff links. Stephen couldn't believe the amount of money sitting here unattended all morning. He thanked God all of the boxes were accounted for and hoped the other delivery items were of lesser value. Once word got out about tonight's delivery, and he knew it would, he feared the other items might not be safe. Not that they were bad guys, but everyone is tempted at some time, and this may prove to be too much temptation for the guys he knew were struggling to get by.

"Are they all this expensive?" Stephen managed to ask around the growing lump in his throat.

Donna casually waved a hand in dismissal. "You didn't think they would be giving out rubber duckies and magic eight balls, did you? Everything they do is expensive."

"I noticed there is only fifteen of everything, but there are eighteen of you here." Jessica commented.

"Only the execs get gifts. Maggie, Paige, and I are just honored to be here." Donna replied with a roll of her eyes. "For tomorrow night, you will need these," Donna pointed to three more boxes.

Stephen and Jessica worked together to group the deliveries by day as Donna directed. Thirty minutes later, they were organized and ready to go. Stephen looked around the storage room uncomfortably. Bellmen had been coming and going the entire time they worked, making Stephen acutely aware of how insecure this location was. Maybe he would be better off moving everything to Lizzie's office so they could be locked up.

Donna glanced at her watch and gave a loud sigh. "I have to get back upstairs. I'm supposed to do a walk-through of the dining room at four-thirty and there won't be time to change before dinner. If you have any problems call me, not Renee." She handed Stephen her business card with her cell phone number written on it, then let herself out.

"Can you believe these gifts?" Jessica asked when they were alone.

"I wish they'd given me a heads up on the value. Think of how bad it would have been if one of these boxes went missing. I think we should move them into Lizzie's office." Stephen spotted a luggage cart and went to get it.

"Do you think they will all fit in there? And how will we distribute them to the bellmen from there?" Jessica asked.

"I'll find a way to make them fit. I don't want these out of our control a minute longer. We will load them into the office with deliveries at the end of the week in the back and working forward. There aren't so many that we can't have the bellmen come to the office door and get them from there." Stephen started loading the cart, making sure to keep them in order. "I want one of us with each of the bellmen making the deliveries as well."

"Don't you think that's a bit of overkill?" Jessica asked.

"I think we will do whatever it takes to make sure these gifts reach their intended recipients," Stephen replied, annoyed with Jessica's lack of support. "It also protects us if someone tries to claim they didn't receive their gift." A bellman entered and stopped in surprise.

"What are you guys doing?" the bellman asked.

"We need to move all of these to the front office. Would you mind calling a couple of other guys and helping us out?" Stephen requested. The bellman looked over his shoulder and waved at a couple of the other bellmen.

With all of the boxes were loaded, Stephen led the caravan of four luggage carts across the lobby to the front office. He fished out the extra key Lizzie had given him and directed the bellman on how to stack the boxes inside. The bellmen grumbled when Stephen told them they weren't being paid for this little move, but he shot them a look that made them quiet down and retreat with their carts.

"What's next?" Jessica asked as she filled a paper cup at the water cooler.

It was already four o'clock and Stephen was supposed to meet with Chef Gustave to walk through the dinner. "If you could try to find Lila Harding's direct phone number that would be great. Lizzie might have it in her files. If not, try Jonathan."

"Why can't I just call the corporate office?" Jessica sounded annoyed.

"If you think they will put you through to Lila, go ahead, but from what I understand, she doesn't talk to anyone less than a general manager. I'll be back as soon as I can." Stephen scooped up the group binder from the desk and left before Jessica could respond.

The kitchen seemed more chaotic than usual. Stephen could hear Chef Gustave before he could see him. When he rounded a corner, he saw the chef berating Marco, his arms flying in two directions at once. The young cook had his head down and nodded occasionally as the chef yelled. Stephen considered turning around, but found himself more afraid of Renee Therriault than the chef.

"How's dinner looking?" Stephen called over the clatter of dishes and the clang of pots.

Chef Gustave looked at Stephen with a piercing gaze, irritated he'd been interrupted. Marco took that moment to escape. Chef Gustave threw up his hands in a gesture of defeat and approached Stephen.

"That louse was using a paring knife to chop vegetables. A paring knife! Can you believe this?" The chef wiped his hands on his apron.

"No?" Stephen replied, unsure if this was the correct answer.

"See! Even this child knows you don't use a paring knife for chopping," Chef Gustave called out to no one in particular. The rest of the cooks continued about their business, accustomed to these outbursts.

Stephen offered a weak smile. "Other than that, how are things coming along?"

"Why don't you have a look?" Chef Gustave led Stephen to the far end of the kitchen where the banquet staff worked. A dozen cooks worked furiously over pots of vegetables, soups, and sauces; the smell of baking fish emanated from the two large ovens. Two pastry chefs were kneading dough and another was stirring a thick white chocolate sauce.

"One of those hoity-toity women was just down here checking out the banquet room," the chef said. Stephen had to suppress a laugh, considering Chef Gustave was fairly hoity-toity himself.

"Did she say anything?" Stephen asked, trying to suppress a chuckle.

"Not to me. You should talk to Oscar; he's in charge of the dining room tonight." Chef Gustave lifted a spoon of shrimp bisque to his lips. A second later, he was shaking salt and pepper into the pot and chiding the cook standing over it. Stephen left them and entered the banquet room.

The room was quiet after the discord of the kitchen. A long table sat in the middle of the room covered by a plain black cloth. Each setting was built upon a gold charger, topped by a Lennox china plate bearing a delicate gray-green leaf pattern around the edge; a cobalt blue crystal water glass and Wedgewood crystal wine glass flanked the plate, and Reed and Barton classic rose silverware was tucked into a pocket made from a napkin of pure white linen. Three centerpieces of candles surrounded by ivy and white roses were spaced evenly along the length of the table. The chairs were covered in black muslin with a gold bow on the back of each.

Stephen gave a crisp nod to Oscar, the banquet manager, delighted with the elegance of the room. Oscar was equally impressive in a black suit and starched white shirt; his dark black hair curling around his forehead made him look younger than his forty-five years.

"The room looks great," Stephen said. Oscar smiled and crossed the room toward him.

"I just completed the walk through with Ms. Katanis. She asked for a few minor adjustments, but otherwise seemed happy." Oscar turned at the sound of a door opening. Three more staff members entered the room, pushing a metal cart. They scurried around the table, reordering the silverware and folding the napkins into swans.

"Is your team ready for this?" Stephen asked.

"As ready as they can be. They are pretty good about adapting to change, which I think will be their greatest attribute this weekend." Oscar chuckled. "All groups have their quirks."

"I'm learning that," Stephen responded with a sigh. He twisted his arm to look at his watch. "They should be arriving any time now. I'll get out of the way."

Stephen left through the front door into a quiet hallway. The resort had four conference rooms along the hallway before it curved around to join the lobby. Stephen felt drained as he made the short walk to the office, unable to comprehend it had only been a few hours since the guests had arrived; it already felt like a week.

"Hey, I think I might have something," Jessica said as Stephen entered the office.

Stephen frowned and sank into a chair.

"A way to reach Mr. Kingsley," Jessica said.

"Really?" Stephen tilted his head. "How?"

"I've been going through all of Lizzie's cards. She knows a lot of people, and I came across a card for a real estate agent. I thought that was a little odd, so I looked her up online. Turns out she is primarily into commercial real estate and brokered several deals for Mr. K." Jessica spoke fast, barely taking a breath. Stephen nodded for her to go on, but she just stood, smiling.

"Did you speak to her? Does she have a number for Lila or Mr. Kingsley?" Stephen asked.

"Well, no. I didn't think she would give any information to me." Jessica's smile faded.

"And you think she'll give it to me?" Stephen asked. Jessica handed him the business card. Victoria Birmingham, the card read. He noticed it was a local number and reached for the phone. A minute later, he was listening to Victoria's voice mail instructing him to leave a message.

"Good afternoon, Ms. Birmingham. I know it may be after hours, but I am really hoping you can call me back today. My name is Stephen Longbottom and I work at Hotel Lago. I would like to speak to you about Mr. Darren Kingsley." Stephen left both his work and cell phone numbers.

"What do you think the chances are she will call you back?" Jessica asked.

Stephen shook his head. "If nothing else, maybe her curiosity will make her call. I guess we need to keep looking for a way to reach him. Are you sure there wasn't a number for Lila in Lizzie's cards?"

"Not that I saw, but then again, I don't know what category Lizzie might have placed it in. I went front to back though."

Stephen pulled the Rolodex toward him and started flipping through the cards. Florists, car companies, airlines, restaurants, theme parks, hotels, entertainment, everything a guest could possibly want, but nothing for Lila Harding or Darren Kingsley. Stephen dropped his head into his hands and tugged on his hair.

The office door swung open and Ben entered with a bounce in his step. "Jess, you've got to see Marco. He hooked us up good tonight." Ben paused when he saw Stephen. "Oh, hey, Chef wants to see you, Stephen."

Stephen looked up. "Is he mad?" he asked.

"How can you tell? I don't think he can speak without yelling." Ben laughed.

Stephen stood, giving Ben a withering look, and set off for the kitchen.

# CHAPTER TEN

Jeffrey didn't bother turning on any lights when he entered the bungalow. All the hurricanes over the summer had put construction of The Plaza weeks behind and Jeffrey had struggled to get back on schedule without paying overtime. For the past two months, the investors had dogged him relentlessly, but today he'd been happy to report to them that work was back on track.

Now he just wanted to collapse in front of the TV for a few hours. He flopped down on the couch and grabbed the remote off the coffee table. He squinted at the glare as the TV came to life. The local news was on and he was about to turn the channel when the news anchor teased an upcoming story.

"Up next, a brutal murder at a prominent downtown financial investment firm."

Curious, he decided to stay tuned. While the commercials were playing, he rooted around in the kitchen, opening cabinet doors in search of something to eat. He settled on cereal and shoveled Cheerios into his mouth until the news returned. A scene of downtown appeared on the screen and Jeffrey traded his bowl for the remote control when he recognized an office building not far from his construction site. He turned up the volume.

"A young woman was found bludgeoned to death in the bathroom of her office early this morning. Amanda Barnes, age thirty-one was discovered by a coworker, brutally beaten and possibly sexually assaulted."

Jeffrey nearly choked as a picture appeared on the screen of Amanda. He remembered the night he'd met her back in August at a bar in Winter Park. She'd thrown herself at him, but he'd turned her down cold. Immediately his thoughts turned to Michelle.

He met Michelle that same night and felt an instant connection. They went out a couple of times, but one night he'd been drunk and a little too possessive of her. He remembered the shame he'd felt the night he'd tried to apologize for his behavior. Michelle hadn't been glad to see him. He had seen fear in her eyes. That had been the night he'd turned his life around. The night he'd ended up on Lizzie's front porch asking her to tell him about God.

After that night, Jeffrey's feelings for Lizzie had grown stronger. She was kind and understanding. She got the pain he'd been going through since Camylle, his fiancée, died, and she understood why he'd been trying to drown his pain with alcohol. She hadn't judged him and she'd been there to keep him out of the bars those first couple of months after giving his life to Christ.

It hadn't been easy and most of his friends didn't understand the change in him. His best friend, Wally, told him it was a phase and he'd get over it in a few weeks, but when weeks turned into months and Jeffrey's faith grew, even Wally had to admit Jeffrey was a different person. His friends stopped asking him to join them at the clubs and he was spending more time with Lizzie, but when he realized he was getting in the way of the romance struggling to bloom between Lizzie and his friend Ian, he knew it was time to find new friends with the same Christian values. People he could call on when he felt the old urges to party or when he felt the loneliness and grief he still felt over the loss of Camylle. These feelings grew less each day and he knew he was well on the way to a better life.

The news footage switched to a video of the police exiting the building with the woman said to have discovered the body. Jeffrey swallowed a mouthful of air at the sight of Michelle being escorted to an unmarked police car. He reached for his cell phone and pulled up his contact list. Finding Michelle's number, he punched it in and waited for her to answer.

"Hey, this is Michelle. Leave a message." The voicemail beeped. Jeffrey thought a moment before speaking.

"Hey, Michelle, it's Jeffrey Robbins. I just heard about Amanda and I wanted to see if you are okay. I know we weren't really friends, but, well, I just wanted to let you know I am thinking about you. Give me a call if you need to talk." Jeffrey hung up feeling stupid. Why would she call him? She thought he was a possessive creep. She didn't know about all he'd gone through the past four months, but he couldn't stop thinking he needed to see her.

I wish Lizzie were here, Jeffrey thought. The old feelings of self-pity came creeping in and Jeffrey found himself craving a drink. He thought about calling Wally, one of his old drinking buddies, to see if he wanted to go out. He flipped open the phone again and dialed.

"Hello?" a tired male voice answered.

"Hey, Stephen, it's Jeffrey." There was a moment of silence on the other end.

"Oh, hey, how you doing?" Stephen replied, evidently surprised by the call.

"Did I catch you at a bad time?"

"No, what's up?"

"Have you had dinner yet?" Jeffrey asked.

"No, it's been one of those days."

"Want to grab a burger or something? You can tell me about it," Jeffrey replied.

"Um, yeah, I guess we could do that. I need to finish a few things. Can we meet in an hour at Houlihans?" Stephen asked.

"Sure, that sounds good. See you then."

Stephen hung up the phone, puzzled by Jeffrey's call. He rose to make one final check on the dinner for the Silken Pleasures group. In the kitchen, Stephen was surprised to find Chef Gustave in his office. The chef rarely left the kitchen during meal times. Stephen knocked on the doorjamb and entered apprehensively.

"I will not have these women telling me what to do," the chef said in such a cold tone Stephen felt goose bumps prickling his skin.

"What happened?" Stephen asked.

"The executive assistant had the nerve to come into my kitchen and tell me that the soup was wrong." Chef Gustave spat the words with contempt.

"I am so sorry, chef. I will tell her she is not allowed in here," Stephen apologized profusely as if he had committed the crime himself. "I'm sure the meal is perfect."

"Of course it is," Gustave bellowed. "That is what I do, create meals that delight the palate and change the way you think about food."

Stephen stifled a smile, knowing the chef would interpret it as mockery.

"We all know you are the best at what you do and could cook in any restaurant in the world. We are honored to have you here." This was a line he'd heard Lizzie use several times and it always seemed to calm the temperamental chef. Chef Gustave glared at Stephen for a moment, then sighed, and stood.

"I have work to do." Chef Gustave left the office and within seconds, Stephen could hear him calling out orders to the rest of the cooks.

Stephen let out a sigh of relief and a quiet chuckle escaped him. He looked around quickly, hoping no one had noticed, but the cooks were all busy putting the finishing touches on their assigned dishes. Stephen ducked out of the kitchen and went to meet Renee Therriault and the rest of her group.

Renee and her vice president, Heidi Pullerton, were crossing the lobby when Stephen appeared from the service corridor. He hurried to meet them, his stomach doing flip-flops at the sight of Heidi in a skintight gold evening gown. Her silky hair was piled on top of her head with wispy tendrils around her oval face. When she noticed Stephen staring, Heidi offered him a coy smile and a flutter of eyelashes.

"Good evening, ladies," Stephen greeted them. "You both look stunning." He offered the compliment to them both despite not even noticing what Renee wore.

"How are you progressing on my request?" Renee asked curtly.

"I'm still working on it." Stephen tried to swallow the fear this woman instilled in him. "Would you like to wait for the rest of your group or may I escort you to the dining room?" Stephen asked.

Renee glanced behind her and saw three more women and a handsome middle-aged man moving towards them. "We'll wait a few minutes."

When everyone except her assistant, Donna Katanis, had arrived, Renee motioned Stephen to lead them to dinner. Outside of the banquet room, they found Donna speaking with Oscar. With a curt nod to Oscar, Donna turned to offer Renee a wide smile.

"I was just giving the banquet captain your instructions regarding the order of service," Donna reported. Renee nodded and swept into the room. Inside Stephen recognized the president's eyes taking a visual inventory of the room as she moved to the table. She took the seat at the center of the table on the far side of the room with her back to the kitchen.

Stephen stood off to the side and waited as the rest of the executives took their seats. Three servers started pouring wine as soon as the guests were seated. Stephen watched until he felt confident everything was going as planned, then quietly left the room.

Ben and Jessica waited for him in the office. They looked up from the patchwork of business cards on Stephen's desk as Stephen entered and dropped into a chair.

"How's dinner going?" Jessica asked.

"So far so good. I just hope chef doesn't choose this weekend to finally quit. It's bad enough I have to make these women happy, but now I have to worry about Gustave's feelings getting hurt by all of their crazy demands. " Stephen glanced at his watch, then looked at Ben.

"Why are you still here?" Stephen asked. "You were off almost an hour ago."

"I know, but I didn't have any plans tonight so I thought I'd stick around and see if Jessica and I could find a way to reach Mr. Kingsley. Lizzie is so meticulous I couldn't believe she wouldn't have information like this."

"I appreciate that. Did you come up with anything?"

"We found one card, it wasn't in any of the categories; it was actually on the bottom of the file when we removed all of the cards. It's for L.D.K. Enterprises. Maybe the L is Lila?" Jessica suggested.

A light bulb flashed in Stephen's brain. "No the L is for Louis. Mr. Kingsley's first name is Louis but he prefers to go by Darren. Good work guys. Where's the card?"

Jessica handed it to him. It was a plain white card, with no address or phone number, only the name L.D.K. Enterprises, and an email address. Stephen exhaled loudly.

"Well, its better than nothing." Stephen pulled the keyboard toward him and opened his mail program.

*Dear Mr. Kingsley, my name is Stephen Longbottom with the concierge team at Hotel Lago. We have the executive board of Silken Pleasures in-house this weekend and Mrs. Renee Therriault, owner and president of the company, would very much like to meet with you before she leaves on Tuesday. I understand this is an unusual request, but she is quite insistent. I know you may not be in Orlando at this time, but would truly appreciate it if you would let me know if you are available for a meeting.*

Stephen read the email several times before clicking the send button.

"Now we wait and see," Stephen said.

A blanket of fresh snow covered the ski slopes and walkways of the Black Bear Lodge. Lizzie stood by the French doors of her suite, gazing out at the pure beauty as twilight settled on the mountains.

"You're thinking about work, aren't you?" Emma's voice came from behind and Lizzie turned to see her emerging from the bedroom. Emma crossed the spacious living room and pulled Lizzie into a warm hug.

"The boy will be fine. I'm sure you've trained him well," Emma reassured her. Lizzie nestled in Emma's arms, thankful she and her husband Ron had come into her life. Lizzie's own parents had died five years ago. She'd met Emma and Ron at church when she was still recovering from the loss and they'd become like family. It meant the world to her, having them here this weekend, as she met Ian's family.

"I know, but I can't help thinking I should be there, or at least be in town. He has to go out on his own sooner or later, but maybe the Silken Pleasures group wasn't the best choice for his solo flight." Lizzie moved to the couch, curled up with her feet underneath her, and ran a hand through her blonde curls.

"You're only a phone call away if he needs advice." Emma poured a glass of iced tea before taking a seat next to Lizzie. "You need to relax and enjoy your time here. Ian's family seems very nice."

Lizzie smiled. The first six weeks of her relationship with Ian had gone from easy and comfortable to strained when their mutual friend Jeffery Robbins admitted his own feelings for her. Lizzie had felt torn between the bond of shared grief she had with Jeffrey and the intense attraction she had to Ian. Four months later, she was thankful Ian had waited for her to sort her feelings out.

There was a knock on the door and Lizzie jumped up to answer it. Ian stood on the other side, wearing a pair of jeans and a thick gray sweater. Lizzie felt her heart skip a beat when he smiled and pulled her into a warm hug.

"Are you guys ready for dinner?" Ian asked as they walked into the living room. Ron came out of one of the bedrooms, buttoning the cuffs of his white dress shirt.

"I'm ready," Ron replied.

"You're always ready to eat," Emma teased, giving her husband a peck on the cheek.

Ian wrapped an arm around Lizzie as the two couples left the suite, making their way to the hotel restaurant where Ian's parents were already waiting. The lobby was full of families and couples, laughing and catching up on the day's activities. The falling snow deterred many guests from venturing into town for dinner. Fortunately, Cassandra and Colin had been able to secure a table for their party, and the hostess seated them immediately.

Lizzie had only met Ian's parents the previous evening, but she already felt comfortable around them. They were kind and obviously adored their only son. She gave Cassandra and Colin each a hug before taking a seat between Ian and Emma.

"How was the skiing today?" Colin asked after their orders had been taken.

Lizzie laughed. "It was quite obvious I am a Florida girl. I came down on my butt more than my skis."

"Don't let her fool you," Ian chuckled. "She was getting quite good by the end of the day."

Lizzie felt herself blush at Ian's compliment. "I won't be competing any time soon though. What did you guys do today?"

"We wandered around town," Cassandra replied. "There is this wonderful bakery; you and Ian have to visit it before we leave. They have a chocolate croissant that is to die for!"

"Two of my favorite words," Lizzie smiled, "chocolate and croissant."

"There is a good outdoors store too," Colin said. "Weren't you saying you needed some new hiking boots, Ian?"

"Actually, I do." Ian turned to Lizzie. "You up for some shopping tomorrow?"

"Now *there* is my most favorite word. Have you known me to turn down a chance to go shopping?" Lizzie asked, causing the whole table to laugh.

"Ron and I just hung out in the lobby most of the day. He read one of those espionage thriller novels and I watched people while I was knitting," Emma chimed in.

Their meals arrived and they ate in silence for several minutes, savoring the culinary delights. Ian noticed Lizzie picking at her veal and leaned over to whisper in her ear.

"Everything okay?"

"Fine," Lizzie replied.

"Do you want to go call him and see how the arrival went?" Ian asked, knowing she was thinking about work.

"I do, but I'm not going to." Lizzie was both grateful and amazed at how well Ian knew her. "I don't want to undermine his confidence. Stephen can handle this; I know that, I just remember how hard my first solo run was."

Ian looked deep into her eyes and she felt like he could see to her very core, to the places inside where she kept her deepest fear and insecurities. He tucked a curl behind her ear and ran his thumb across her cheek. She couldn't help smiling at him.

Emma watched the exchange and felt tears in her eyes. She had grown to love Lizzie as her own child and prayed God would bring the right man into her life. Watching the two of them in moments like these, she believed her prayers had been answered.

Jeffrey's truck rolled into the crowded parking lot right at eight o'clock and he saw Stephen stepping out of his SUV. Jeffrey found a parking spot and jogged to the front door where Stephen was waiting.

The men greeted each other awkwardly. This was the first time they'd been out together alone. Lizzie was their common bond and they'd gone out a number of times as a group, but Jeffrey felt at a loss without her here now, and regretted making the call.

"How are things going with Lizzie out of town?" Jeffrey asked when they were seated.

Stephen shook his head and then covered his face with both of his hands.

"I have no idea how I am going to make it through this weekend," Stephen muttered.

"That bad?" Jeffrey asked mustering a tone of interest when all he really wanted was to talk about his own problems. Stephen was quiet for a moment, then his words burst forth as though a floodgate had been opened. He spent the next ten minutes relieving himself of the worries of the day sparing no detail.

"And then there is this woman, the vice president of the company, for crying out loud. She's just gorgeous and I think she might like me," Stephen finished.

"Really?" Jeffrey arched an eyebrow, suddenly intrigued. Stephen had never seemed very interested in women when they'd been out before.

"I know, I can't believe it myself. I mean she could be, in fact she probably has been, a model, but I swear, something about the way she looks at me." Stephen's eyes gleamed as he spoke of Heidi.

"She's the vice president? How old is she?" Jeffrey asked.

"Forty-three, I looked her up online. She's never been married either, which I find hard to believe."

"You looked her up?" Jeffrey tried hard not to laugh.

"Well," Stephen's face reddened, "I created profiles on all the execs. Lizzie told me to know everything I could about VIP guests."

Jeffrey took a long drink of water to hide his amusement.

"She's probably one of those women married to her work. She'd have to be to have made VP." Jeffrey took a large bite of his burger.

"True," Stephen replied somewhat distractedly. "What's going on with you?"

"Did you hear there was a murder at an office downtown?" Jeffrey asked.

"If it didn't happen in the hotel I haven't heard about it."

Jeffrey filled him in on what he'd learned from the newscast. "And this girl Michelle, I went out with a couple of times. She's a good person."

"Sounds like you have a thing for her," Stephen suggested, sticking a thick french fry into his mouth.

Jeffrey shrugged, surprised to realize he hadn't been on a date since he and Michelle last went out.

"Maybe I do still have feelings for her." Jeffrey shrugged noncommittally, reached for the ketchup, and pounded the bottle until a large glob plopped onto his plate.

"You should call her," Stephen said.

"I did, it went to voicemail. Everyone she knows is probably calling since seeing her on the news."

"It's up to you, but I'd keep calling if I were you." Stephen replied.

"Says the man who hasn't been on a date since I met you." Jeffrey laughed.

Stephen looked wounded. "How do you know?"

"Well, I just meant, um, you don't ever have a girl with you when we go out with Ian and Lizzie."

"Neither do you," Stephen retorted.

"Good point. It's hard to find a nice girl these days." Jeffrey's voice trailed off.

"Why did you call me?" Stephen asked after several minutes of quiet.

"I needed to hang out with someone who wouldn't let me drink," Jeffrey admitted. "With Lizzie and Ian out of town you were the only person I could think of."

"I'm glad you did."

"All right, enough talk about women, are you going to watch the Magic play this weekend?" Jeffrey turned the subject to more manly topics.

"I'll be at the hotel all weekend," Stephen replied. "I may be able to catch snippets though. I certainly hope they can pull it together and get out of this losing streak.

"No kidding," Jeffrey agreed. The men finished their dinners over conversation about sports and work. Outside, they shuffled awkwardly for a few moments, unsure how to end the evening.

"Thanks for hanging out with me," Jeffrey said without looking at Stephen.

"Thanks for calling. It was a nice break from all the women at work." Stephen smiled, realizing he didn't have many guy friends.

"I guess I'll see you around." Jeffrey pulled his keys from a pocket.

"Yeah." Stephen started to walk towards his car then turned back. "You should call her again."

Jeffrey stared at Stephen's back as he crossed the parking lot and climbed into his SUV. Traffic rumbled past him on Colonial Drive; a constant noise of accelerating engines, tires hitting dips and gaps in the pavement, the occasional car horn, but he didn't hear any of it, just Stephen's parting words.

As he climbed into his truck, Jeffrey again felt the old longing for a drink, for the company of the fun-loving crowd he used to hang out with. It was only nine thirty, but he figured he might be able to find someone he knew at one of the clubs. He'd just stop in and have one drink. Maybe he'd even run into Michelle.

He threaded his way through the parking lot to a side exit onto Bumby and turned left. In less than ten minutes, he was walking down Orange Avenue towards the Loaded Hog.

# CHAPTER ELEVEN

When the dinner dishes were cleared away and they were waiting for their desserts to arrive, Cassandra turned to Lizzie.

"Ian tells us that you are a concierge. I bet you have some great stories," Cassandra said. She placed her elbows on the table, laced her fingers together, and rested her chin on her knuckles, giving Lizzie her whole attention.

Lizzie blushed. "I'm sure you don't want to hear about my job."

"Oh but I do. In my office, we don't get much entertainment. Accountants aren't known for their sense of humor." Cassandra smiled.

"I have to admit I have seen some bizarre things, and it's true what you hear about the full moon bringing out the crazy in people." Lizzie glanced at Ian and knew which story he wanted her to tell.

"Last summer, it was the week of the full moon and we had a man come to the front desk, freaking out about the Bible in the bedside table. He wanted to know why it was there and the front desk agent said they were in all the rooms. The man then wanted us to remove the Bibles from all the rooms."

"Why on earth would he want that?" Cassandra asked.

"He seemed to think there was something in it telling people to kill him," Lizzie replied, shaking her head. "We took it out of his room, which seemed to appease him somewhat, but he was edgy the whole time he was there, always looking over his shoulder as if he thought he was being followed."

Ian shook his head. "I was worried the entire time he was there. I thought he might be a serial killer."

"That's awful. Surely that's a rare case." Cassandra leaned forward and placed her palm under her chin.

Lizzie laughed and spent the remainder of the dinner regaling them with tales of guests who had asked for escort services, children flushing green army men down the toilet, demands for foods not to be touching on dinner plates, and one guest who sent a twenty-page booklet of recipes for the only foods she could eat.

"I thought for sure Chef Gustave was going to quit when he received the recipes. He's very sensitive about people telling him what to do in his kitchen." Lizzie paused and finished the last bite of her chocolate lava cake.

"I don't know how you do it," Colin shook his head. "I would have to keep a lawyer on retainer if I had your job."

"It was tough at first. Some guests can be so vicious and seem to think it is my personal mission to ruin their lives, but after a while you begin to see how ridiculous they are. Whenever I think I've seen it all and can't be surprised anymore, something new happens, but every once in a while there will be a really sweet guest who's so appreciative of the things we do for them.

"We had a couple over the summer that was so sweet. She was getting chemo treatments and I received a postcard from them a couple weeks ago letting me know she is now in remission."

"I still say you are a saint." Cassandra folded her napkin and scooted her chair back. "We brought some board games. Would you all like to come back to our room for a while?"

"That sounds like fun," Lizzie agreed. The group rose and followed Cassandra and Colin to their suite. On the way, Ian caught Lizzie sneaking a peek at her cell phone.

"Any messages?" He asked quietly.

Lizzie shook her head, embarrassed at being caught.

"Good. That must mean things are going well. Stephen would call if he needed something."

Lizzie returned the phone to her purse and pushed thoughts of Hotel Lago out of her mind. Cassandra pulled several games from a cabinet in the living room and they quickly agreed on a game of Monopoly.

Loud music battled on the sidewalk, live bands versus deejays. At the Loaded Hog, a band Jeffrey didn't recognize was playing and he stepped inside, scanning the crowd. He spotted Wally on the far side of the bar and waved. Wally was absorbed in conversation with a slender blonde in a black mini skirt, tight white sweater, and boots that came to her knees. Jeffrey stopped at the bar to order a beer, then made his way over to Wally.

"How you doing?" Jeffrey yelled over the loud music, pounding Wally on the back.

Wally turned around, startled. At the sight of Jeffrey, he smiled and gave him a bro hug.

"Mary Ann, this is my friend Jeffrey," Wally introduced his lady friend.

"Nice to meet you," Mary Ann replied with a flutter of her eyelids.

"What are you doing here?" Wally asked. "You haven't been out in ages."

"I know, I know." Jeffrey shook his head sheepishly. "I've had a lot going on," he lied.

"Really?" Wally asked with surprise. "I thought you were just too good for us nowadays."

"You know that's not the case." Jeffrey was beginning to wonder if this had been a mistake.

"Would you like me to leave you boys alone to catch up?" Mary Ann asked.

"No, no, no." Wally slipped an arm around her waist and pulled her to him. He nuzzled her neck and whispered in her ear.

Mary Ann ran a finger along Wally's cheek, down his chin, gave him a light jab in the chest, and sauntered away.

"Where's she going?" Jeffrey asked.

Wally gave him a wicked grin. "To find you a friend."

"I don't need that," Jeffrey said. "I just wanted to hang out, have a drink, see who might be out."

"Come on, don't be a kill joy. You're here, have some fun. Look, here comes Mary Ann now." Wally nodded toward the blonde, now flanked by a red head and a brunette.

"Jeffrey, I'd like you to meet Fiona and Diane." Mary Ann pointed to the red head and then the brunette. Fiona's green eyes locked on Jeffrey's and he felt his pulse quicken.

"Hi," Jeffrey said.

"You look familiar. Have we met before?" Fiona asked.

"I'm pretty sure I would remember if we had," Jeffrey replied. He hadn't even acknowledged Diane, who now stepped in front of Fiona.

"You want to dance?" Diane asked with a slur. Before he could answer, she had grabbed his hand and was pulling him. Jeffrey gave Wally a helpless look before they disappeared into the crowd.

Jeffrey's dancing lacked enthusiasm. Diane moved closer and cupped the back of his head with one hand while placing the other on his chest. Jeffrey studied her face just inches away. She was attractive, with almond-shaped brown eyes, a tiny nose that reminded him of a cat's, and straight hair that swung just below her shoulders. The song ended and the band announced they were taking a break. Jeffrey took a step back from Diane, freeing himself from her embrace.

"I need a drink," Jeffrey mumbled. He got the attention of the bartender and ordered another beer. Diane appeared at his elbow.

"Aren't you going to order me a drink as well?" she asked.

"Uh, sure, what would you like?"

"Cranberry and vodka," Diane replied.

When the bartender returned with Jeffrey's beer, he ordered the drink for Diane and turned to look for Wally. Some of the crowd had thinned out when the band stopped and he quickly spotted Fiona's fiery red hair. She and Mary Ann were laughing about something, as Wally looked bored. Jeffrey grabbed his beer and moved towards his friend, forgetting about Diane.

Fiona looked him up and down as he approached the group and Jeffrey wished he had worn something different. His jeans were baggy and his sweatshirt was old and worn.

"Jeffrey Robbins," Fiona said. "I knew you looked familiar. I saw an article about your father a few months ago and there was a family photo. He had a heart attack this summer, didn't he? How's he doing?"

Jeffrey felt his stomach clench at the mention of his father. Until recently, he hadn't spoken to his father for years, and they still didn't have much of relationship. Neither man seemed able to forgive the other for past mistakes.

"He's doing well," Jeffrey replied. The heart attack had slowed Edward Robbins for a couple of months, but by Christmas, he was back to his old self, ruling his company with an iron fist.

"You work in construction don't you?" Fiona asked.

"Yeah, I'm the project manager over at The Plaza." Jeffrey was uncomfortable that she seemed to know so much about him.

"I'm surprised you aren't part of the family business." Fiona cocked her head and gave him a quizzical look.

"I tried it but it wasn't for me," Jeffrey told her. "You know, I think I'm going to head out." Jeffrey sat his untouched drink on a nearby table.

"The night's still young," Wally protested.

Jeffrey shrugged and shot Wally an annoyed look. "Where's Tim tonight?" he asked, referring to Wally's teenage son.

"He's camping with some friends this weekend." Wally shifted his weight, and glared at Jeffrey.

"Who's Tim?" Mary Ann asked.

"Wally's son." Jeffrey retorted, then walked away. Outside, Jeffrey took a deep breath of the cold air. Groups of twos and threes passed him on the sidewalk, laughing and chattering. Jeffrey shuffled down the busy street to the parking garage. Inside the truck, he pulled down the visor and stared in the mirror.

What had he been thinking? Why did he still feel like partying would make things better? He knew he should call his sponsor, let him know what had happened tonight. He'd been sober for three months and now here he was back where all his troubles had started. He didn't want a lecture from his sponsor though; he wanted to talk to Lizzie.

Lizzie, Ian, Emma, Ron, Cassandra, and Colin sat around the coffee table, a Monopoly board covered with hotels between them. Lizzie laughed loudly as Ian's game piece landed on Park Place.

"You owe me $1,500," Lizzie gleefully announced. Ian thumbed through his small stack of money.

"I seem to be a little short." He gave her a mournful look. "Would you consider a trade?"

"What did you have in mind?" Lizzie's eyes sparkled.

Ian looked thoughtful. "How about $200, a get-out-of-jail-free card, and this?" He pulled a small box from under the table.

Lizzie caught her breath. She reached for the box, but Ian pulled it back.

"You have to accept the trade, before you open the box," Ian said.

"But what if the box is empty? Then I am losing $1,300."

"I can assure you it's not empty," Ian replied with a smile.

Lizzie flicked her gaze to Emma and Ron. Emma wore a broad smile and gave Lizzie an imperceptible nod. Lizzie opened her mouth to speak when her cell phone rang. She recognized the ring tone designated for Jeffrey and hesitated. She looked at Ian, whose smile had slipped.

"Go ahead, take it," Ian said. "I need some hot chocolate, anyone else want some?" he asked as he stood. The rest of the party accepted and Ian pulled mugs from the cabinet in the small kitchenette. Lizzie answered the phone and moved out into the hallway.

# CHAPTER TWELVE

"Hello," Lizzie said quietly.

"Hey, Lizzie. I'm sorry to bother you, but…" Jeffrey didn't know what to say. How could he excuse calling her when he knew she was with Ian and his parents, that this was an important weekend for them?

"It's no bother," Lizzie said. "Is everything okay?"

Jeffrey didn't answer right away. He watched a couple making out against a silver sports car two rows over from him. Their hands roved up and down each other's bodies. The woman pushed the man back and he bumped against a neighboring car, setting off the alarm.

"Jeffrey? Are you there? What's going on?" Lizzie's voice sounded panicked.

"I'm here. Just a car alarm."

"Where are you?" Lizzie asked.

"In a parking garage downtown. Lizzie, I…I screwed up." Jeffrey leaned his head back against the seat.

"What happened?"

Jeffrey could hear a door opening and he paused before speaking again, imagining her walking away from Ian and his parents.

"I had a drink," Jeffrey finally said.

"Why?" Lizzie asked, obviously surprised.

Jeffrey told her about Amanda's death, calling Michelle, dinner with Stephen, and his decision to look for old friends. Lizzie listened without interrupting.

"When Fiona started asking about my family I wanted nothing more than to slam down the drink I had and chase it with another. I wanted to forget everything. I don't know why I thought I could change," Jeffrey finished.

"But you have changed. Why did you leave instead of having that next drink?" Lizzie asked.

Jeffrey didn't want to answer this question. He knew the truth would make Lizzie uncomfortable.

"Jeffrey?"

"I'm here. It was stupid of me to call you. I'm fine. I'll see you when you get back"

"Stop it. You don't get to call, tell me you are drinking again, and then just drop it."

"I'm not drinking again," Jeffrey yelled. "It was one drink."

"You've only been sober three months. One drink leads to another very quickly."

"I put that second drink down because of you," Jeffrey yelled before he could stop himself. The line was silent for a full minute before Lizzie replied.

"I thought we had talked about that." Lizzie's voice trembled.

"We did, but it's not like that. I just remembered the day you were telling me about how you prayed when you felt the urge to do something stupid and I realized I had to get out of there." Jeffrey held his breath, waiting for her to respond.

"Did you try to call Michelle again?" Lizzie shifted the conversation.

"No. I can understand if I'm the last person she wants to talk with right now. I just wish she could understand things are different now." Jeffrey ran a hand through his hair and massaged his temples. The car alarm still blared. He started the truck and pulled out of the parking space.

"She'll never know if you don't show her." Lizzie replied. "Call her again tomorrow."

"Yeah, we'll see. Anyway, I'm sorry for calling. I'm going home; you should get back to whatever you were doing."

"I was beating everyone at Monopoly," Lizzie replied with a chuckle. "We'll talk when I get home."

Lizzie set the phone on the table, but she didn't return to Ian's suite right away. She fished her wallet out of her purse and retrieved a picture, worn and wrinkled. It was a photo of her parents taken at a Valentine's Day party a week before they died. She ran a finger over the faces as she had so many times before. A knock at the door interrupted her thoughts. The door opened and Ian slipped in.

"Emma gave me her key," Ian said, concern in his eyes. He noticed Lizzie shoving her wallet back into her purse and sat down beside her. "Everything okay?"

"Yeah," she replied wiping away a tear. "Jeffrey just needed to talk. You remember that girl Michelle he went out with a few times?"

Ian nodded.

"One of her coworkers was killed last night and he's been trying to reach Michelle. I guess it stirred up some feelings he had for her."

Ian rubbed her back tenderly and she leaned over, placing her head on his chest. He smelled of pine and rain. He wrapped his arms around her and rested his chin on her head.

"We should get back to your parents." Lizzie's voice was muffled by his thick sweater.

"No rush. Emma and Ron were telling them about their latest trip to Sudan when I left," Ian replied.

"But I haven't found out what you are offering as payment for landing on my property." Lizzie smiled up at him. Ian looked into her tired eyes and kissed her forehead.

"We'll finish the game tomorrow. You should get some rest." Ian loosened his arms and allowed her to sit up.

"You aren't upset with me are you?" she asked.

"Why would I be upset? You were just being a good friend. Jeffrey doesn't have many of those." Ian tipped her chin up and kissed her lips. It was a long, tender kiss that made Lizzie's heart race, then Ian stood.

"I love you," Ian said.

"I love you too," Lizzie replied. She stood and wrapped her arms around him, one of her hands caressing the back of his neck. He stood five inches taller than her and she laid her head on his shoulder.

"Get some rest," Ian whispered. "We have a big day tomorrow." He kissed her cheek and moved toward the door. He turned and smiled before closing the door behind him.

Lizzie suddenly realized how tired she was and how much her legs ached. She wandered into the bathroom and filled the tub with hot water. Lowering herself into the tub, she resolved to push any worry about Jeffrey out of her mind for the rest of the trip.

# CHAPTER THIRTEEN

Just before eight o'clock Saturday morning, Stephen's SUV came to a screeching halt in the Hotel Lago parking garage. Twenty minutes earlier, he'd received a call on his cell phone from Victoria Birmingham, Mr. Kingsley's real estate agent, advising that she had a meeting with Mr. Kingsley that morning. Incredibly, she'd agreed to call him while she was with Mr. Kingsley so Stephen could plead his case.

The murmur of voices and clanking dishes wafted up from the restaurant area, but the lobby was surprisingly empty when Stephen stepped through the side door. He considered the itinerary for the Silken Pleasures group, burned into his memory from days of revisions, and remembered they had their own private breakfast planned for nine thirty. He would need to check in with Chef Gustave soon.

In the office, he stowed his messenger bag under the desk and powered up the computer. The message light on his phone was illuminated and he punched some buttons to retrieve the voicemails. He breathed a sigh of relief when none of them were from Renee Therriault or Heidi Pullerton. He made notes to follow up on later and rushed to the kitchen.

The tantalizing smells of eggs, bacon, and fresh bread filled his nostrils as he pushed through the swinging door. His stomach responded with a loud growl, reminding him he'd forgotten to eat breakfast after Victoria's call.

Chef Gustave held a large stainless steel bowl in the crook of his left arm and vigorously worked a whisk with his right. Occasionally, a splatter of egg would escape the bowl and land on his arm. Stephen weaved around the prep stations and large stoves until he reached the chef.

"Bonjour, Stephen," Chef Gustave cried with a warm smile.

"Good morning," Stephen replied, taken aback by the jovial greeting from the usually surly chef.

"So happy to see you," Chef Gustave beamed. "Mrs. Therriault is such a charming woman. I do not know why you have been so worried about her."

Stephen's mouth dropped open in surprise, sending the chef into peals of laughter.

"Are we talking about the same woman you were cursing just two days ago because she kept changing the menus?" Stephen asked.

Chef Gustave gave a dismissive shrug. "She wants perfection and that is what I give her. We understand each other."

"I see. When did the two of you come to this understanding?"

"Last night. After dinner." The chef set down the bowl of eggs and dabbed at his face with a corner of his apron.

"Billy! Where are my cranberries?" Chef Gustave demanded, startling Stephen, who was still trying to understand the change in the chef's attitude. A scrawny cook scurried over with a glass-measuring cup filled with the dried berries. Chef Gustave tasted one before pouring them into a bowl of flour.

"So the dinner went well?" Stephen asked.

"Of course it did." Chef Gustave seemed tired of this conversation. "Now go; I have to finish these scones before Mrs. Therriault arrives for breakfast." With a dismissive wave, Chef Gustave turned his back on Stephen and focused on adding the beaten eggs to the flour and cranberries.

Stephen turned and wandered out of the kitchen. Guests milled about the lobby as he passed through, but he barely noticed them. When a well-dressed, elderly gentleman called his name, he continued walking, until he felt a hand on his shoulder.

"Mr. Hamish, so sorry, I was-- How can I help you?" Stephen pushed aside all other thoughts and focused on the guest before him.

"I just wanted to thank you for the recommendation of Chez Ambra. The missus and I had the best meal and they certainly made our anniversary a night we won't soon forget." Mr. Hamish pressed a bill into Stephen's palm.

"I'm so happy to hear it," Stephen responded sincerely. "Please let me know if there is anything else I can do to make the remainder of your stay more enjoyable."

Mr. Hamish thanked him again and loped off towards the front door. Stephen shoved the cash into his pocket without looking at it and returned to the front office.

For the next hour, Stephen remained at his desk, praying Victoria Birmingham would call. By nine fifteen, he was beginning to worry she had forgotten.

"Morning boss," Ben said as he took a seat across from Stephen. "How are things looking this morning?"

Stephen ran a hand through his hair and leaned back in his chair. "I may have a line on Mr. Kingsley, and apparently Renee Therriault has charmed Chef Gustave with her feminine wiles. I have never seen the man so happy."

"Well, I'll be," Ben chuckled. "I didn't know old Frenchie could be happy."

"Would you mind popping down to the dining room and making sure everything is ready for Mrs. Therriault and her group? They should be down any minute."

"Sure thing." Ben rose to leave.

"And would you mind sticking around for a few minutes once they get their food, to make sure they are happy?" Stephen asked, feeling awkward giving direction to his peers.

"No problem. I can't wait to see what a happy Gustave looks like." Ben was out of the office in a flash.

A reminder popped up on Stephen's computer screen and he slapped the desk with his palm. He was supposed to be in a managers' meeting in fifteen minutes. He looked around the office, hoping to find Jonathan nearby to beg off from the meeting. He wasn't the manager anyway; why did he need to be there? It wasn't like everyone didn't know Lizzie was out of town.

I'll just wait until the absolute last minute and maybe Victoria will call before I have to leave, Stephen thought. The minutes seemed to fly and before he knew it, the reminder was flashing again advising him the meeting was scheduled to start. He clicked on the dismiss button and locked the computer. He was no more than five feet from the desk when the phone rang. He raced for it, diving for the receiver and answered in as calm a tone as he could muster.

"Good morning, Stephen, it's Victoria Birmingham." Her voice sounded like the most beautiful music he'd ever heard.

"Ms. Birmingham, thank you so much for calling. Are you with Mr. Kingsley now?"

"I'm sorry, but Mr. Kingsley just called to cancel our engagement." She sounded truly sorry, but Stephen didn't need sorry, he needed action.

"I don't suppose you would be willing to give me his phone number?" Stephen asked dejectedly.

There was silence and Stephen realized he wasn't breathing. "If you promise not to let him know where you got it," she replied hesitantly.

"Really?" Stephen exclaimed. He grabbed a pen and scribbled furiously as she rattled off the number.

"Thank you! Thank you so much," Stephen gushed.

"Just remember, you didn't get this from me," Victoria cautioned.

When Stephen hung up the phone, he could barely contain himself. He jumped up and danced around the office. Jonathan appeared from the lobby and scowled at Stephen, stopping him in his tracks.

"Were you planning to attend the staff meeting?" Jonathan asked, trying to sound authoritative but coming off more like a sniveling teenager.

Stephen believed Jonathan's lack of confidence in confrontational situations was a large reason Lizzie had been promoted. She had a way of tackling things head on, and managed to resolve difficult situations diplomatically.

Stephen smiled and hugged the thin front office manager. "I'm happy to attend the meeting." Scooping his notebook off the desk, he practically skipped to the small conference room where the rest of the managers were waiting.

"So sorry I'm late," Stephen apologized as he entered the room. "I had to take a call."

Jonathan took a seat at the head of the table and shuffled some papers.

"Now that we are all here," Jonathan said with a pointed look at Stephen, "why don't we start with a food and beverage report?"

Stephen tried to focus on the reports from each department, but he was anxious to contact Mr. Kingsley. His mind drifted, as he planned exactly what he would say when he reached the hotel owner.

"Stephen, would you mind giving us an update on Concierge and Group activities?" Jonathan asked.

Stephen dragged his thoughts back to the meeting and read off a list of activities for the Silken Pleasures group over the next two days. With them in-house, there were very few concierge rooms available, but he gave an update on the three other guests who would be arriving that afternoon.

"Fortunately, they don't have any special requests yet, as we are stretched pretty thin," Stephen said as he wrapped up his report.

"That about covers it," Jonathan said. "Everyone have a great day."

The meeting broke up and the managers shuffled off to their respective areas. Stephen raced back to the front office and pulled the slip of paper with Darren Kingsley's phone number on it from his coat pocket. He took several deep breaths, trying to slow his racing heart, and dialed the number.

# CHAPTER FOURTEEN

It was after ten in the morning when Michelle rolled out of her bed and rubbed her sleep-crusted eyes. She stumbled into the kitchen and started a pot of coffee. The light on her answering machine blinked angrily. She considered just hitting delete, her finger hesitating over the button, and then pushed play instead.

A stream of concerned friends who had heard about Amanda's murder left messages of encouragement and offers of whatever help she might need. It should've been nice to know so many people cared, but somehow it just made things worse.

Before she'd left the police station, Dr. Mendenhall had recommended a therapist who specialized in trauma. She'd taken the card with no intention of using it, but this morning she wondered if it might not be a good idea to talk to someone. Her dreams had been filled with flashes of the crime scene. Now she could remember almost everything that had happened upon arriving at work Friday morning.

The coffee pot released a hiss of steam as the last of the water dripped into the carafe. She filled a large mug and took a tentative sip of the black liquid, savoring the bold flavor. Grabbing her cell phone off its charger on the kitchen counter, she returned to her bedroom and curled up on the bed.

A message on the screen of the cell phone told her she had fifteen missed calls. She dialed into her voicemail and quickly deleted eight calls, duplicates from her answering machine. On the ninth call, she allowed the whole message to play, then played it again. She saved the message and proceeded to clean out the remaining messages. She wasn't ready to call anyone back yet, so she opened her laptop and composed a group email, thanking everyone for their concern and assuring them she was fine. Then she played the saved message one more time.

She was surprised Jeffrey had called, that he even still had her number, but she was more surprised by the tone of his voice. He sounded concerned for her, as if they were close friends rather than the estranged acquaintances they were. She thought about the last time she had seen him.

She'd been so angry, not just at him, but at herself. Angry she had allowed herself to open up to Jeffrey, believe he might be different from the other guys she'd dated. Ever since she'd broken up with DJ, she'd been more cautious, to the point of not dating at all for nearly two years. She'd felt an instant connection with Jeffrey the first time they met. When he had turned down Amanda's advances, Michelle was sure he was different from the guys she'd dated in the past, but that thought was short lived when his possessive side came out on their second date. Unconsciously, she rubbed the tiny scar above her right eye.

With a groan of frustration, Michelle tossed the cell phone to the other side of the bed and pulled the covers up over her head. In the quiet darkness under the blankets, she willed herself to sleep.

Fifteen miles away, Jeffrey jogged up the driveway to his bungalow, chest heaving from his morning run. Since giving up the party life, he'd taken up running to occupy the excess time he now seemed to have. His thin t-shirt clung to his chest and sweat poured off his face. He walked in several circles around the front yard before performing some cool down stretches.

Inside, he guzzled a bottle of water before peeling off the wet clothes and jumping into the shower. He emerged from the steamy bathroom ten minutes later, feeling refreshed, but still restless, unable to get the picture of Michelle being escorted out of her office to a police car out of his mind. There hadn't been any mention on the news that she was a suspect, but she'd looked so scared and vulnerable.

In the kitchen, he rummaged through some drawers, looking for the phone book. Not finding it there, he started pulling open drawers throughout the small house. Finally, under a pile of architectural magazines, he found it.

He flipped through the pages until he found Michelle's name and scribbled down the address. Then he turned to the yellow pages looking for a florist. He hesitated when he found the listing he wanted. Were flowers the right thing? Was there a card that said, "Sorry you found a dead body?" What woman doesn't like flowers, though? Jeffrey dialed the number.

"Hi, I'd like to order a dozen, um, flowers, roses I guess," Jeffrey said when the phone was answered, realizing he didn't know what kinds of flowers Michelle liked.

"What color, sir?" a bored-sounding voice asked.

"Um, well, I, what colors do you have?" Jeffrey stammered.

"White, red, pink, yellow, and purple," was the rather annoyed reply.

"White, I think. Maybe yellow. Wait, could you do half white an half yellow?" Jeffrey had ordered flowers before, but hadn't realized it would be so hard in these circumstances.

"Yes, sir. Is this for delivery?"

"Yes." Jeffrey supplied the name and address. "On the card, would you just write, '*Thinking of you, Jeffrey*'?"

"Of course. That will be $65.70. We take Visa, American Express, and MasterCard." With an actual sale confirmed, the clerk sounded the tiniest bit friendlier.

Jeffrey fumbled with his wallet before providing his credit card number.

"Thank you, sir. Your flowers will be delivered before three o'clock. Thank you for calling Fields of Bloom."

The line went dead, leaving Jeffrey staring at the phone before clicking off himself. It was done, no turning back now. Either Michelle would call to thank him or she would call the police and report him as a stalker. He might as well go about the rest of his day.

# CHAPTER FIFTEEN

With every ring of the phone, Stephen felt his chest tighten. What if Mr. Kingsley didn't answer? Would he return the call if Stephen had to leave a voicemail? The ringing stopped and Stephen held his breath.

"You've reached Darren Kingsley. Please leave a message and I will get back to you." An automated voice came on telling him to press five to leave a call back number or one to leave a message. Stephen's heart sank as he pressed one.

"Good morning, Mr. Kingsley, this is Stephen Longbottom, acting concierge manager at Hotel Lago. I sent you an email about one of our guests, Mrs. Renee Therriault, of Silken Pleasures, who is very insistent about meeting with you while she is in town." Stephen left his work and cell phone numbers and hung up, defeat weighing him down.

"Wow, seeing chef so happy is kind of a scary thing," Ben said as he breezed back into the office. "It almost turns the whole world upside down. I mean what's next. Peace in the Middle East?" Ben laughed and plopped into a chair.

"Everything going well with the breakfast, then?" Stephen asked, trying to forget Darren Kingsley and focus on the work at hand.

"Sure. Mrs. Therriault has him eating out of her hand. Apparently, her grandmother is French and his cooking reminds her of childhood visits to grandma's house." Ben smiled.

Stephen nodded. "I remember something about a French grandmother in all the reading I have done about her."

Stephen couldn't stop wondering about Mrs. Therriault's request. Why did she want to talk with Mr. Kingsley? Was she planning to manipulate him in some way? Maybe he should do some more research on Mrs. Therriault.

"Ben, can you manage things for a few hours? The board meeting starts at eleven thirty and they have lunch being brought in at one. They are scheduled to work until five and then they are going out to dinner at seven thirty. I just need you to make sure their cars are here no later than six forty-five. Jessica can handle the three check-ins we have this afternoon." Stephen opened his notebook and searched for a page as he spoke.

"Sure, boss. What are you going to be doing?" Ben asked.

Stephen shot him an annoyed look. "How many times do I have to tell you to stop calling me boss? I'm going to do some more digging on Mrs. Therriault and see if I can figure out why she wants to talk to Mr. Kingsley."

"All right." Ben stood. "I'm going to mingle in the lobby for a bit."

Stephen nodded absently, his fingers already flying over the computer keys to access a website. Over the next two hours, Stephen did search after search on Renee Therriault, but found very little about her personal life.

She rarely gave interviews, and those she had were completely focused on the company. He was able to confirm her marital status by a records search of marriage licenses in the state of New York, but no photos of Mr. William Therriault were available, much less any mention of his profession. Stephen decided to run a search on what he thought was her maiden name, Johnson, and learned that was actually her name from a previous marriage to a Mr. Ronald Johnson. Unfortunately, this name was so common; he seemed to hit a brick wall.

Stephen leaned back in the chair and cracked his knuckles. Every new obstacle made him more convinced there was something Renee was hiding and more determined to find out what that was.

"Hey, Stephen, I think you might need to come out to the lobby." Ben's voice startled Stephen, who hadn't heard the office door open.

"What's wrong?" Stephen asked.

"A couple of the women stormed out of the board meeting and are arguing in the lobby." Ben tried to contain his delight at the possibility of two women engaging in a physical fight.

"What?" Stephen jumped up and ran out the door into the lobby. There he found Donna Katanis, and another woman whose name he couldn't remember, in the middle of the quiet lobby, screaming at each other.

"I am not your lackey! I work for Mrs. Therriault and Mrs. Therriault alone," Donna screamed.

"You work for Silken Pleasures and as such you will do what I tell you," the other woman bellowed, a thick blue vein swelling in her temple.

"Ladies," Stephen said softly, hoping to get their attention without yelling himself. "Why don't we take this discussion someplace more private?"

"Unless your name is on the president's office, I don't have to do a single thing for you!" Donna continued to yell.

Several other guests had left the dining room to see what the commotion was. Stephen cringed at the growing crowd and stepped closer to the women.

"Ladies," he said again in a gentle tone.

"I will have you fired for insubordination! You don't see Renee here fighting for you, do you?" Ellen, that was her name, Stephen finally remembered. He stepped forward and placed a hand on each woman's shoulder.

"Donna, Ellen, please, let's take this conversation to my office." Stephen spoke with more confidence then he felt. "I'm sure Mrs. Therriault would frown upon such a public disagreement."

The women paused and looked at him for a moment, then simultaneously brushed his hands away.

"I can't allow you to continue behaving this way." Stephen spoke before they began arguing again. He waved for two bellmen, who appeared at his side in seconds.

"Will you please escort these ladies to the office?" Stephen asked. The bellmen each hooked an arm around one of the ladies as if they were escorting them to a ball, rather than detaining them. Ellen resisted at first, but gave in when the bellman gave her a tight squeeze. Stephen turned to see Ben standing ten feet away, a smirk on his face.

"Why don't you offer these folks some coffee?" Stephen gestured to the handful of onlookers and turned for the office.

When Stephen entered, he found the two bellman standing guard over the women, glares of hatred flashing from their faces.

"Thanks, guys, I'm sure we will be fine," Stephen said with a pointed look at the two women. The bellmen nodded and left.

"All right ladies, why don't you sit down and tell me what seems to be the problem?" Stephen said, directing them to some chairs.

"She thinks she can boss me around," Donna growled.

"She is an employee of the company, not of—" Ellen started to retort, but Stephen lifted a hand to stop her.

"I got that much in the lobby. Donna, what is it that Ellen wants you to do that has you so upset?" Stephen asked.

Donna looked uncomfortable and dropped her gaze to the floor.

"All right, Ellen, what did you ask Donna to do?" Stephen was growing impatient.

Ellen shifted in her seat and wouldn't make eye contact. "It's really an internal matter. I don't think we should be discussing this with you," Ellen finally replied.

"I understand. Would you like me to go get Mrs. Therriault or Ms. Pullerton for you to speak with?" At the mention of the company president, both women went rigid. Then Donna looked up at him and smiled.

"Yes, perhaps you should get Mrs. Therriault. She should know what her employees are doing," Donna said with a vehemence that surprised Stephen.

"No wait" Ellen exclaimed, jumping to her feet and grabbing Stephen by the arm. "You don't need to get Renee or Heidi involved."

Stephen thought Ellen looked panicked and his suspicions about grew. He removed Ellen's hand from his arm and motioned her to sit back down.

"Obviously, neither of you wants your boss to find out what has happened here, and I respect that, but one more public outburst and I will get her involved." Stephen gave each woman a stern look until they both nodded in compliance.

"We should get back. The lunch break is almost over," Donna said softly.

Stephen watched them cross the lobby until they disappeared down the hallway to the conference rooms. When they were gone, he returned to the desk and began a search on Ellen Cartwright.

# CHAPTER SIXTEEN

After a hearty breakfast of eggs, pancakes, bacon, blueberry muffins, and lots of coffee, Lizzie felt too full to move, but Ian was ready to hit the slopes again.

"I promise you will do better today, and it's good for you to keep moving. It helps with the pain." Ian's energy was contagious, so despite a feeling of drowsiness and aching legs, Lizzie pulled on her ski suit, gloves, and knit cap. Ten minutes later, they were on the lift to the intermediate trail.

"I spent most of the day on my butt on the beginner's trail. I don't know why you think I can handle the intermediate trail today," Lizzie said.

"Trust me, this slope won't be as crowded. I think part of your challenge yesterday was all the other people. The beginner and the black diamond slopes are always the most congested. This way you can take your time and find your groove." Ian kissed the only thin sliver of her face not covered by the knit cap, scarf, and sunglasses.

"We'll see," Lizzie replied, still unconvinced. "Hey, what was in that box you were going to give me last night?" she asked, suddenly remembering their interrupted game of Monopoly.

Ian grinned. "What box?"

The lift reached the top and the couple scooted off their seats. It took Lizzie a minute to regain her balance and she was thankful the lift was empty behind them as far as she could see.

They swooshed their way to the top of the run. When they reached the edge, Lizzie gaped in awe. The snow dazzled in the morning sun, ice crystals in the scattered trees glittered, and below it all sat the rustic lodge, curls of smoke rising from the four chimneys.

"It's absolutely gorgeous," Lizzie said, feeling overwhelmed by it all.

"It certainly is," Ian replied, but his gaze was focused on her, not the landscape.

Lizzie couldn't help smiling. Ian had a way of making her feel like the most beautiful woman in the world.

"You ready for this?" he asked, clearly excited.

"I don't know," Lizzie replied. "Maybe you should go first and wait for me at the bottom."

"Not a chance. We do this together."

"I guess I'm as ready as I'll ever be."

"On three then. One. Two. Three." Ian pushed off, starting a graceful descent. Lizzie hesitated, then gave herself a much more tentative push. She only moved a few feet before coming to a stop. Ian sliced to the left and brought himself to a halt, turning back to wave her on. Taking a deep breath, Lizzie dug her ski poles in and gave a mighty push.

In seconds, she was flying past Ian, hands tucked into her sides with the poles parallel to the ground, just as he had taught her. She bent her waist and leaned slightly to the left to make a small turn, then back to the right. Ian slipped in behind her.

When they reached the bottom, Lizzie felt exhilarated.

"That was amazing," she breathlessly exclaimed as she pulled the scarf away from her face.

"I told you, you could do it." Ian slid to a stop and side stepped toward her. "You want to go again?"

"You couldn't stop me." She secured the scarf around the lower portion of her face again and started the awkward march to the lift.

They completed five more runs before Lizzie surrendered to exhaustion. They turned in their skis and boots and returned to the lobby.

"Why don't we have some hot chocolate and sit by the fire for a little while, then we can go into town and find that deli my mom was telling us about?" Ian suggested.

"That sounds good. Do you mind if I go sit down while you get the drinks?" Lizzie stretched her arms above her head and tried to suppress a yawn.

"Sure." Ian leaned in and kissed her cheek. "I'll meet you in a few minutes."

Lizzie found a spot on one of the green and burgundy striped love seats in front of the large fireplace. She held her hands out to the fire. Despite the insulated gloves she'd been wearing, her fingers felt frozen. She tugged at the sleeves of her parka until she was free of it and curled her feet up under her on the sofa.

Ian crossed the lobby, carrying two large Styrofoam cups of hot chocolate. He watched Lizzie lean back and rest her cheek on the edge of the sofa. Her curls were squashed tightly around her head from the knit cap she'd worn all morning. Rounding the end of the loveseat, he smiled and offered her a cup. She wrapped her hands around the cup, absorbing the warmth and inhaling the sweet scent.

"Now, aren't you glad we did the intermediate slope?" Ian asked.

Lizzie gave him a playful slap. "You don't have to say 'I told you so.'"

As Ian took a seat next to her, she scooted over and rested her head on his broad shoulder. Ian slipped an arm around her and held her tight. Moments like this were hard to come by in Florida when she always seemed absorbed with work.

"We don't have to go to town if you would prefer to take a nap," Ian said quietly.

"No, I want to go. We have so little time here, and I want to see everything," she replied sleepily.

Ian ran his hand up and down her arm and they sat in silence for several minutes, gazing at the flickering flames. Ian felt Lizzie's body relax and heard her breathing become more even, and knew she'd fallen asleep. He set his cocoa on the end table, took her cup from the loose grasp of her hand, then rested his head on hers and closed his eyes.

Ian was far too happy to fall asleep, though. He wanted to savor every second of this time, knowing with each passing minute, he was losing more of his heart to this woman. He thought about the box back in his room and smiled.

Ian felt Lizzie stirring in his arms and returned from his thoughts of their first days together.

"Are you awake, sleepy head?" he whispered into her hair.

Lizzie rubbed her eyes. "Why'd you let me go to sleep?" she asked groggily.

"It's not often I get to watch you sleep," he replied with an impish grin.

"What time is it?"

"A little after two."

"Do we still have time to go into town?" Lizzie asked hopefully.

"We have all the time you need. I told my parents this morning they were on their own today."

"Oh, but you don't get to see them very often." Lizzie gave him a distraught look, which caused Ian to laugh.

"Relax. We can get together with them after dinner if we want to, but they understand we need some time together too. They're already crazy about you, by the way."

"I doubt that. They've only known me a day." Lizzie blushed.

"A day and a half, thank you very much, and it doesn't take more than an hour to love you." Ian leaned in and gave her a tender kiss.

"I'm guessing you've had a plan all along, then," she said.

"You know me too well. Why don't we get out of our ski clothes and head into town?" Ian stood and pulled Lizzie to her feet.

"How should I dress? Will we be back for dinner?"

Ian's gave her a mischievous smile. "Jeans and a sweater are fine, and no, we won't be back for dinner, but that's all I'm telling you."

"Race you to the stairs," Lizzie said and took off running, leaving Ian behind. He watched her run for a minute before taking off after her, easily overtaking her ten feet from the stairs, but she brushed past him when he paused on the third floor.

Breathless, they reached the fourth floor with Ian leading by half a flight. At the door to her suite, he pulled her into his arms and kissed her again, then released her.

"See you in fifteen?" he asked.

"Okay." Lizzie, eyes dreamy, opened the door and floated into the bedroom.

# CHAPTER SEVENTEEN

Michelle awoke to knocking on her front door. She stumbled into the living room and looked through the peephole. When she saw a short Hispanic man with a vase of roses, she opened the door, certain he had the wrong address.

"Can I help you?" she asked.

"Delivery for Michelle Burton," the man replied.

"That's me," she replied.

The man extended the vase with one hand and a clipboard with the other. Michelle took the vase, surprised at the weight. She tried to hold it in the crook of her arm so she could sign for the delivery.

"Can you hold on a minute while I set this down?" she asked.

"No problem."

Michelle backed into the living room and set the vase on the coffee table.

"Who are they from?" she asked, taking the clipboard from him.

"I don't know, but there is a card." The man took the clipboard back and turned to leave.

Michelle closed the door and moved to the table to read the card. I hope this isn't from some kind of weird crime sicko, she thought, just what I don't need.

*Thinking of you, Jeffrey.*

She read the card three times, unsure if she should be angry or touched. She thought she'd been quite clear the last time she'd seen him; she didn't want anything to do with him, and she hadn't heard from him since. Why now? Just because he'd heard about Amanda's death? That didn't seem like the Jeffrey she knew, or thought she knew. Had she been wrong about him?

She picked up the phone and dialed.

"Hello?"

"Matt, it's Michelle."

"Hey! How are you? Have you heard any news?" Matt's words came fast, with barely a breath in between them.

"Slow down. No, I haven't heard anything, but that's not why I called. I just received flowers, from Jeffrey." She paused, waiting for her friend to answer, but he didn't.

"You know the guy from this summer, the one who got all mad that I wanted to hang out with *Wonderland*."

"Oh, yeah. Why's he sending you flowers?" Matt asked.

Michelle sighed, wishing Matt were a girl who would understand things without having to be told, but he was her best friend. They'd been playing together for almost four years and he knew her better than anyone else did.

"I don't know why he sent them. You're a guy. Why would you send flowers to a girl you haven't spoken to in nearly six months?"

"I wouldn't," Matt replied. "What did the card say?"

"Just, 'thinking of you.' Why is he thinking of me?"

"Maybe he saw you on the news."

"A lot of people saw me on the news, but they didn't all send flowers." Michelle was growing exasperated. "Think about it. Is there any reason you would send flowers to a woman you barely know?"

"I can think of one reason, but it's not one you will like." Matt offered a sly chuckle.

"Matt!"

"You asked." Matt continued laughing. "What does it matter anyway?"

"It matters, because, well, because…"

"Because it doesn't matter. Either you call and thank him or you just ignore it." Matt replied matter-of-factly.

"It's not that simple."

"Why not?"

"Because he left me a voice mail too." Michelle was beginning to feel she might be making a bigger deal of this than she needed to.

"Then call him, or don't. It's your choice. If I remember right, you were pretty mad at him. Why would you want to invite him back into your life?"

"I don't know. He sounded different. Maybe I misjudged him. We were on a date and I did kind of bail on him. He did apologize." Michelle twisted a lock of hair around her finger until it pulled at her scalp.

"Then call him."

"You've been absolutely no help," Michelle replied with a heavy sigh.

"What did you expect? I'm a caveman." Matt paused. "So, you gonna tell me what it was like finding a dead body?"

"Ugh, too soon, Matty. I'll talk to you later." Michelle hung up and reached for the card again, rubbing her fingers slowly over the writing as if trying to divine Jeffrey's motives. What harm was there in calling him? She didn't have to see him. She found the paper where she had scribbled his number and dialed.

"Hey, I'm so glad you called," Jeffrey answered on the second ring.

"I wasn't sure I should," Michelle admitted.

"How are you doing?"

Again, he sounded sincere, as if he'd stopped everything he was doing and his full attention was focused on her.

"I'm okay, mostly I'm tired." Michelle sank onto the couch.

"I can't imagine how awful it must have been for you," Jeffrey replied. "I know we didn't leave things on the best of terms, but if there is anything I can do, I hope you'll let me know."

"Thanks for the flowers. They're beautiful, but you really shouldn't have."

"Would you have called me back otherwise?" Jeffrey asked.

Michelle was surprised his tone was more teasing than accusatory, and felt guilty.

"No, I probably wouldn't have," she admitted.

"There you go then. I had to send them. I hope they find whoever did this soon. Are they putting any extra security measures into place in the meantime?"

"I don't know." The thought hadn't even occurred to her and the idea frightened her. Jeffrey must have sensed the fear in her words.

"I'm sure things will be fine. It's not as if it happened during business hours. Does anyone know why she was in the office so late anyway?"

"No. She and a couple of the other girls had come to see *Tangled Web*, we had a gig opening for *Wonderland*." Michelle felt a twinge of guilt as she mentioned the band's name. "The girls said she left on her own."

"You opened for *Wonderland*? That's great! So things must have worked out with you and Andy."

Jeffrey surprised her again by his support and his apparent lack of jealousy.

"Well, Andy and I are friends, yes, but that's all. He's been dating an actress for the past two years." Michelle suddenly wanted to make sure Jeffrey knew there had never been anything romantic between her and Andy.

"Really? I'm happy to see things seem to be going well for the band. Still the same gang?"

Did she detect a sense of relief in his tone? "We replaced Tina, but other than that, I still play with Jonesy and Matt. We've had a few big gigs, and we don't play at the Loaded Hog anymore. I don't think we will be getting a recording contract anytime soon, but we have fun."

"That's good to hear. By the way, I'm sorry if you aren't crazy about roses. I didn't realize how little I knew about you when I placed the order. What is your favorite flower?" Jeffrey asked.

"The roses are fine," Michelle replied, embarrassed to answer his question.

"But what kind of flowers do you like?" Jeffrey pressed.

"You'll think it's ridiculous."

"Not at all. Every woman is entitled to her opinion on flowers."

"Daisies," Michelle whispered.

"Those big, bright ones? Gerbera, I think they are called, or the old-fashioned white and yellow ones?"

"The old-fashioned ones. They are what my mom had in her wedding bouquet." Michelle felt her face flushing, certain that Jeffrey was laughing at her on the other end of the phone line.

"That's good to know," Jeffrey replied without a hint of derision. "I should let you go. I just wanted to make sure you were okay. Like I said, call me if there is anything I can do for you."

"Jeffrey..." Michelle wasn't ready to hang up yet.

"Yes?"

"Never mind. Thanks for calling and the flowers." Michelle didn't know what else to say. After they said their goodbyes and Jeffery had hung up, Michelle sat on the couch, staring at the roses. She seemed to be seeing them for the first time. They aren't daisies, but at least he got the colors right, and they truly are beautiful she thought.

# CHAPTER EIGHTEEN

The search on Ellen Cartwright was proving quite fruitful. In a couple of hours, Stephen had compiled a biography on the woman that had him on guard. He was surprised a woman with Ellen's background had risen to be an executive in any company, much less one as protective of its image as Silken Pleasures. Her short bio, available on the corporate website, covered her place of birth, college education, husband, and children, along with two previous jobs that apparently made her fit for her current role. It left out her attempts to sabotage one of her former employers when they passed her over for a promotion and her affinity for being in the wrong place at the wrong time, landing her in jail three times, although there had been no convictions.

The scene between Ellen and Donna was starting to take on a more sinister air in his mind, especially in light of both women wishing to keep Renee Therriault uninvolved. Was Ellen plotting against Renee? If so, why didn't Donna want to expose her? Was she involved?

"Afternoon," Jessica greeted the few employees in the back office as she entered. Stephen quickly shut his notebook, unwilling to share his suspicions with the team yet.

"Looks like it will be a quiet night for you, Jessica." Stephen smiled and waited for Jessica to sit down beside him.

"That's good news. I could use the free time to study; art history exam on Wednesday." Jessica pulled a thick textbook from her bag.

Stephen frowned at her. "I didn't hear that. You know how Jonathan feels about us doing anything personal on the clock."

"What else am I supposed to do when it is dead around here? Twiddle my thumbs?" Jessica demonstrated how proficient she already was at this task.

"Believe me, I know how quiet the night shift can get. We only had three concierge check-ins today and two of them are already here." Stephen shuffled some file folders until he found the one he wanted.

"Here's the one still left to arrive. Their flight lands at six and they are renting a car, so who knows when they will show up."

"Got it." Jessica took the file and scanned the first page with all of the pertinent details of the couple. "This is their third visit this year isn't it?"

"I believe so," Stephen replied.

"It's not even Valentine's Day yet. What has them coming here so often?"

"I'm sure it is our warm hospitality and smiling faces that bring them back," Stephen tried to sound serious, but couldn't help laughing.

Jessica smiled as well. "I guess I should be on my best behavior then. Where's Ben?"

Stephen glanced around the office. "I don't know. I asked him to check on the board meeting, but that was hours ago." Stephen began to worry. "I hope something hasn't happened with them and he didn't want to tell me."

Stephen stood and tucked his notebook under his arm. As he was reaching for the door handle, the door flew inward, smacking Stephen in the face. There was a loud crack and he felt warm blood oozing down his face.

"Oh man! I am so sorry." Ben stepped back from the door. Jessica jumped up and ran to Stephen.

"Tilt your head forward," Jessica instructed, guiding him to a nearby chair. "Ben, go get some paper towels."

Tears burned Stephen's eyes from the excruciating pain, but he wasn't about to let his coworkers see him cry.

"We need to get you to a hospital," Jessica said.

"No, I'll be fine. I just need to get the bleeding to stop," Stephen said through clenched teeth.

"Stephen, your nose is broken. You have to get that taken care of," Jessica insisted.

"Just get me some ice," Stephen said.

Jessica shook her head and took the paper towels from Ben, who came running back into the office. She wiped the blood from Stephen's face, but when she touched his nose, he jerked away.

"Ben, will you get some ice please?" Jessica asked. Ben took off at a run for the kitchen. Jessica tried to dab at Stephen's nose again, where the blood continued to flow, but he jerked away again.

"Don't touch it," Stephen growled.

"Someone is going to have to touch it eventually," Jessica replied, tilting his head further forward, hoping to slow the blood flow.

Stephen gagged, reached for a paper towel, and coughed up blood.

"That's it. I'm taking you to the hospital." Jessica pulled him to a standing position and grabbed her purse.

"Not the hospital, but you can take me to the urgent care center," Stephen conceded.

Ben came rushing back with a bag of ice. Jessica took it, wrapped it in the few remaining towels, and handed it to Stephen, who immediately held it to his already swollen nose.

"I'm taking him to the walk-in clinic. Can you manage things around here?" Jessica asked Ben.

Stephen caught Ben's look of remorse out of the corner of his eye and tried to smile.

"Don't worry, it was an accident," Stephen said. "I'll be fine."

"I am so sorry," Ben apologized again.

Stephen patted his shoulder as he walked past. Jessica guided him through the lobby and service corridors to the parking garage. When they reached her car, she opened the passenger door and helped guide him into the seat.

"I don't want to bleed all over your car," Stephen said.

"No biggie, I'll just submit an expense report for the detailing I have done this weekend. " Jessica shut the door and jogged around to the driver's side.

In a matter of minutes, they were parked at the urgent care clinic and Jessica was leading Stephen into the small waiting area.

"Oh my, what have we here?" The gray-haired receptionist asked as they approached her desk.

"Workplace accident, door versus employee," Jessica tried to joke, but the receptionist gave her a disapproving look. "Broken nose, ma'am," Jessica said more seriously.

"I just need you to fill out some paperwork." The receptionist handed Jessica a clipboard with a pen attached. Jessica guided Stephen to a chair.

"I guess I'll fill these out," Jessica said after taking a seat herself.

"Ask away." Stephen gave a tired sigh.

"Date of birth, wow, can't believe I don't even know that." Jessica scratched down his answer and moved through the rest of the questions as quickly as possible.

"I feel like I should ask you on a date now," Stephen joked when they finished the paperwork. "You already know everything about me."

"Stephen, come on back," a short, round nurse called from a door to the left of the reception desk. Jessica helped him stand and pointed him toward the door.

"I'll wait out here for you," Jessica said.

"All right," Stephen replied. He could sense Jessica watching the nurse escort him down the hall until the door fell closed.

The nurse settled Stephen in a quiet room and lifted the bag of mostly melted ice from his nose.

"You did quite a number on this," the nurse said cheerfully. "What happened?"

"I was too close to a door when it was thrown open," Stephen mumbled.

"How long ago?"

"About twenty minutes or so."

"Has it been bleeding the whole time?" The nurse peeled off the pile of tissues Jessica had stuck on his face when they got in the car.

"Yes, ma'am."

"Don't you worry, the doctor will get you all fixed up. You sit tight and he'll be right in." The nurse patted Stephen on the shoulder and left the room.

Without the ice to numb it, a throbbing pain gripped his face, making his eyes water. He could taste blood running over his lips and he desperately wanted to lie down. Before he could get comfortable, the door opened again.

"Good afternoon, Stephen, I'm Doctor Ryan. Let's see what we've got." The doctor's gloved hands pressed on Stephen's nose, causing him to scream out.

"Yep, definitely broken, no x-rays needed for this one," Dr. Ryan announced. "I'm going to try to splint it and see if that helps stop the bleeding, but I may have to go in and cauterize the bleeding veins."

The nurse handed Dr. Ryan a towel. "First, I want you to blow your nose into this towel. It's going to hurt, but we need to clear out any mucous that may be in there before I reset the bone."

Stephen did as he was told and the towel quickly turned bright red.

"Now, I am going to shift the bone back into position." Dr. Ryan formed a triangle with his hands placing all four finger pads against one another, and settled them on the top of Stephen's nose.

"I want you to take a deep breath through your mouth, and when I start squeezing my hands together, you are going to slowly exhale."

Stephen tried to brace himself for the pain as he watched the doctor's hands descend on his nose like a claw. Before he knew it, the doctor's hands were squeezing and he forced himself to exhale. He felt the bone crack again and squeezed his eyes closed against the pain.

"There we go, back in place and the blood seems to be slowing. I'm going to pack this nostril with some gauze since that seems to be where the majority of the blood is coming from." The nurse removed the top of a glass canister and pulled several gauze pads out, which Dr. Ryan then rolled up and slowly pressed into one side of Stephen's nose.

Stephen gripped the sides of the exam table and bit his tongue against the pain.

"There," Dr. Ryan said when he had finished inserting the gauze. "Now, we're going to leave you in here to rest for half an hour, then we'll come back and check on the bleeding. If it hasn't stopped, I'll try to cauterize. I'll have the nurse bring you some Tylenol for the pain."

Dr. Ryan pulled the bloodied gloves off and dropped them in a nearby biohazard trashcan. When the door closed behind him, Stephen let loose a jumble of words, his alternative to curse words, which would mean nothing to anyone within earshot.

"Here you are." The nurse appeared with a paper cup of water and two Tylenol. Stephen took the medicine, wishing it were something stronger, then laid back on the exam table. He closed his eyes and tried to relax, to focus on anything other than the throbbing pain. He thought about Ellen Cartwright and wondered what she might be plotting against Renee Therriault. He reflected on the tidbits of information he'd gathered so far, trying to find a pattern. His brain shifted facts around like pieces of a puzzle and he was starting to form a theory when Dr. Ryan returned.

"Very good," the doctor said when he found the gauze was still relatively dry. "Leave this in overnight, and be careful removing it in the morning as the blood may have dried up around the gauze. If it starts bleeding again when you remove the gauze, come back to see me. You can put some ice on it, but don't leave it on for more than fifteen minutes at a time, and don't take any Ibuprofen or Aleve for the next forty-eight hours." Dr. Ryan smiled. "Any questions?"

"How long is it going to hurt?" Stephen asked.

"A few days I'm afraid, and you will probably have some bruising," Dr. Ryan advised.

"Great." Stephen slid off the table, but as soon as his feet hit the floor, he grabbed for the table, overwhelmed by dizziness.

"Oh yeah, you will probably be woozy from the trauma. I wouldn't recommend driving for the next hour or two." Dr. Ryan reached over to help steady Stephen. "Why don't I help you out?"

Stephen leaned on the doctor's arm and took a couple of baby steps forward, slowly becoming more balanced. At the door to the waiting room, the doctor passed him off to Jessica, who escorted him to the car and helped him in.

"Do you want me to take you home?" Jessica asked.

"No, take me back to the hotel. I'll stay there until I feel up to driving. There are a few things I need to do there anyway," Stephen replied.

"You said yourself it's going to be a quiet night. Why don't you let me take you home?"

"I'm fine. You and Ben can handle the guests. I just need to finish some paperwork." Stephen appreciated Jessica's concern, but he wanted to look at his notes on Ellen Cartwright and see if his theory could be right.

# CHAPTER NINETEEN

Stephen sank into his desk chair and flipped his notebook to the pages of scribbled notes about Ellen Cartwright's past exploits. There had never been enough proof for one of her former employers to press charges against her for sabotage, but she had been let go, very discretely.

He found her arrest record and learned she had been caught breaking and entering the offices of another employer, but a lawyer was able to make a case that there had been a misunderstanding and the charges were dropped. She'd also been suspected of embezzlement at a third company, but again, the charges were dropped. Stephen couldn't understand how a woman with her history had been hired as the Creative Director for Silken Pleasures.

An alert appeared on his computer screen and he groaned. The fundraising dinner for Eli's Hope was in two hours and he'd completely forgotten about it. He looked around the office, but Ben and Jessica were not in sight. He dialed Jessica's cell and waited.

"Hello?" Jessica sounded distracted.

"Jessica, I need some help," Stephen replied.

"Eli's Hope, I know, already on it," Jessica said.

"Really?" Stephen was surprised by her initiative. She'd been the team member who seemed completely happy to wait for an order to be given rather than thinking for herself.

"I didn't think you were presentable enough to be meeting people." Jessica laughed. "With that roll of gauze sticking out of your nose, you would have scared them all away."

Stephen chuckled. "You're right. Thanks, I appreciate you being on top of things."

"No problem. How are you feeling?"

"Better. I'll stick around until things get under way in case you need anything, then I'm going to head home."

"You don't have to stay for me. Chef has things under control in the kitchen and Oscar has the service staff ready to go. All I'm going to be doing is shaking some hands," Jessica replied.

"I'm finishing up a few things anyway. I'll send you a text when I leave." Stephen felt uneasy about leaving Jessica alone, but Lizzie had taught him, sometimes you have to be given the chance to stand or fall on your own.

"Have a good night." Jessica hung up.

Stephen ripped the scribbled pages from his notebook and started a clean sheet with a basic timeline of the facts of Ellen Cartwright's professional life. It may not be any of his business, but he felt an obligation to let Renee Therriault know of his suspicions.

# CHAPTER TWENTY

Ian slid the jeep into a spot along Main Street and cut the engine. His gaze passed over the signs hanging from the colorful awnings as he rounded the car to open the door for Lizzie.

"Is there anything in particular you would like to shop for this afternoon?" Ian asked.

"No, I just want to stroll and stop when something catches our fancy," Lizzie replied.

Ian reached for Lizzie's hand. Even through their gloves, he could feel how delicate it was in his large palm.

They started down the street, pausing to look into shop windows. At the Gourmet Pantry, Lizzie paused and Ian opened the door. He followed her up and down row after row of the tiny store. She stopped every ten feet, picking up some new cooking gadget.

"Look at these tart pans. Aren't they just darling?" Lizzie asked, holding up a pan not much bigger than her palm.

Ian smiled and nodded. One of the first things he'd learned about Lizzie was her love of cooking, especially baking. She loved to entertain guests and the more food involved the better. At Thanksgiving, Ian had been amazed at how she managed to prepare an entire feast for ten of her friends who weren't able to go home for the holiday, and she took what was left over to the hotel for everyone who was working. If anyone had asked him what Lizzie's ministry was, he would have said feeding people.

A meal with her was never just a meal, though. It was an event, with cloth napkins and themed china. She put as much thought into the presentation of the food as in the preparation.

"What do you think of these?" Lizzie asked, holding up a set of cookie cutters in the shape of a dove, a cross, and some kind of flower.

"For Easter dinner, I'm guessing." Ian smiled.

"I was thinking more for Easter cookies, but I could roll out croissant dough and have fun shaped rolls also." Lizzie took the cookie cutters to the register and checked out.

The sun was starting to sink behind Bear Mountain when they returned to the sidewalk. They turned so the sun was at their backs and continued down the street. When they came to an outdoors store, Ian veered off toward the entrance.

"Do you mind?" he asked.

"Of course not." Lizzie stepped inside and followed Ian as he rummaged through racks of sweatshirts and jackets, studied packs of dehydrated trail food, and admired several snowboards. Lizzie found a pink and gray plaid hat with earflaps and put it on.

Ian laughed, and cupped her face with both his hands. "You look adorable. We have to get it."

"When would I ever wear this at home?" she asked, tugging it off

"We get a few cold days. Anyway, you can wear it when we come back here next year." Ian leaned down and kissed her, sneaking the hat from her hands while she was distracted.

"What are you doing?" Lizzie asked, laughing as he held the hat out of her reach. When he reached the checkout counter, he handed the hat to the clerk before Lizzie could snatch it.

"I don't need a bag," he told the cashier, handing him several bills. The cashier gave him the change, removed the tag, and returned the hat to Ian.

Outside, Ian put the hat on Lizzie and positioned it so that the flaps covered her ears and the brim covered her forehead. Her blonde curls flipped up under the edges of the hat and he felt his breath catch in his throat. Lizzie turned to look at her reflection in the mirror and burst out laughing. "See, you are now the fashion plate of town and everyone will be sporting one of these by the end of the week." Ian wrapped an arm around her waist and pulled her close as they wandered on down the street.

"Aside from the ridiculousness of it, I guess it doesn't look half bad," she admitted.

When they reached a small alley with white lights crisscrossing overhead, Lizzie followed as Ian turned and they walked toward a small courtyard. Snow crunched under their feet, not having been cleared after yesterday's shower. The narrow walls of the alley made it impossible to see anything in the courtyard other than a fountain, now silent, with icicles hanging from the three levels. When they emerged into the courtyard, Lizzie was surprised to find an elegant bistro at the far end. Topiaries stood on either side of the large plate glass window in the shape of hearts, with red silk roses woven into the greenery. *Bistro Amore* was written in black letters across the front door.

"I hope you're hungry," Ian said, stopping in front of the bistro.

"Famished actually," Lizzie replied, stepping through the door he held open for her. Inside, the restaurant was dimly lit with hundreds of white, votive candles in small glass vases scattered on the tables and tall pillar candles perched in sconces along the walls, but only one table, in the center of the room, was set, ready for service.

"It doesn't look like they are open yet," Lizzie whispered, turning back to Ian.

"I don't know, maybe you should ask the hostess." Ian pointed.

Lizzie turned back around to find a young woman with long black hair, wearing a red velvet skirt that flowed to her ankles coupled with a white blouse standing before her, holding two menus.

"Good evening, Ms. Reynolds, Mr. Cavanaugh. Your table is ready for you." The hostess led them to the center table and pulled the chair out for Lizzie, waiting until Ian was seated to hand out the menus. When she did, Lizzie gasped.

The front of the menu had Lizzie and Ian's names on it, with the date, and a photo from their first date at the Samba Room.

"Happy Valentine's Day, Lizzie," Ian said.

"But Valentine's Day isn't until Monday." Lizzie gave him a confused look.

Ian reached across the table and took her hand. "I know you aren't the biggest fan of this Hallmark holiday, but I wanted to do something special for you. I thought maybe if it wasn't on the actual day, you wouldn't think it was just part of the commercialism."

Lizzie felt walls built up over years of disappointment crumble in her heart. She wrapped his hand in both of hers and gazed into his eyes, hoping he understood how much his words meant to her.

"Do you want to look at the menu?" Ian asked

"I don't know if I can take my eyes off you," Lizzie whispered.

"Maybe I should read it to you then. There aren't many choices, though. To start, a butternut squash soup, followed by a Caesar salad, then maple glazed salmon, mashed potatoes, and asparagus, and for dessert, well, I'll let that be a surprise."

"My favorites," Lizzie said, her heart racing.

"I'm happy to hear that," Ian replied with a laugh.

"How did you do this?" Lizzie asked.

"I just made a reservation," Ian replied innocently. "Isn't that something you do all day at work?"

Lizzie looked around the restaurant and laughed. "Hardly. I don't think I have enough pull to get an entire restaurant for one guest."

"I guess you just don't know all the right people then."

"Come on, you have to tell me."

"I went to school with the owner, and I have to be honest, they will open to everyone else at eight. He agreed to open early for me as a favor."

"Very impressive favor."

"A high compliment coming from the queen of making the impossible happen," Ian replied.

A waiter approached with a tray containing their soup and a bottle of wine. Lizzie leaned over the bowl of soup and breathed in the warm aroma, feeling any lingering chill in her bones fade away. The server poured a taste of wine into Ian's glass. He swirled it around, gave it a good smell, swished a bit in his mouth, and gave his approval. When their glasses were filled, the waiter retreated. Ian raised his glass.

"A toast. To the first of many Valentine's Days together." They clinked their glasses and took a sip of the chilled Riesling.

Lizzie slurped at the hot soup, her taste buds going wild as the liquid slid over them. She closed her eyes, allowing her sense of taste to take over as she picked out the flavors of saffron, nutmeg, and cinnamon.

"You can never repeat this, but this soup is so good, I may have to suggest Chef Gustave visit your friend for some pointers." Lizzie opened her eyes to find Ian watching her with pleasure.

"I'm glad you like it," Ian said, dipping his own spoon into the creamy yellow soup.

The salad and then the main course were served, each bite seemingly better than the last. Lizzie cleaned each of her plates and sat back with a sigh of contentment as the waiter removed the empty dishes.

"I know you said there was dessert, but I don't think I could eat another bite," Lizzie said and dabbed at the corners of her mouth with her napkin.

A look of disappointment clouded Ian's face and Lizzie regretted her words.

"But, I could probably share with you," she quickly added.

"I understand if you are too full. We can always have something later. The night is still young." Ian pushed his chair back. "Wait here a minute." He turned toward the kitchen and slipped through the door.

Lizzie rubbed her stomach as if that would speed along her digestion, and glanced around the restaurant. She could see twenty other tables, each covered in a black cloth. She could hear more voices from the kitchen as they prepared to open to the rest of their patrons. Without warning, the hostess appeared at Lizzie's side.

"How was everything?" the hostess asked.

"It was perfect. Please send my compliments to the chef. I can't remember a better meal." Lizzie smiled and extended her hand. "Thank you all for making this such a memorable evening."

"It has been our pleasure. Ian has been such a good friend to my husband. When he called us, we were happy to help him."

"You and your husband are the owners?" Lizzie jumped up from her chair and pulled the woman into a hug that nearly knocked them both over. "This truly has been the best night of my life."

The woman's eyes sparkled. "Ian is always full of surprises." With that, she faded into the darkness.

Lizzie sat down again and pulled her phone from her purse. As she was typing a text message to Emma, Ian returned and pulled her to her feet, wrapping her in his arms and holding her close to his chest. She rested her ear over his heart and listened to the steady thump.

"Where to next?" she murmured.

"That would ruin the surprise wouldn't it? Let's just see where our feet take us." Ian led her out of the restaurant back to Main Street.

# CHAPTER TWENTY-ONE

The streetlights, shaped like old-fashioned gas lamps, were illuminated when Ian and Lizzie left the bistro and returned to Main Street. Ian clasped Lizzie's hand as they joined the flow of tourists and locals filling the sidewalks.

"I need to pick up some gifts for everyone back home," Lizzie said as they approached a little boutique.

"Sure." Ian held the door open and watched as Lizzie was drawn to a table of black bear themed dishes.

"These will be cute for the Concierge Club," she said, holding up several coffee cups.

"Let me help you." Ian reached for a shopping basket and gently placed the collection of cups inside. He followed Lizzie around several displays and suppressed a smile each time she fingered a serving dish, knowing she was trying to come up with a reason why she might need it.

"Why don't you get one for yourself?" he finally asked when Lizzie returned to the same platter for the third time. It was oval, with several trees and a large black bear on it.

"When would I ever use it?" she said with a trace of longing.

Ian picked up the dish and studied it. "Maybe you could use it to serve s'mores or at Christmas you could fill it with cookies." He paused and his gaze locked with hers. "Or you could just put it on display as a reminder of this trip."

Lizzie nodded and leaned in to kiss him as he added the dish to the basket. They moved to the counter and the sales clerk carefully wrapped each piece in thick paper.

"What do you think of these?" Ian asked, holding up a pair of earrings shaped like skis. "I think I will get them for Mom."

"She will never wear those." Lizzie giggled.

"Oh, you don't know my mother very well yet. She loves stuff like this," Ian replied in a serious manner. "She has a whole collection of jewelry inspired by whatever sport I was interested in at the time."

Lizzie doubled over with laughter. "You were the kid who gave his mom the soccer ball charm for her birthday and matching earrings for Christmas, weren't you?"

Ian pouted. "What's wrong with that? She's always been very supportive of my athletic endeavors."

Lizzie's laughter shook her shoulders and seemed contagious. Ian struggled to keep a straight face, but soon he succumbed to his own laughing fit.

"Okay, so she doesn't have a whole collection, but she will like these. She can wear them while she is skiing, won't be completely devastated if she loses them, and they do represent her favorite pastime." Ian tucked the box into his coat pocket and rubbed a finger over the similarly sized box already there.

"How about we get some coffee," Ian suggested. He led her down a side street, into a bakery that smelled of cinnamon, fresh bread, chocolate, and fresh ground coffee.

"What? No private table here?" Lizzie asked.

"Sorry, we will just have to slum it with the rest of town," Ian replied and pulled her into a hug, inhaling the scent of rosemary and mint from her hair. "You can have whatever you want, though."

"I'll have a vanilla chai latte, please," Lizzie placed her order. Ian studied the menu and the display cases, rubbing his chin thoughtfully.

"I think we will also have two glasses of Banfi Rosa Regale and two red velvet cupcakes." Ian pulled out his wallet.

Instead of pulling a cupcake from the display case, the cashier disappeared into the back of the shop. Another employee handed Lizzie her latte and took the next customer's order.

"Where did he go?" Lizzie wondered as she and Ian moved aside.

"Probably had to go get the champagne," Ian replied.

"I don't even see that on the menu. How did you know they would have it?"

"What self-respecting bakery that serves all of this chocolate wouldn't have it?" Ian replied. Lizzie could tell from the attempt at innocence that he was up to something.

The cashier returned and opened a small swinging door at the end of the counter.

"Right this way, sir," the cashier directed.

"Thank you," Ian replied, taking Lizzie by the hand he led her through the kitchen to a small patio. A small table covered with a red cloth and a curved wicker loveseat sat in the middle of the patio, flanked by two large, outdoor heaters. An arrangement of tulips sat in the middle of the table, two champagne flutes dipped in chocolate, and a bottle of the Banfi Rosa.

"Ian, this is too much," Lizzie whispered, gripping his hand. She had never received such attention and knew she didn't deserve it.

Ian tilted her face up, capturing her eyes with his own.

"It can never be too much, Lizzie. There is not enough time in this life for me to give you all the things you deserve."

Lizzie wanted to melt and cry at the same time. This was the stuff that fairy tales were made of, and real life was far from a fairy tale.

"Why? Why do you keep doing these things? I don't deserve them. I don't deserve you." Tears glistened in Lizzie's eyes. Ian led her to the loveseat and sat beside her, taking both of her hands in his.

"Why don't you deserve it?" Ian asked.

Lizzie just shook her head, unable to speak over the tears tightening her throat.

"You have to stop beating yourself up for things that have happened in the past. Just because you made some bad choices doesn't mean you don't deserve happiness now; that you don't deserve to be treated with respect." He leaned forward to brush a straggling curl from her pale cheek. "I know you aren't perfect, but none of us are. I'm not going to stop doing things like this just because you can't forgive yourself."

His last words stung and she dropped her eyes from his gaze. Until she'd started dating Ian, she'd thought she had forgiven herself. When her friends asked her why she wasn't dating, she always blamed it on how busy she was, focusing on work, and didn't have time for a relationship. Now she wondered if Ian was right, if the real reason was she didn't trust herself not to make the same mistakes again. Had she really not forgiven herself for the choices she'd made?

"Elizabeth, look at me." Ian rarely used her full name; doing so now returned her attention to him. She looked up and saw pain in his eyes.

"I know we've had problems. I admit I get jealous of the time you spend at work and your relationship with Jeffrey, but I also know I've never met anyone like you. You are kind, generous, dedicated, loyal, and merciful. You give so much to others and your faith in God has made you stronger than you know. I love you, and I always will, but I can't make you let me in, can't make you forgive yourself."

"Ian, I'm sorry," Lizzie replied, ashamed of how selfish she suddenly felt.

Ian her put a finger to her lips. "We don't need to talk about it now. This was supposed to be a memorable night. Just think about what I said."

He poured them each a glass of champagne. Lizzie took a sip of the sweet champagne, the taste of the chocolate mixing with the bubbly strawberry. She tried to savor the flavors, but found herself reflecting on Ian's words. Could she ever have a healthy relationship? One without guilt, without doubt.

They drank in silence and Lizzie picked at her cupcake while Ian simply pushed his aside. When they finished their glasses, Ian stuffed the cork back in the bottle and stood up.

"Maybe we should head back to the hotel, it's getting late," he said, reaching for her hand. On the way out, he stopped to speak with the cashier. Lizzie stood by the window watching couples pass by, smiling, laughing, whispering, cuddling.

Less than an hour ago, she had looked like them. Were any of them battling the same feelings of inadequacy? Would any of those couples end the night alone, feeling like they had lost the only bright and shining part of their lives?

Ian returned to her side and they walked back to the car. Tiny snowflakes began to fall as they left the lights of town behind. At the lodge, Ian walked Lizzie to her room and held her in a prolonged embrace for several minutes, before kissing the top of her head and walking away.

# CHAPTER TWENTY-TWO

Emerson spent Saturday night trying to recreate Amanda's last hour by watching video surveillance from cameras along Orange Avenue and the lobby of the office building.

Based on the information from Michelle's friends, Wendy and Tiffani, he'd been able to pick Amanda up leaving The Social a little after eleven. The video footage allowed Emerson to follow her the entire way to the high-rise office. He believed she might have returned to the office for her keys or something similarly important, as he'd watched her rummage through her purse outside the club.

Once Emerson established a timeline for Amanda leaving the club and arriving at the office, he rewound the tapes and searched the crowded streets for anyone who appeared to have been following her. A minute behind her on each camera, he saw a tall man of average build, wearing a gray hooded sweatshirt and dark jeans. The man was able to catch the door before it closed behind Amanda.

Emerson watched as the suspect stood in the lobby, studying the bank of elevators, his face hidden in the shadows of his hoodie. When the lights above Amanda's elevator car stopped on the sixth floor, the suspect darted onto another car. Emerson pushed the fast-forward button until the suspect returned to the lobby twenty minutes later.

While the suspect didn't run from the scene, as Emerson would have expected, he did look over his shoulder a number of times as the footage showed him retracing his steps until he turned down a side street and the cameras lost him. Emerson called to request video footage from all the area parking garages, hoping to get an image of his license plate number.

None of the video had provided a clear view of the suspect's face, but they were still waiting for footage from the floors belonging to the investment firm. The fact that they seemed to be dragging their feet was beginning to appear suspicious to Emerson. If he didn't receive it today, he would have to take a closer look at everyone in the company.

"Why don't you take a break Detective?" the tech who'd spent the night running the footage asked. "I can try to put together some kind of composite sketch of the subject from different camera angles."

Emerson rubbed his tired eyes. "That would be great. You want some coffee?"

"No thanks. I'll get you the sketch as soon as I can."

"Call if any additional footage comes in."

"Will do." The tech worked several buttons and began getting screen shots of the suspect.

Emerson left the dark video room and poured a cup of thick, black coffee. He took a sip and grimaced at the bitter flavor. He took one more gulp and chucked the half-full cup into the garbage. He shuffled through the quiet halls of the police station and glanced at his watch, surprised to find it was a little before eight in the morning.

"McDonald," he called when he caught sight of the young detective. "Anything come back on Michelle Burton's prints?"

"Not a match to anything in the system, but I ran the background check like you asked. She was involved in a car accident a couple years ago. Her boyfriend was driving and he hit an oncoming vehicle. In the report, Burton stated she and the boyfriend had been arguing when the wreck occurred. She sustained the most injuries; her head went through the passenger window, and her face was cut up pretty bad. The other driver was in a Hummer. The accident photos could be used in a commercial for the safety of Hummers. Barely a dent, and it was hit at close to sixty miles per hour." McDonald pulled a folder from a pile on her desk and handed it to Emerson.

"Thanks." Emerson took the folder and skimmed a few pages.

"Were you here all night?" McDonald asked.

"There was a lot of video to go through."

"Why don't you go home, get a shower, catch a few winks?" McDonald asked in a motherly fashion, which caused Emerson to smile.

"I'm fine," Emerson replied.

McDonald held up a mirror, causing Emerson to flinch at the reflection he saw. His hair was sticking up from running his hands through it so many times, his eyes were bloodshot, and his face wore several inches of stubble, thickly peppered with gray.

"Okay, okay, just put that thing away. I'll go get cleaned up." Emerson held up his hands in surrender. He went around to his own desk, unlocked a drawer, removed his 9mm Glock, and clipped it to his belt.

Interstate 4 was clogged with morning rush hour traffic as he headed west. He considered using the lights and siren to clear a path, but worried it might just as easily cause a wreck, then he'd have to stick around for an accident report. He just wanted to shower, shave, get a decent cup of coffee, and get back to work. The more time he allowed to pass, the colder the trail became.

It took forty-five minutes to reach his one-bedroom apartment off Conroy Road. He crossed the small living room in three long strides and entered the bathroom. He turned on the hot water and waited for the shower stall to fill with steam before stepping in.

After showering and dressing in a fresh suit, he heated a breakfast sandwich in the microwave and poured a cup of coffee. He switched on the local news, to see if they were running anything on the murder. They were showing footage from Friday morning, with a brief comment that police had no new leads.

Traffic had cleared up some and he was able to make it back to the precinct in twenty minutes. He found a note on his desk that the parking garage video had arrived, and made a beeline for the viewing room. A different tech sat at the controls, scanning the footage.

"Hey, Tony. You looking at video for the Amanda Barnes case?" Emerson asked.

"Yes, sir. Parking garage footage arrived ten minutes ago. Nothing so far, but I'm still on the first garage. Have a seat." The tech turned back to the monitor and sped up the frames.

"What times are you looking at?" Emerson asked, rolling the chair closer to the screen.

"I started at six, thinking we might see him entering the garage. He wasn't dressed like someone who worked in the area, so I thought he might have come down for dinner before hitting the clubs," Tony replied.

"Good idea. I suppose we'll have to watch until close to three, after all the clubs closed. He could have ducked down the side street and hit another bar after the murder, although that seems risky. He had to have blood on his clothes from the spray."

Emerson tried to think like the killer. Was he rattled after the attack or was he ruthless enough to be unfazed by it? The way he hadn't tried to avoid all the street cameras seemed to indicate he was inexperienced. Did he know the victim and was it a crime of passion? The brutality of the attack seemed to indicate a great deal of rage.

The door opened behind Emerson and McDonald entered with a manila envelope.

"Video from the investment firm just arrived," she said waving the envelope.

"Great." Emerson snatched the envelope from her and removed the compact disc. "Mind if we switch over to this?" he asked Tony.

"Not at all." The tech took the disc and popped it into the computer.

"They only sent video from the elevator lobby. They don't have cameras on the hallway the bathroom is in," McDonald explained.

Emerson cracked his knuckles, wishing he could wrap his hands around the neck of the security agent who'd chosen the footage sent to the police.

"Let me fast forward to the time they would have arrived on the sixth floor," Tony said as he worked some more buttons. Streams of people flew in and out of the elevators, until it became a trickle, and then no one passed through for several hours.

"There, that's Amanda." Emerson pointed and the tech slowed the video.

They watched as Amanda stepped off the elevator, moving quickly out of view. A minute later, a second elevator opened, but when the suspect emerged, his back was to the camera, his hands shoved in his pockets and shoulders hunched, making it hard to determine his height.

An agonizing fifteen minutes passed, but they were afraid to fast forward and miss their man. The suspect ran back into the picture, his hood back around his shoulders providing a clear view of his face.

"Gotcha," Emerson exclaimed and jumped from his seat. "Print that!" A surge of adrenaline flowed through him, erasing all thoughts of sleep.

"What do you do now?" McDonald asked.

"We hit the streets and see if anyone from the clubs recognizes him" Emerson replied.

"I'll print out several copies," Tony offered, quickly working the controls to clean up the image.

"Thanks, Tony," Emerson said as he left the video room to update the captain on the new lead.

# CHAPTER TWENTY-THREE

Michelle pulled a photo album from the bookcase and took it to the couch. She tucked a pillow behind her back as she opened it. Pictures of her and several friends filled the first pages, a record of her first band and their performances at dive bars and backyard parties. Farther in, she found what she was looking for, a strip of photos from one of those photo booths at the mall. Her face was pressed to DJ's; his brown eyes reminded her of a puppy's even now.

She remembered the day well. They'd been Christmas shopping, laughing all day long. When they'd seen the booth in the food court, DJ had insisted they have their picture taken. There were the obligatory funny photos; eyes crossed, mouth pulled with fingers, and rabbit ears, but the last one had caught them kissing. Michelle rubbed a thumb over this photo as she thought about the rest of the day.

After shopping, they'd gone to dinner at the Cheesecake Factory. It had been a wonderful day until they got up to leave the restaurant. Michelle caught DJ checking out one of the waitresses, and saw a flicker of recognition on her face. In the car, she had asked DJ about it, but he'd denied knowing the woman, although he admitted to finding her attractive. Michelle continued to press, accusing him of cheating on her. DJ didn't respond, he just drove faster, weaving in and out of traffic. Michelle wasn't wearing a seat belt and begged DJ to slow down or pull over. Instead, he turned onto Kirkman Road and he hit the accelerator. When the Hummer turned in front of them, DJ didn't have time to stop or swerve and barreled into the tank-like vehicle. Michelle was flung forward through the windshield, a large shard of glass lodging in her forehead, barely missing her eye.

The impact knocked her unconscious. When she awoke, she was in the emergency room. Amazingly, DJ had only sustained minor cuts. The doctors asked Michelle if she wanted a plastic surgeon to stitch her up to limit any scarring, but she had declined. She wanted to remember what had happened.

This wasn't the first time DJ's temper had put her in a dangerous situation, but she swore it would be the last. When the police came to take her statement, she told the truth about the argument, and her lack of judgment for starting it while they were driving.

Michelle flipped the page in the photo album and found a picture taken shortly after the accident. Her face was still bruised and she still had stitches splitting her eyebrow in half. She studied the picture and rubbed the scar on her forehead. She always seemed to pick guys who were bad for her in some way, whether it was physical abuse, drugs, or lack of fidelity. After DJ, she'd sworn off men, until meeting Jeffrey.

She closed the album and returned it to the shelf. Her stomach grumbled and she realized she hadn't eaten anything all day. She looked in the freezer, but didn't find anything appealing. Grabbing her keys, she headed out. Her cell phone rang as she started the engine.

"Hello?" she answered, slipping the car into reverse.

"Ms. Burton, it's Detective Emerson. We were able to obtain a photo of a suspect and would like you to come in, see if you recognize the man."

Michelle was nearly out of her parking spot, but slammed on the brakes at this news, sitting motionless until another car honked for her to get out of the way.

"Are you still there?" Detective Emerson asked.

Michelle shifted into drive and pulled forward. "Yes, I was just surprised. Of course, I'll come in. I was on my way to grab something to eat."

"Would you mind stopping here first? The sooner we can ID this guy the better," Emerson pressed.

"Of course. I'll be there as soon as I can."

"Just ask for me when you get here," Emerson said and hung up.

The drive seemed to take forever. Michelle ran through everyone she knew, unable to believe that any of them were capable of murder. She feared she wouldn't be much help making an identification.

At the police station, Emerson stood up when he saw Michelle and went to meet her.

"I appreciate you coming in so quickly." Emerson led her to his desk and offered her a chair. "Would you like something to drink?"

"No, I'm fine," Michelle replied.

"All right, we'll get right to it then." Emerson opened a folder and pulled out the photo the computer tech had printed from the screen shot and handed it to Michelle. He noticed her hands shaking as she took the photo.

Emerson waited as Michelle studied the picture for several minutes.

"He does look vaguely familiar. He may have been at a few of our performances, but I don't know his name." Michelle handed the picture back to the detective.

"Do you think any of your band mates might recognize him, maybe even know his name? If he's a fan, perhaps one of them has talked with him," Emerson pressed.

"It's possible. I can give you their phone numbers," Michelle offered.

"You already did," Emerson reminded her. "How are you doing?" his tone softened. Now that she wasn't a suspect, he felt bad for her, remembering how tough seeing his first dead body had been.

"I don't know when I'll have a good night's sleep again, but I'll survive," Michelle replied.

"Have you given any thought to calling the counselor Dr. Mendenhall recommended?"

"Yeah, I may call her on Monday," Michelle replied.

"You don't have to wait till then, if you need to talk. She's very understanding, and is on call twenty-four/ seven. She works with us a lot and understands that crime doesn't just happen during regular office hours. She'd be happy to talk to you this evening or tomorrow." Emerson returned the photo to the file and closed it.

"Do you think you are going to find this guy?" Michelle asked.

"I'm going to do my best." A thought popped into Emerson's mind and he pulled his notepad from a coat pocket. "When are you performing again? If he's a fan, he may be at the show."

Michelle's eyes went wide with fear, and Emerson kicked himself for not being subtler, but subtlety was definitely not his thing.

"I didn't mean to scare you. If there is a chance he could show up to watch you play, we would like to have some officers on the premises to apprehend him." Emerson hoped this would help allay her fears.

"We don't have any gigs for the next couple of weeks." Michelle's body stiffened and she turned fearful eyes on Emerson. "You don't think he will come after me or any of the other members of the band, do you?"

"Right now, he probably thinks he got away clean, There's no way for him to know we have a photo of him. As long as he thinks we don't have any leads, he should continue about his normal routine. Can you think of any other times you might have seen him, maybe at another concert?"

Michelle wrinkled her brow in concentration, then shook her head.

"Well, if you think of anything, please give me a call." Emerson escorted her back to the entrance and watched as she got into her car.

At his desk, Emerson found the phone numbers for the other members of *Tangled Web* and called them each to come in to view the photo.

Heavy clouds hung low in the sky when Michelle emerged from the police station, reminding her of impending snowstorms back in Boston. The gloomy weather fit her mood. Seeing the picture of the suspect had completely unnerved her. She checked her rearview mirror as she turned onto the highway, watching for anyone following her.

A few blocks from her apartment, she slid across traffic and turned into the Burger King drive-thru, where she ordered a burger, fries, and large shake. As she pulled away from the restaurant, she felt her body relax the tiniest bit, the smell of the food awakening her appetite.

When she reached the apartment, she shoved the bag of food into her large purse and raced up the steps to her door. After finishing her food, Michelle pulled the card Dr. Mendenhall had given her from her wallet. She studied the number for several minutes before making the call.

"Dr. Tushton," a female voice answered on the third ring.

"Um, hi." Michelle felt her heart begin to race as she spoke. "Dr. Mendenhall gave me your card yesterday. My name's Michelle." She felt ridiculous making this call and almost hung up, but the counselor responded quickly, in a warm and comforting tone.

"Yes, Michelle, I am so happy you called. Dr. Mendenhall told me you might. How are you doing?" Her voice was kind and made Michelle feel at ease.

"Honestly, I wish people would quit asking me that," Michelle replied. "How am I supposed to be doing? I just found one of my co-workers murdered in our office."

"That's good," Tushton replied encouragingly. "I want you to feel like you can tell me anything that is bothering you. Would you like to come into my office?"

"I'm actually more comfortable doing this over the phone right now if you don't mind," Michelle replied. She needed to take control of all that was happening to her and this seemed like one thing she could control.

"Of course. Do you want to talk about what you saw?"

"Will talking about it make the nightmares go away?" Michelle asked.

"Dreams are often our mind's way of dealing with unresolved issues. Sometimes talking about them helps us understand those issues so we can deal with them."

"I don't think I need any help understanding these dreams," Michelle retorted.

"I'm sorry. I didn't mean to imply you did. What would you like to talk about?" Tushton asked.

"How do I go back to work after this? How do I go back into that bathroom?"

"What are you afraid will happen when you go back?"

"I don't know," Michelle replied, thinking about it for the first time. "I guess I'm afraid something like that could happen to me."

"So you are feeling vulnerable, maybe feeling like you have to face your own mortality?"

Michelle was beginning to remember why she didn't like therapists. They never had answers, just more questions.

"Isn't it natural to question your own safety when you have been exposed to a brutal crime?" Michele countered.

Tushton laughed. "You would make a good therapist."

"It's not my first time playing this game," Michelle mumbled.

"I see. Would you prefer to talk about that?"

"Ancient history," Michelle replied. "I'm talking to you because I want to know how to forget what I saw."

"Why do you want to forget it?" Tushton asked.

Michelle was growing impatient with the questions. "Really? Wouldn't you want to forget it if you went to the bathroom and found a dead body?"

"From what I understand, it was dark in there. What did you actually see?"

Michelle was ready to yell at this woman, but she stopped. She closed her eyes, trying to remember everything.

"It was dark. The lights wouldn't come on and there was a metallic smell. I held the door open to let light in and saw the body. The tiles were stained and then I saw her face, black and blue, swollen." Michelle felt her stomach clench and she feared her dinner was about to return.

"What happened next?" Tushton asked.

"I threw up, then I called the police." Michelle took several deep breaths as she spoke.

"Did you see Amanda again after that?"

"I took the police to the bathroom when they arrived, but I didn't look inside. I went to the break room and served scones."

"Scones?" Tushton asked, her voice rising in surprise.

"I was so wound up after our gig, I couldn't sleep so I was up baking. I had brought the scones in for my coworkers, but when the police arrived, I don't know. Things got pretty crazy in my head."

"Have you experienced severe trauma situations before?" Tushton asked.

"I guess that depends on what you mean by severe trauma." Michelle rose from her couch and paced the living room.

"Why did you talk to a therapist before?"

"I told you I don't want to talk about that. It's done and in the past," Michelle replied defensively.

"I understand, but I'd like to be able to determine what your coping mechanism is for stressful situations."

"Why does that matter?"

"Because it sounds to me like you disassociate yourself from the situation, which can end up causing more stress. Then things you think have been dealt with end up becoming ticking time bombs waiting for the next stressor." Tushton's reply was gentle but insistent.

Michelle thought for several minutes about the last therapist she'd seen. He hadn't been nearly as patient or willing to answer her questions as Tushton seemed to be. Maybe the woman had a point. Maybe she hadn't dealt with the past issues and that was why she was so quick to judge Jeffrey.

"I had a couple of bad relationships," Michelle said quietly. "One guy nearly beat me to death, and another, well, I went through the windshield of his car. I went to a shrink to find out why I was so attracted to these types of men. I figured two near-death experiences were all I could risk."

"How did you end the relationships?" Tushton asked and Michelle could almost picture her sitting on the edge of her seat in anticipation.

"The first guy, I let beat on me a few times, then I moved, changed my number, and didn't tell him." Michelle paused.

"What about the second guy?"

"Same thing, almost. I told him about a week after the accident that it was over, then I moved and changed my number."

"Hmm," Tushton replied.

"Hmm, what?" Michelle asked.

"Do you really have to ask?" Tushton replied.

"Are you saying by moving I was disassociating myself?"

"Weren't you?"

"I had to move. They wouldn't have gone away otherwise."

"There are things you could have done. Gotten restraining orders, for instance, but instead you picked up your whole life and moved. Where were you living when the first incident happened?"

"I didn't change states or even towns, if that's what you are getting at."

"Well, that's good. That means at least a part of you knew running wasn't the answer."

"I wasn't running away, I was saving myself," Michelle protested.

"Did you remember to have your new phone numbers unlisted?" Tushton asked.

Michelle could hear paper rustling in the background.

"I, uh, no, I didn't," Michelle admitted, all fight leaving her.

"So that means you are currently living on Cypress Woods Drive?" Tushton inquired.

"Yes."

"How are you any safer from these guys? If they decided tonight they were still angry with you, all they'd have to do is look you up in their phone book."

With this comment, Michelle realized that must have been how Jeffrey knew where to send the flowers. She didn't remember telling him where she lived. She stopped pacing and went to make sure her door was locked.

"Okay, you've made your point. Where does that leave me?" Michelle wandered through the apartment as she talked, checking each of the windows.

"First, you can sit down and stop worrying someone is trying to get into your home," Tushton replied.

Tushton's uncanny knowledge of Michelle's reaction was unnerving, but she did return to the couch.

"How long has it been since the car accident?" the therapist asked.

"A little over two years."

"If he hasn't come looking for you in that time, he isn't going to. Have you moved since then, or was that your last move?"

"I haven't moved since then."

"Good. Why don't we meet for coffee tomorrow? We can talk about better ways for you handle these stressful situations."

"I'm not sure I'm ready to see you yet," Michelle replied uncertainly.

"Michelle, the minute you decided to call me you admitted there was a problem. Seeing me in person doesn't make that any more real than it already is. I'll see you at the Roasted Bean at one o'clock," Tushton said authoritatively.

"How will I recognize you?"

"Don't worry. I saw you on TV, I'll recognize you."

# CHAPTER TWENTY-FOUR

Stephen awoke, groaning with pain. His nose felt the size of a grapefruit and his whole head throbbed. He stumbled into the bathroom and grimaced at his reflection. Deep black and blue bruises covered his nose and most of the right side of his face. How am I going to face Renee and Heidi this morning? he thought. He soaked a washcloth in hot water, laid it across his face until it grew cold, and repeated this several times.

Slowly the throbbing ebbed. He gingerly pulled the gauze from his nose and waited, watching to see if the blood would start flowing again, but it did not. After a long shower, he dressed in a dark blue suit and red tie, almost finding it humorous that his face matched the outfit. He downed a glass of water and a couple of Tylenol, sticking the bottle in his pocket.

Arriving at the hotel, he kept his head down as he ducked into a side entrance, slinking down the service corridor, hoping to avoid being seen. He was surprised to find Jessica in the office when he arrived. She wasn't in the business suit uniform they had adopted when Lizzie was promoted to manager; instead, she wore baggy jeans, a gray thermal shirt, and a baseball hat. A look of horror crossed her face when she saw him.

"It's not that bad," he tried to joke.

"Of course not," she replied, "but I'm glad I came prepared." She pulled a toiletry bag from behind her back.

"What's that for?" Stephen asked with a sense of dread.

"You can't be talking to guests looking like that." She opened the bag and started pulling cosmetics and brushes from it. "I will cover up the bruises and see if I can't distract from the swelling."

"Oh no, you aren't putting make-up on me." Stephen held up his hands and slowly backed away.

"What choice do you have? If Renee or Heidi sees you like this there are going to be questions."

"So I'll tell them what happened. Accidents do happen."

"They do, but we don't usually wear them on our faces. Now sit down and take this like a man." Jessica pointed at the chair and gave him a stern look.

Stephen approached the chair like a disciplined dog with his tail between his legs. Jessica gently rubbed foundation on his cheeks, using the lightest touch possible as she neared his nose, covering the medical tape used to hold the splint in place. He flinched several times and she paused, giving him a chance to catch his breath.

Once she had a coat of foundation on, she picked up a compact of pressed powder and dusted his face, then stood back to assess her work.

"Are you finished?" Stephen asked.

"I haven't decided yet. You want to take a look?" She rummaged through the bag and found a small mirror. He took it from her and held it up. The bruising was still faintly visible, but she'd managed to camouflage the splint fairly well.

"Not as bad as I thought it would be," Stephen replied grudgingly.

"If you don't have to get too close to anyone today, you should be fine. From a distance you don't even notice the bruises, but up close..."

"Up close they will be able to tell I'm wearing make-up. Got it, keep a good distance." Stephen returned the mirror. "Thanks, Jess."

"Do you need me to work this afternoon?" Jessica asked as she put her tools away.

"No, it's your day off. Have fun. I'll see you on Tuesday," Stephen replied.

"When does Lizzie get back?"

"She flies back Tuesday, but she isn't coming in to the office until Thursday."

"Have you heard from her at all?" Jessica asked.

"Only an email Friday morning wishing us luck with Silken Pleasures. I'm kind of surprised she hasn't checked in."

"It's good she is disconnecting from this place. She spends too much time here." Jessica dropped the toiletry bag into her even larger purse and slung it over her shoulder.

"She's dedicated," Stephen agreed.

"Hope everything goes smoothly today," Jessica said.

"Oh, that reminds me, how did dinner go last night?" Stephen asked.

Jessica flashed him a brilliant smile that lit up her whole face. "It was fantastic. I had no idea how many children they help each year. I had a chance to talk with their community relations director and he is just amazing. I signed up to help out with their Spring Fling in April."

"Really?" Stephen arched an eyebrow at her.

Jessica blushed. "I like helping kids," she replied.

"Uh huh, I hear ya. Now get out of here. Have a good day off." Stephen shooed her out of the office and turned to the day's itinerary. The message light on his phone was illuminated, so he dialed into his voicemail. There was a message from Jackson Compton, checking to make sure the flowers had been acceptable, one from the president of Eli's Hope thanking him for an excellent evening, and then Stephen nearly dropped the phone.

"Stephen, this is Darren Kingsley. I received your message and email. I'm impressed you managed to get my number. Call me so I can learn more about this guest who wants to meet me."

When the voicemail ended, Stephen checked the clock. It was nearly nine. Certainly a man like Darren Kingsley would be up by now. He began to dial, then paused. It was Sunday, should he wait a little longer? He shook his head and dialed.

He was afraid he was going to get voicemail again, but Mr. Kingsley answered on the fifth ring.

"Hello?"

"Mr. Kingsley, it's Stephen Longbottom at Hotel Lago. I just received your message."

"Good morning, Stephen," Kingsley gave him a hearty greeting. "Fine bit of detective work getting my number. How'd you do it?"

"I promised I wouldn't reveal my source, sir," Stephen replied, hoping he wouldn't offend the man.

"Well, I can admire that. It's good to know I have employees who are willing to go the extra mile for our guests and stand behind their word. So, tell me more about this Renee Therriault. Do I know her?"

"I'm not sure sir. You might have met at a social function, she didn't say." Stephen gave Kingsley a brief bio of Mrs. Therriault.

"Hmm, do you happen to know what her maiden name is?"

"No, sir, she's been married several times, I was only able to trace her back to her marriage to Ronald Johnson," Stephen supplied.

"Not ringing any bells, but I meet so many people, and honestly I'm terrible with names; much better with faces. Did she mention why she wanted to meet with me?"

"No, sir. I'm sorry, I should have gotten that information, but she made it seem very personal." Stephen felt like an idiot.

"Personal, hmm. Well, now I'm intrigued. When does she check out?"

"Tuesday morning. Their plane leaves at eleven."

"I'm in Colorado right now, but I can fly in tonight. Do you know what her schedule looks like tomorrow?" Kingsley asked.

Stephen flipped the itinerary to the next day. "She has a meeting from nine to eleven, then they are free the rest of the day. I know several of the women have spa appointments and the two men are golfing. Looks like Mrs. Therriault has a massage scheduled at one."

"All right, set up a lunch reservation for us. I'll have my assistant call you later today for the details."

"Yes, sir," Stephen could barely contain his relief.

Hanging up the phone, Stephen jumped from his chair and did a victory dance around the office. Mrs. Therriault and her group were scheduled to have breakfast in the dinning room, so he set out to find her and give her the good news.

Renee sat at the head of a long table, with Heidi on her right hand and Donna on her left. Stephen noticed Ellen Cartwright sat at the far end of the table and remembered he wanted to talk to Mrs. Therriault about the argument between Ellen and Donna. He paused self-consciously, realizing he would have to get close enough to Renee for her to notice his make-up. Maybe he should have one of the servers deliver her a note.

Just as he was turning to leave, Renee noticed him and waved him over. Stephen weaved through the scattered tables and stopped three feet from Renee's chair.

"Good morning Stephen. I was hoping you could settle a debate for us," Renee Therriault said.

"I'll certainly try," Stephen replied, instantly on guard.

"What year did Walt Disney World open?" Renee asked.

Stephen relaxed. "The Magic Kingdom was the first of the four theme parks and it opened in October 1971."

Renee smiled. "Thank you very much. You owe me ten bucks, Ellen."

Stephen tensed at Ellen's name. Why would she be wagering about something as silly as this? Was she trying to lure Mrs. Therriault into a false sense of security, believing that Ellen was something less than she really was?

"Was there anything else you wanted to tell us?" Renee asked.

"Oh, yes, forgive me. The matter you asked me to look into. I have some good news. Are you free for lunch tomorrow?"

"Really?" Renee sounded surprised. "Yes, I am free from eleven thirty to twelve forty-five. Please make the arrangements and I will call you later this afternoon."

"Very well. Enjoy the rest of your breakfast." Stephen felt like he should bow before leaving, but he managed to remain upright as he turned and hurried out of the room.

Back at his desk, he arranged a table for two at the Lakeview Inn, a few blocks away. He spoke with the manager, who guaranteed him a prime view in a private location, and his most discrete server. In return, Stephen promised to get him VIP tickets to *Oliver!*, which was coming to the Bob Carr Performing Arts center in March. Stephen had learned the art of trading quickly, but made use of it only in the most important circumstances.

# CHAPTER TWENTY-FIVE

Detective Emerson rolled over in his bed and squinted at the clock on the bedside table. He shot up when he saw it read nine twenty-five. Wrestling a shirt and a pair of pants off their hangers, he flew into the bathroom where he splashed his face with warm water. He dressed rapidly, applied cologne liberally, and sped out the door, running until he was behind the wheel of his black Crown Victoria. His cell phone rang six blocks from the office.

"Where are you?" McDonald asked when he answered the phone.

"Almost there. I must've forgotten to set the alarm. Anything new turn up?" Emerson asked, crossing two lanes of traffic to make a right hand turn.

"Looks like you have a voicemail. Maybe the drummer called you back last night."

"Hopefully he can tell us something about our suspect. I'll be there in a few minutes." Emerson hung up and swung the sedan into a parking spot. When he reached his desk, McDonald was waiting for him, a fresh cup of coffee in her outstretched hand.

"Thanks." Emerson took the cup and slurped at it. He listened to the voicemail and smiled.

"Yep, it was Matt. He said he could meet with us between ten and twelve."

Emerson dialed Matt's number and arranged to meet him in fifteen minutes at a coffee shop near the Mall at Millennia. He unlocked his drawers, retrieved the case file, made sure the photo was in it, and looked up at McDonald.

"Want to come along?" Emerson asked. He'd been a loner since his last partner had been killed two months ago, but knew eventually he'd have to take on a new partner. Maybe it wouldn't be so bad to team up with McDonald. She seemed to have a level head and wasn't jaded by the job yet.

McDonald eagerly nodded. She followed Emerson to the car and quietly slipped into the passenger seat.

"Why don't you read this over on the way," Emerson said, handing her the case file. "See if there's anything I've missed."

The young detective took the file, shuffling through the gruesome crime scene photos and statements provided by Amanda's coworkers. When they reached the coffee shop, she trailed Emerson inside, both cops looking for a man fitting the description Michelle had provided.


Matt stood at the counter, waiting for his coffee to be made. His gaze turned to the door as the sound of traffic increased. He watched a burly man with gray hair enter, followed by a slender woman with auburn hair, easily twenty years younger.

Matt recognized them as cops by their walk and alert eyes. He thanked the barista who handed him his drink and moved towards the detectives.

"Detective Emerson?" Matt asked as he approached them.

"You must be Matt." Emerson extended his hand. "Thanks for meeting us. Let's take a seat." Emerson motioned towards a table in the back corner, isolated from the other patrons.

Matt felt Emerson studying him as they moved to the table.

"As I said on the phone, Michelle said the guy we are looking at seemed familiar. Maybe he was at some of your shows. If you could just take a look at this photo…" Emerson didn't finish the sentence, but removed the photo from the case file and slid it across the table.

Matt studied the picture for several minutes, holding it with one hand and rubbing the back of his neck with the other. "Yeah, I think I've seen him at a couple of shows. I seem to remember him sitting with Marty and Elliot at the last couple of gigs we had at the Loaded Hog, but that was three months ago." Matt handed the picture back to Emerson.

"Do you happen to know his name?" Emerson asked and Matt caught a glimmer of hope in the female detective's eyes.

Matt shook his head. "I wish I did. Not many fans want to talk to Jonesy or me after the shows, they are only interested in Michelle and Jenny, the pretty faces of the group, you know." He offered the detective a half-hearted grin.

Emerson laughed. "Surely you have female fans too."

"A couple," Matt admitted shyly. "I do have Marty's phone number, though. He and Elliot have been fans since the beginning and we've hung out a few times. He might know the guy's name."

"I'd appreciate that."

Matt pulled out his cell phone and scrolled through his contact list, then jotted down the number on a napkin. "Is there anything else I can do to help out?"

"Not at the moment, but if you recall anything else about this man or anything out of the ordinary that may have happened Thursday night give me a call." Emerson handed Matt his business card. Matt shook their hands and watched them leave over the rim of his coffee cup.

Before starting the car, Emerson dialed the number Matt had given them, hoping to catch Marty. When it went to voicemail, he left his information and hung up with a sigh.

"Too much waiting around for me," Emerson said, starting the car and revving the engine as if to emphasize his impatience.

"Maybe Doc Robinson will have something on the DNA when we get back," McDonald said with the hope of a rookie.

Emerson chuckled. "DNA never comes back that quick. Heck, sometimes we don't even get DNA results until we've already caught the guy and he's confessed. It's a great tool for supporting your case in court, but not always that useful in catching the bad guys."

"It can't be that bad." McDonald's eyes widened in surprise.

Emerson shot her an amused look before turning onto the highway. "It's not like on TV where they get samples and appear to know right away what the results are. Sure, it can break a case wide open when there isn't a lot of other evidence, but it can sometimes be months before those samples get processed."

"That's just crazy," McDonald said, shaking her head. "What about the crimes that person is out there committing in the meantime?"

"Then we hope we can prosecute them for those crimes as well. Until there is more funding for crime labs, we just have to keep fighting crime the old fashioned way." Emerson thought back to his first days as a cop, when they still did paperwork by hand, in triplicate, and a search was conducted on foot, not on the internet.

When they arrived back at the station, McDonald went to check on another case she was assisting on, and Emerson added his notes from the conversation with Matt to the file. With the file up to date, Emerson spread the crime scene photos on his desk and studied them, trying to get inside of the mind of the man who had done this.

Amanda's coat had obviously been ripped open and her skirt hiked up, but there had been no evidence of sexual assault. Maybe her attacker realized she was dead before he could get her undressed. Maybe murder wasn't his intention, but things got out of hand when she fought back.

Emerson's stomach growled and he realized it was almost noon. He shuffled the pictures into the file folder and stood, stretching his aching back. He looked around the room and saw McDonald seated at her desk.

"Want to grab some lunch?" Emerson asked as he approached her desk.

McDonald looked up, glanced around as if to see if he was talking to someone else, then pointed a finger at herself. "Me?" she asked.

"Of course you. Come on, I know this great burger joint." Emerson turned, expecting McDonald to follow. When he didn't hear her footsteps behind him, he stopped and looked over his shoulder. "You coming?"

McDonald jumped up, grabbed a small purse from her desk drawer, and followed Emerson outside.

# CHAPTER TWENTY-SIX

Snow fell all through the night, late into Sunday morning. Lizzie sat in a window seat, gazing out at the landscape completely shrouded in three feet of snow. The limbs of the evergreens bowed low under the weight. The drifts were pristine, unmarked by human or animal footprints, yet occasionally a bit of rock still protruded from the deep fluff. Growing up in Florida, Lizzie had only seen pictures of winter scenes like these. Sitting here now, she wondered why so many people complained about the snow. It was the most beautiful thing she'd ever seen.

Startled by a hand on her shoulder, she turned to find Emma in one of the hotel's plush bathrobes, a concerned look in her eyes.

"Are you okay, honey?" Emma asked softly.

"Of course. Why wouldn't I be?" Lizzie replied.

"You were awfully quiet when you came in last night and I heard you up before the sun this morning."

Lizzie turned back to face the window. "I couldn't sleep. Sorry if I woke you."

"You know I don't mind. If there is something you need to talk about..." Emma let her words trail off.

Over the years, the women had developed an unspoken language, knowing when the other needed space or a shoulder to cry on. Emma gave Lizzie's shoulder a squeeze and padded out of the bedroom.

Lizzie appreciated her friend's understanding. She still needed time to think about all that happened the previous night. Ian had planned such a special evening and she had ruined it by allowing old fears to rise up and control her. Slowly, she uncurled her legs from underneath her and stretched for a moment before crossing to the bedside table and reaching for her Bible. She'd been up most of the night reading it, seeking answers to questions she still hadn't fully defined. The one thing she did know, she and Ian could never have a lasting relationship until she dealt with her own demons.

She returned to the window seat, propped her back against one wall and her feet against the other, allowing the Bible to open on her lap. The cover was worn, the pages bent, passages underlined or highlighted, with notes in the margins. She'd had this Bible for only four years, since she'd returned to church after the dark year following her parent's funeral. In that time, she'd read it cover-to-cover three times, and each time she was amazed to find something new.

She loved the letters of Paul to the new believers and found herself returning to them now. She poured over Philippians, drinking in the apostle's words. Lizzie knew the book of Philippians was made of a series of letters written by Paul from a Roman prison to the members of the church he had started in Philippi. The letters were sent to provide practical advice on how to live the Christian life and now, thousands of years later, they were still sound instruction.

When she turned the page again, she continued into Colossians. Halfway through the first chapter she stopped, re-reading the thirteenth and fourteenth verses. *"For he has rescued us from the dominion of darkness and brought us into the kingdom of the Son he loves, in whom we have redemption, the forgiveness of sins."*

How many times had she read this verse? How many times had she shared with others the power of God's forgiveness? And yet, she read these words as if for the first time. As well as her mind had comprehended the idea of God's forgiveness, as much as she knew intellectually that her past sins had been separated from her as far as the east is from the west, something in her heart hadn't allowed that to sink in.

She realized now that by continually punishing herself for her past, she was trying to make herself bigger than God. She was diminishing His power and grace. Tears poured down her face, dripping on the thin pages of the Bible. She pulled her knees up to her chest and hugged them close, bowing her head until it rested on her knees.

"Oh Lord forgive me for my arrogance," she moaned. "Forgive me for trying to put you in a box and believing I somehow knew more about the punishment I deserve than you. I know your grace washed me clean the moment I first confessed my sin to you and you remembered it no more."

She couldn't find the words to complete her prayer, so many thoughts filling her mind. She gently rocked back and forth, an occasional groan escaping her lips. Lizzie didn't know how much time had passed, but she slowly opened her eyes, feeling so humbled, a peace filling her whole being.

Several drops of water hit the windowpane. The icicles on the roof were beginning to melt. She watched as the liquid slipped down the window, leaving tracks in the frost. Lizzie closed her Bible and set it on the window seat as she stood. Voices reached her from the living room along with the smells of bacon and fresh coffee.

Emma met Lizzie with a hot cup of coffee when she emerged from the bedroom. She accepted it with a grateful smile and took a seat at the small table where she found a bowl of scrambled eggs, a plate of bacon, and a carton of orange juice. Half-empty plates sat in front of Emma and Ron. Lizzie reached for the bowl of eggs and spooned out several mounds before speaking.

"What are your plans for the day?" Lizzie asked as she picked up a couple of pieces of bacon.

"I don't know," Emma replied.

"I can't take another day of shopping," Ron chuckled.

"You guys haven't been skiing yet. Why don't you give it a shot?" Lizzie asked.

Both Emma and Ron laughed. "I don't have good balance walking. What makes you think I could keep myself upright on skis?" Emma replied.

"It really isn't as hard as you may think," Lizzie replied. "I was getting pretty good at it with Ian's help." At the mention of Ian's name, Lizzie's gaze dropped to table and she became very quiet.

"You are just a wee bit younger than us, remember," Ron replied teasingly. "I'm pretty sure I would end up rolling head over feet down the mountain, creating a giant snowball that might take out this whole resort."

Emma burst into laughter and reached over to grasp Ron's hand. Lizzie looked up at her friends and she could see the love in their eyes. She ached to have that type of relationship for herself. Someone she could laugh with and cry with, see the world with or never leave home. Had she ruined her chance with Ian?

"Oh, I almost forgot." Emma stood and moved to the coffee table. "Ian left this for you a little while ago." She returned with a small envelope.

Lizzie felt her stomach tighten with fear as she took the envelope. "When did he come by? I didn't hear him. Didn't he want to see me?"

Emma put a comforting hand on Lizzie's. "I opened the bedroom door to get you, but you were praying, and I thought it best not to interrupt."

Lizzie turned the envelope over in her hands several times, afraid to open it. Was this how he was going to break up with her? Would Ian and his parents be gone by now?

"Aren't you going to open it?" Ron asked.

Lizzie turned her attention from the envelope to her adoptive family. She knew she should tell them about what had happened last night, but she was embarrassed to admit how badly she had screwed up. Reluctantly, she slid a finger along the seal of the envelope, tensing with each ripping sound. She pulled out a note card with the lodge's logo on it. Tears welled in her eyes as she read the message.

*My dearest Elizabeth,*

*I know you don't feel like you deserve my love, but I believe God brought us together for a reason and I am not willing to give up on you yet. You are everything I never even knew I needed in life. Please don't sell yourself short and settle for less than all the blessings God has in store for you. Meet me in the lobby at eleven.*

*Love Always,*

*Ian*

Lizzie felt the tears running down her face, but couldn't let go of the note to wipe them away. Emma came around the table and wrapped her arms around Lizzie, who laid her head against the woman's stomach. Emma cooed reassuringly and rubbed Lizzie's back.

"He really loves me," Lizzie murmured into the folds of Emma's dress.

"Of course he does," Emma replied. "Haven't you known that?"

"I don't think I ever believed it until now."

Emma pulled back and took Lizzie's face in her hands, tilting it up to meet her gaze. "Why not, child? He adores you; everyone can see that. Don't you feel the same way?"

Lizzie didn't respond for a minute. When she did speak, her words were quiet, causing Emma to lean closer. "I have been waiting for him to leave, to get bored with me like Kevin did."

"Oh, honey, that isn't going to happen. You and Kevin didn't have a relationship; you had sex. You aren't in that place of darkness anymore, where you found comfort, however fleeting, in his arms. Now you find your comfort in God."

Ron rose from his seat and came to embrace both women. "It is never easy for us to forget our past, Lizzie. Satan has a way of making us dwell on our mistakes, to make us feel unworthy of God's love."

Ron's deep voice resonated in Lizzie's soul.

"That is how he separates us from God and makes us vulnerable to spiritual attack. You have been freed from that darkness to live in the light of God's love for you. All you have to do is accept that freedom, in all aspects of your life."

Lizzie smiled weakly. "That is what I was reading this morning in Colossians. I don't know why I haven't understood it before."

Ron patted her shoulder and stepped back. "God works on us one piece at a time, like putting together a broken vase, because we are all broken when we come to him. He works with patience and tenderness, fitting the pieces back together. Sometimes a piece needs extra time for the glue to dry so it will stay in place, but He will hold onto that piece until it does finally stick, so today one more piece of your vase has been repaired."

Lizzie allowed the imagery to sink in, seeing herself in pieces, imagining the parts already put back together and those still scattered on the ground, unsure if she was even close to being halfway repaired, knowing she would never be complete until she reached heaven.

"Thank you," she choked out around the growing lump in her throat. Lizzie didn't know what she would have done if Ron and Emma hadn't come into her life, and she realized they had played a vital role in repairing the first piece of her brokenness.

"So are you going to meet the boy or not? It's already ten-thirty," Ron broke into Lizzie's thoughts.

"I better get dressed." Lizzie jumped up from her chair, hugged Ron and Emma, and ran to her bedroom.

At exactly eleven o'clock, Lizzie ran down the stairs into the lobby, her eyes scanning the large room for Ian. She found him sitting by the fireplace and approached him, breathless from her hurried dressing and the rush to meet him on time. His face brightened with a smile as wide as the Mississippi at the sight of her. He stood and she rushed into his arms.

"I didn't know if you would come," Ian whispered as he kissed the top of her head. Lizzie's cheek, pressed against his chest, could feel his heartbeat, a strong thump-thump that seemed to slow as they stood in silence, clinging to each other.

Ian loosened his grip first, and turned Lizzie's face up to his. He brushed her lips with his own, then dusted her eyes, her cheeks, her nose, her chin, and her forehead with kisses. When he finished, he gazed down at her, waiting for her to open her eyes again.

Lizzie's eyelids fluttered, opening to find Ian's deep blue eyes watching her intently. She ran her fingers through his thick hair, twirling several strands around her finger before releasing them.

"I am so sorry. I've been a fool," Lizzie said, her eyes never leaving his.

"Sshh." Ian placed a finger on her lips. Lizzie kissed his finger and felt a fire building inside her. She wanted to crush Ian in her arms, wishing they could melt together into one being so she would never have to be apart from him.

Ian smiled as if he understood what she was feeling, but took a step back from her, pulled her hands from around his neck, and clasped her right hand in his. Without speaking, he led her to the front door, down the steps, to the parking lot. All of the cars were buried in several feet of snow, so Lizzie had no idea where he was taking her. Then she saw it. A sleigh pulled by two chocolate brown horses. Bells tinkled in the stillness as the horses trotted towards them.

The sleigh stopped in front of them and Ian helped her to step up into it. A pile of thick blankets awaited them; the driver stepped off the forward box to assist them with arranging the blankets around themselves. When all was settled, he returned to his perch and with a shake of the reins, they were moving. Lizzie took the scarf she had worn and wrapped it around her head, making sure to cover her ears. Ian laughed when she turned to look at him.

"You look like a Russian babushka," he said, which caused Lizzie to laugh as well.

"I hope that isn't a bad thing," Lizzie replied.

"Not at all. You are the most attractive babushka I have ever seen."

"Seen many have you?" Lizzie was grateful for how easy it had been to fall back into a comfortable rhythm, all the tension of the previous night gone.

"Only in old movies," Ian replied.

"Where are we going?" Lizzie asked, turning to watch the trees slipping past them. She glanced behind them, surprised at how far they had already travelled, the lodge diminishing to a small dot in the distance.

"Haven't you learned by now, not to question my surprises?" Ian replied.

Lizzie sighed. "Hard habit to break." She leaned over and nestled her head on his shoulder, her hand searching under the covers for his hand.

The scent of pine filled the air as they passed through a thick forest. When they emerged into a clearing, they slowed in front of an old stone church. The church stood alone within the circle of trees. Drifts of snow filled in the crevices of the roof and all around the ancient structure. Ian pushed back the blankets, not waiting for the driver to unbundle them, and stood, extending a hand to Lizzie. She took it and they stepped down into the unblemished snow, sinking up to their calves.

Ian laughed. "I should have thought to bring snowshoes." He shuffled toward the church, supporting Lizzie. Ian pushed the old wooden door open with a loud creak. Inside, squares of yellow light fell through the windows, long devoid of any glass. The stone floor was scattered with a fine dusting of snow that had blown in during the night. There were five rows of wooden benches on each side of the church, facing a small raised platform. Ian led her to front row and sat on a wobbly bench.

"How did you find this place?" Lizzie asked.

"This is where my grandparents were married," Ian replied softly. "My grandfather brought me here the summer I turned thirteen and told me the story of how he met my grandmother and their wedding. I wonder now if he knew that he would die just a few weeks later. It seemed so important to him that I know how special it is to find the right woman, but I was just a teenager. I thought it all was pretty lame at the time. I wish you could have met him."

Lizzie slipped her arm around his waist and leaned on his shoulder. "Their wedding must have been beautiful."

"It was simple. My grandmother's sisters gathered flowers from the meadow for her bouquet and wove some in her hair. She wore a dress her mother made for her and my grandfather wore his regular church suit. His brothers played the guitar as she walked down the aisle. Grandpa said he couldn't take his eyes off her as her father escorted her to front of the church."

Lizzie and Ian both gazed at the small platform. Lizzie could almost hear the guitar playing as she envisioned a man not much different from Ian standing there waiting to greet his bride. The spell was broken when one of the horses outside whinnied as if frightened by something. The bells on the harnesses jingled and the driver gave a shout.

Ian and Lizzie leaped to their feet, racing to the doorway, just in time to see the sleigh disappear into the trees.

Lizzie clutched his arm. "What are we going to do?"

"I'm sure he will be back. Something must have spooked the horses. He just has to get them turned around," Ian replied confidently. "Why don't we build a snowman while we wait?"

Lizzie hesitated, then smiled. "Why not?" she replied.

They waded through the snow in separate directions, each rolling a ball toward the other, laughing when they met, their rolls each the same size.

"He will be quite disproportionate if we put these together," Ian said. "Why don't we use yours for the base and I will carve mine down some. You go ahead and start forming his head, but not so big this time."

"This *is* my first snowman, you know." Lizzie feigned a pout.

"Then it will be one you always remember." Ian kissed her cheek and set about thinning his ball of snow.


Half an hour later, the snowman was complete with rocks for eyes and mouth, twigs for arms and nose, and even some pine needles for hair, and still the sleigh had not returned. Ian was beginning to get worried, but he continued to put on an air of confidence so Lizzie wouldn't panic.

After admiring their snowman and snapping a couple of photos, the couple returned to the church to sit on the benches and wait.

"Shouldn't he be back by now?" Lizzie asked.

"I would have thought so," Ian admitted and pulled his cell phone from his jacket pocket. "I don't have any signal out here, do you?"

Lizzie checked her phone and found she had half a bar. "Not much, but we can give it a shot."

Ian took the phone from her and dialed, but the call didn't go through. "I'm going to walk outside and see if there is any better signal."

Lizzie grabbed his hand. "Don't leave me here alone," she pleaded.

"I'm not, I'll be right outside." Ian stepped outside, holding both phones up toward to the clear blue sky, walking to the right and then the left, slowly moving further from the church.

Ian stopped when he noticed the signal bars jump slightly on Lizzie's phone. He dialed again, careful to hold the phone in the same spot. He put it on speaker as it began to ring. There was a pause, a garbled voice, then the line was quiet.

"Hello? Dad, can you hear me?" Ian called into the phone, held two feet above his head.

"Ian? Where..." The phone crackled and the rest of his words were lost.

"Dad, Lizzie and I are at the old church." Ian didn't know if his father had heard him or not and was starting to speak again, when the call was lost. He tried to dial again, but couldn't get a connection.

"Try sending a text," Lizzie said behind him, causing Ian to jump. She placed a hand on his back and offered a brave smile. "Sometimes if you can't get a voice signal, you can still manage a text message."

"Good idea." Ian handed Lizzie her phone and they each began texting. "Now we wait and see if they reply."

"Do you think we should start walking back?" Lizzie asked, giving a nervous look toward the woods.

"No, I'm sure the text went through and someone will be around to pick us up before you know it." Ian slipped his arm around Lizzie's waist and gave her a squeeze. He hoped that he was projecting more confidence then he felt. He couldn't understand why the sleigh driver hadn't returned yet. A brisk wind shook the trees, sending snow swirling in the air around them.

Ian looked up and noticed that the sky that had been so clear when they left the hotel was filling with heavy gray clouds. "Maybe you should go back inside and I will see if I can gather some wood for a fire."

"Won't it all be wet from the snow?" Lizzie asked.

"Maybe not. The snow hasn't melted any and it is more of a dry fluff than the icy wet stuff. Go on, I'll only be a few minutes." Ian turned toward the woods, leaving Lizzie alone in front of the church.

Ian trudged into the forest, unsure how he would find wood under the thick snow. After digging in several spots and finding no dead twigs or branches, he was sweating and breathing hard. The cold air, so refreshing when they left the lodge now burned his lungs. He looked up at the drooping trees and considered pulling some of the low hanging branches from the trees. While burning green wood would create a smoky fire, it would keep them warm, and perhaps someone would see the smoke.

With new resolve, he reached for the nearest limb and pulled until he heard it splinter. Allowing his body to sink toward the ground, using all of his weight, he pulled again and the limb gave way. Ian repeated this process until he thought he had enough to sustain the fire for at least an hour. Surely, help would arrive before then.

He dragged the limbs back to the church where Lizzie helped him break the branches into smaller pieces.

"Maybe we can strip some of the needles off to cover the floor. All this stone seems to absorb the cold," Lizzie said, her teeth chattering.

"Not a bad idea," Ian replied. He searched his pockets until he found his pocketknife, and began cutting bunches of the fragrant needles free. While he was cutting, he noticed a pile of debris on one of the benches.

"I gathered anything I could find in here, a couple of old bird's nests, some scraps of paper," Lizzie replied to his questioning look. "I thought they would make good kindling to start the fire."

"How did you think of that?"

"My dad and I used to go camping. He taught me about making fire and some edible plants."

Lizzie had a far off look in her eyes and Ian wished he could wipe away the pain she must be feeling at the loss of her father. The moment passed quickly and Lizzie returned to cracking the tree limbs.

The smell of pine and spruce filled the small church, and somehow just the scent warmed them. When all of the branches had been stripped of their needles, Ian made a tepee of sticks outside the door, placing one of the dried up bird nests in the center. He'd found a pack of matches in his coat pocket, a souvenir of a visit to a jazz club year ago, and prayed they still worked.

He struck the first match, which blazed to life then quickly burned out. Ian's fingers were numb after having removed his gloves to use his knife. He fumbled with another match, striking it several times before it caught. He touched it to the kindling, which ignited immediately. Ian fed a bunch of pine needles into the fire. Slowly, the yellow tongues licked at the needles and smoke rose. He prayed the flames would hold out long enough to catch the green wood on fire as well. He bent forward and cautiously blew on the fire. It flickered, then shot upward toward the peak of the triangle, heating the wood.

They could hear the sap heating up, snapping, and popping as the wood was engulfed in flame. Ian released a sigh of relief and shoved his hands back into his thick gloves. While Ian had worked on the fire, Lizzie had gathered bunches of needles and created a circle on the stone floor, where she now sat, with her back against one of the wooden benches.

Ian sank down on the floor beside Lizzie and pulled her into his arms. She was shivering, and cuddled up to him. They sat four or five feet from the fire, the heat radiating off it working its way through their coats, and clothes, until finally their skin began to warm. Ian kept the fire fed with new branches and smoke billowed into the sky. He wasn't sure if the smoke could be distinguished from the building clouds, but prayed someone would see it.

"I'm guessing your dad didn't teach you anything about surviving in a snow storm, did he?" Ian asked light-heartedly.

"Actually he did. He taught me about snow caves. If you are caught out in a storm, you can dig a cave and no matter how cold it gets outside it will remain 32 degrees inside the cave. I think we are better off inside here, though."

"Why in the world would a girl from Florida need to know about snow caves?" Ian asked in surprise.

Lizzie shrugged. "He thought it was important I know how to survive in different environments. He told me you never know what life is going to throw at you so you better be prepared. I wish he'd prepared me for life without him," Lizzie whispered.

"I'm sorry. I didn't mean to make you sad. You just don't talk about them very much." Ian clasped Lizzie's hands in his own, their gloves fitting together awkwardly. He searched her face for a clue to what she was thinking, but she averted her gaze. For several minutes, the only sound was the crackling fire, then Lizzie looked up, her eyes locking with his.

"Other than Emma, no one has ever asked me about my parents," she said, her voice trembling. "I quickly found out people generally don't want to hear about your dead relatives. I guess it makes them uncomfortable, so I stopped talking about them."

Ian's heart broke as she said this; trying to imagine how many things she had kept bottled inside. "You can talk about them anytime you want with me. I'd really like to know more about your family, what your life was like before they died."

"My parents would have liked you." Lizzie shifted on the bed of pine, moving closer to Ian. She curled into a ball, laid her head on Ian's chest, and closed her eyes.

# CHAPTER TWENTY-SEVEN

The Roasted Bean bustled with well-dressed patrons getting their post-church caffeine when Michelle arrived. She scanned the tables for Dr. Tushton, but didn't see a woman sitting alone. She ordered a soy latte and a slice of banana bread, then settled down to wait at small table with a view of the door. Five minutes later, as she was scraping together the crumbs from her bread, a woman of average height with black hair and green eyes took the seat across from Michelle.

"Sorry I'm late." Dr. Tushton apologized, but offered no explanation. Michelle studied her for a moment before lifting her coffee cup to her lips.

"I was getting ready to leave," Michelle replied.

"I'm glad you didn't." Tushton's glance flicked around the crowded cafe. "I didn't realize it would be so busy this morning."

"So, what sage words of advice do you have for me?" Michelle asked, raising her head, as if going into battle.

Tushton placed her right elbow on the table and rested her head on her hand. "How did you sleep last night?" she countered.

Michelle crossed her arms across her chest and tapped her foot against the leg of the table. "Better."

"Good." Tushton nodded. "Perhaps our talk helped to relieve some of the stress your subconscious was under. I believe talk therapy is more effective than medication in trauma cases. Meds can help stabilize a patient so they are able to talk, but in the end, it is the discussion that heals. Drugs just mask the problem. Fortunately, our talk last night shows you don't need any stabilization."

Michelle laughed. "If I'm stable, I feel really bad for your other patients."

Tushton smiled. "The brain is complex. Tell me about your relationship with Amanda."

Michelle's body stiffened and her eyes narrowed. "What does that have to do with anything?"

"It will help me understand the bigger picture. Might even explain why you reacted the way you did."

"We worked together, not much else to it." Michelle gazed out the window at the passing traffic.

"Wasn't she at your band's performance the night of her murder? Sounds like more than just co-workers."

"Like I told the police, Wendy and Tiffani made her feel guilty for not being more supportive, reminded her how she made us all go see her dog in one of those ridiculous dog shows."

"So there was some social aspect to your relationship?" Tushton asked.

"If you can call it that. She forced herself on Wendy and me a couple of times when she heard us making plans, and then there was the dog show."

"But you wouldn't consider yourself friends with her?"

"No, I wouldn't. Amanda and I couldn't have been more opposite, from our taste in music to clothes to men. She was a spoiled little rich girl, who thought she should always get her way, and did everything she could to make sure she did," Michelle replied bitterly.

"Is it possible you felt some guilt, or maybe relief, when you saw her body on the floor?" Tushton asked.

What? No way." Michelle nearly spilled her remaining coffee as her hand slapped the table. "I'm not a monster. Even Amanda didn't deserve to die like that."

"I'm not saying you're a monster. In fact, it would be perfectly natural for you to have a moment of relief, knowing you wouldn't have to put up with her anymore. However, the moment of relief could have quickly transformed into fear and self-preservation. Did you worry at any time that the police would think you had committed the murder?"

Michelle flinched at the question and turned her gaze out the window.

Tushton reached across the table and placed a comforting hand on one of Michelle's. "You don't have to feel guilty. We all have someone in our lives that we wish we could get away from, whether it's a family member or a co-worker."

"What happened to me that morning? Why couldn't I remember what I saw when the police arrived?" Michelle asked, desperately hoping Tushton would provide some answers.

"Like I said, the brain is complex. Sometimes it shuts things into little boxes to protect itself. Most likely, when you felt the relief that Amanda was gone, then the fear of being accused, your mind couldn't handle all of the conflicting thoughts and emotions. It tried to process the information normally, which is why you were hysterical when the police first arrived, but I'm guessing you are a person who likes to be in control." Tushton paused, looking at Michelle as if waiting for confirmation of this assumption. Michelle nodded and frowned.

"The part of you that likes to be in control wasn't happy with the hysterics and decided to put everything into a box and take control of the situation. You already had the pastries there so you kicked into hostess mode, controlling who you interacted with and what the conversation was." Tushton paused, giving Michelle time to absorb this information.

"Dr. Mendenhall told me there was a picture at the police station you seemed very interested in," Tushton continued. "Can you tell me about it? What did it look like? What did it make you think of?"

Michelle closed her eyes and thought of the large print. "It was a swamp, the Everglades maybe. There was tall grass, dark water, and a blue sky with three large white clouds. On the bank, there were two alligators. One of them was looking right out of the picture, watching me."

"Did the alligator frighten you?" Tushton asked.

"No, the whole scene actually calmed me. When I was looking at it, I forgot where I was. My parents took me to the Everglades our first summer down here. I hadn't thought about that trip in years.

"One night, we went on a boat ride. As we slid across the water, the tour guide was shining a spotlight back and forth. We could see the glowing eyes of the gators all around us. I was so scared I hid behind my dad." Michelle gave a sad smile.

"The painting reminded you of this trip?" Tushton asked. Michelle nodded. "Have you talked to your parents this weekend?"

"My mom called after seeing the news Friday. I told her I was fine."

"Have you talked to anyone besides me and the police about what happened?"

Michelle shook her head. "Who can I tell? What's there to tell?"

"You found a dead body, and not just the body of a stranger, but someone you knew. You need to be able to talk about how that made you feel. How you feel now."

"I guess I feel numb right now." Michelle dropped her gaze to the floor. "And a little nervous about going to work tomorrow."

"Do you have a friend at work you can talk to, maybe one of the girls you mentioned before?"

"Wendy maybe, but I think she might want more of the gruesome details than I am ready to talk about." Michelle swallowed the last bit of cold coffee and crushed the cup. She thought of Jeffrey and wondered if he could understand.

"What about your parents? Are you close to them?" Tushton asked.

"Yeah, but my mom will worry if I tell her everything. She is a bit over protective." Michelle could picture her mother coming over and packing her up to move home.

"If she saw the news then she knows you discovered the body and she has a general idea about how Amanda died. What else are you afraid she will find out?"

"What if she finds out how I shut down, and thinks there is something wrong with me?" Michelle asked timidly.

"If she thinks that then you tell her you are already talking to me and I said there is nothing wrong with you time can't heal."

Michelle shifted in her chair and looked around the now empty café. Tushton waited, but Michelle remained silent.

"Why don't we call it a day? We can get together again later in the week and see how you are doing," Tushton suggested.

Michelle nodded and pushed back her chair, the feet squealing against the tile floor. The women walked to the door and Tushton put a hand on Michelle's shoulder as she turned toward her car.

"You call me anytime if you need to talk," Tushton said kindly, locking eyes with Michelle.

"Thank you," Michelle nodded and slipped into her car.

# CHAPTER TWENTY-EIGHT

After leaving the Roasted Bean, Michelle drove aimlessly for half an hour, until she found herself at a stoplight outside of her office building. She shivered as she looked at the front doors, knowing she would have to pass through them once more in less then twenty-four hours. The thought of returning to her desk, passing the scene of the crime, made her stomach clench. What would work be like without Amanda's radio playing sickening pop songs, without her condescending remarks, without her fashion critiques?

A car honked behind her and she realized the light had turned green. Slowly, she pulled away from the building, turned left onto Jackson Street, and entered a parking garage. The garage was practically empty and she found a spot on the first level. She slipped the car into park and cut the engine, feeling an overwhelming need to talk to someone about her fear of returning to work.

She started to call Wendy, but couldn't bring herself to share the details of Friday morning. Finally, Michelle dialed and waited as the phone rang, holding her breath until it was answered.

"Hey, how are you doing?" Jeffrey asked, his voce bright and cheerful.

"A little freaked out to be honest," Michelle replied.

"What's wrong?"

Michelle heard the concern and felt the knots in her stomach loosen the tiniest bit. "I'm kind of stressed out about going back to work tomorrow," she said, her words rushing out. "How can I go back in there and not see Amanda's body, not worry the killer is watching the building for another victim? The police have a suspect, but no motive. What if he thinks I need to be killed because I found the body?" Michelle's words were lost in sobs as all of the fear she'd been holding back came rushing forward.

"Where are you? I'll come over and we can talk it all out," Jeffrey said.

"I'm downtown," Michelle sniffed and wiped her face with the back of her hand.

"Why don't you meet me at my office? I can be there in fifteen minutes."

Michelle mumbled an agreement before hanging up and rifling through the glove box for a tissue. Finding some crumpled up napkins, she blew her nose and blotted her face before starting the car again. She exited the garage and drove three blocks to The Plaza construction site.

Jeffrey sped down I-4, praying he wouldn't be pulled over. At the exit he barely slowed for the curve, sling-shotting onto Colonial Drive, then yanked the wheel to the right onto Orange Avenue. He sailed through with all green lights until he reached The Plaza. His truck bounced over the curb, into the parking lot, and pulled to a stop next to Michelle. A cloud of dust hung in the air as he stepped out of the truck.

Jeffrey led Michelle up the steps and unlocked the trailer door. They stepped into the chilly interior and Jeffrey turned on a small electric heater before clearing off a chair and motioning Michelle to have a seat.

"It should warm up in a few minutes," Jeffrey said apologetically. "Can I get you some water?"

"No, thanks." Michelle bounced her keys in her hand.

Jeffrey pulled a chair close to her and sat down, unsure what to say. He wished Lizzie were here. She would know exactly what to do. He found himself saying a silent prayer for guidance. He was still so inexperienced at praying, he often felt like a teenage boy trying to ask the popular girl to dance. He cleared his throat and made eye contact with Michelle. She looked at him and the toughness he'd seen the last time they'd met was gone, replaced by uncertainty.

"I'm really glad you called," Jeffrey started. "Why don't you tell me what is going on?"

Michelle looked down at her hands and started cracking each knuckle. "I don't know how I can face going back into the office.

People are going to want to know what it was like to find Amanda, and I don't think I can handle that. What am I supposed to say?"

"You don't have to tell them anything if you don't want to. I think most people will understand it was a terrible experience for you and will respect that. From the little I know about the people you work with, Amanda was the one who would have made a scene about this."

Michelle's lips twitched in a brief smile. "How can I ever go into that bathroom again though?" she said in despair.

Jeffrey rubbed his chin. "That is certainly a more difficult question. I can't imagine going eight hours without using the restroom."

Michelle giggled at his serious tone. "You do have a way of putting things into perspective."

Jeffrey leaned back in his chair and crossed his right leg over left, his foot twirling in circles. "Tell me what's really bothering you."

Jeffrey watched as Michelle's gaze traveled around the cluttered office and felt embarrassed he didn't do more to keep it cleaned up.

"I've been talking to a shrink and she said something the other night I haven't been able to shake." She paused and Jeffrey waited for her continue.

"She asked me if I was questioning my mortality. I didn't think anything of it at the time, but now I'm not so sure."

Jeffrey leaned forward, placed his elbows on his knees, hands clasped together, thumbs touching his chin. "You're feeling vulnerable, maybe a little less invincible than were a few days ago?"

Michelle nodded.

"Why are you afraid of death?"

"Who isn't afraid of death? Aren't you?" Michelle asked.

"Not like I used to be, now I mostly worry about how it will affect my family and friends if I should go before them, and I hope however I go isn't painful, but other than that, I am pretty comfortable with it."

Michelle looked at him, her eyes wide. "How can you be so calm about it?"

"A few months ago, I wouldn't have been, but a lot has changed with me." Jeffrey's heart began to pound. He hadn't shared his newfound faith with anyone and now he didn't know what he was supposed to say. He wondered if this was how Lizzie had felt when he showed up on her doorstep looking for answers. He swallowed and looked Michelle right in the eye.

"The last time you saw me, I was a broken mess. I left the bar so mad at you for pushing me away. I must have gone to ten other clubs, but all of the alcohol did nothing to dull my anger. I found myself standing there, watching the people around me and for the first time, I saw desperation and squalor, where I'd only seen easy opportunities before. I left and went to see a friend who'd been trying to help me see how I was throwing my life away. Before then, I wasn't ready to hear what she had to say, but suddenly I had to have answers.

"She showed me death isn't the end. There is a chance for something more, something better than anything I have ever imagined here on earth." Jeffrey saw Michelle's face darken and hurried on. "I know what you are thinking. Lizzie wasn't the first to try to tell me these things. My friend Ian, you met him, he tried to tell me too after my fiancée died, but I wasn't ready then. I think I listened to Lizzie because I believed she understood what I was feeling more than Ian ever could.

"Lizzie talked to me about God and what having a relationship really means. For me, it was important to know my fiancée wasn't gone forever, that she was in heaven and happier than she'd ever been, and I could see her again if I chose. That night, I gave my heart to God. I won't tell you I changed overnight. It was a struggle to leave my old life behind, but it wasn't as hard as I thought it would be. I did feel more at peace, though." Jeffrey finished, surprised at how easily the words had come once he started. Maybe there was something to what Lizzie said about God giving wisdom in times of need.

Michelle could barely keep up with the thoughts swirling in her head. This man sitting before her was not the man she'd first met. While he had been confident then, perhaps to the point of arrogance, he now exuded an air of peace. He spoke with compassion and empathy so different from the anger and resentment she remembered. But was he really talking to her about God?

"I know, I know." Jeffrey chuckled as if reading her mind. "Hearing me talk about God is pretty bizarre. Outside of Lizzie and Ian, you're the first person I've spoken with about this. I'm still trying to figure things out myself, but I can tell you, I don't fear death anymore. I know now my spirit will live on and I will spend eternity in heaven. What is there to be afraid of when you know what lies ahead of you?" Jeffrey's face glowed and he spoke with confidence.

Michelle couldn't deny he had definitely changed and she found herself envying the peace she saw in him, but she wasn't sure if she was ready to believe what he was telling her.

"I can see that you've changed," she spoke slowly, careful with the words she chose. "I just don't know if this…" she moved her hands in a circle as if trying to encompass not just Jeffrey but everything. "I don't know if this is the answer."

Jeffrey nodded. "I understand. I had to hear it a number of times before I believed. You have to make your own decision, but I am happy to talk to you anytime. If you have questions I can't answer, then I'm sure Ian or Lizzie can. I just want you to know I am here if you need to talk." Jeffrey stood and clapped his hands together.

"What do you say we go get some dinner? We can catch up on all that's happened the past few months."

Jeffrey's manner was so easy going and warm that Michelle couldn't refuse. A normal evening would be nice. She followed him outside and waited as he locked up.

# CHAPTER TWENTY-NINE

"Wake up," Ian said softly, shaking her shoulders. Lizzie's eyelids fluttered and she murmured something unintelligible. He shook her again, more forcefully. "You can't go to sleep." He tried to keep the panic out of his voice, afraid that even with the fire Lizzie might be succumbing to hypothermia.

"What? Just let me sleep a few minutes," Lizzie replied groggily.

"Lizzie, you have to wake up." Ian brushed her curls off her cheek and kissed her. She smiled and opened her eyes a tiny bit.

"Please wake up," he whispered into her ear. She wiggled and sat up, eyelids drooping.

"Why can't I sleep?" she asked with a pout.

"Are you warm enough? Maybe we should move closer to the fire." Ian turned his attention to the fire and realized he'd let it burn down. He leaned over to add some more wood and moved Lizzie closer to the growing blaze. The sky had grown dark with clouds, the sun completely obscured.

"Do you think they got the text messages?" Lizzie asked.

"Yeah, they have probably already sent someone out to get us, and will be here any minute." Ian checked his watch. It'd been a little over an hour since they'd sent the texts. If they had been received, help should have arrived by now.

"I'm getting hungry, aren't you?" Lizzie asked.

"We'll have a nice big dinner when we get back to the lodge. They have an amazing porterhouse steak. Usually my parents split it."

"Mmm, that sounds good, with a loaded baked potato and biscuits." Lizzie's stomach growled, making Ian smile.

"Sounds like you could eat the whole steak by yourself," he said playfully.

"I just might," Lizzie replied. "How long were your grandparents married?"

"Almost sixty-five years," Ian said proudly. "My grandmother died a week before their anniversary. That was tough for Granddad."

"My parents had thirty years together. Sometimes I wonder if it was better that they died together. I can't imagine either one of them without the other. They were devoted to each other."

"Do you know how they met?" Ian asked, leaning back on his hands and stretching his legs toward the fire.

"A blind date actually," Lizzie replied with a giggle. "They had a mutual friend who set them up and two years later they were married. What about yours?"

"According to my dad, the first time he saw my mom was in seventh grade. She had just transferred to the school and he claims it was love at first sight. It took him three years to work up the courage to talk to her though, and even then, they just became friends. It was another year before they went on their first date. Mom told me she didn't think he was ever going to ask her out and had actually started dating one of the football players. The day after her date with Dad she broke up with the football player and started planning her wedding, even though it didn't happen for four more years." Ian chuckled. "Dad's never been in a rush to get things done."

Lizzie watched Ian's face as he spoke, drinking in the micro expressions as he remembered the stories his parents had told him. She wanted to know each of his looks, every inflection of his voice, all the subtleties of his eyes. She knew if she became intimately familiar with these things, she would always know when he was being honest with her. She hadn't missed the fact that he didn't make eye contact with her when he assured her that help was on the way and yet had held her gaze during the story about his parents.

Lizzie stood, reached her arms over her head, and bent down in a swan dive, touching her toes. Her back and shoulders ached from sitting on the floor for so long. She rose slowly, clasped her hands behind her back, and pulled downward, feeling her shoulders pop. She sighed with relief and stepped toward the fire. Her cheeks and nose were numb with cold, her lips cracked and dry.

"Maybe we should gather some more wood," Lizzie said as she looked at their dwindling supply.

Ian's gazed flicked from the small stack of branches to Lizzie and back. "I think we have enough. Someone should be here to pick us up any minute."

"Ian, stop it." Lizzie stamped her foot in frustration. "No one is coming," she yelled, then took a deep breath, and spoke as calmly as she could.

"They obviously didn't get our messages or they would have been here by now. We are going to spend the night here and tomorrow we are going to start walking back to the hotel. Now we need to make preparations to make it through the night."

Ian jumped to his feet and tried to pull Lizzie into his arms, but she resisted.

"You need to gather more wood. I'm going to build up a snow wall behind the fire to help block the wind if it shifts during the night. We will add another layer of pine to the floor to make a sleeping area. We can tip the benches up and put them against the windows to help keep out any new snow and provide a little extra protection from the wind." Lizzie spoke with determination. Ian nodded obediently and skirted the dying fire to gather more wood.

Lizzie followed him outside and surveyed the area outside the church. She could hear her father telling her about how to survive when caught in unfamiliar territory. Her idea was to take advantage of the resources she had, to pile the snow high enough to protect the open door of the church from wind without being so close that it would melt from the heat. She stepped away from the church slowly, gauging the heat as she moved. Five feet out, she shook her head. This far away, she wasn't sure if a wall would help at all.

She looked to the west where the sun hovered just above the tree line. It would be dark in a couple of hours. She scrapped the wall idea and returned to the church where she struggled with the heavy benches, scooting each one across the floor towards a window. When she reached the window, she lifted one end and pushed with all her might until the six-foot long beam stood upright. It took two benches to cover the first window. With five windows remaining and only eight benches, Lizzie studied the small room, seeking the most-strategic windows to block.

By the time Ian returned, Lizzie had covered the four windows closest to the doorway of the church, leaving one window on each side of the building near the altar only partially covered. Ian found Lizzie leaning against the wall, breathing heavily, clearly exhausted from the effort. The fire had burned down to a few hot embers. Ian hauled in the new wood as quickly as possible, then turned his attention to the fire, slowly adding twigs and blowing on it until a tentative flame licked at the kindling.

Lizzie plopped down on the floor beside him and began stripping the new branches of needles, then broke them into manageable pieces. The sweet fragrance of pine and fir reminded her of the last time she and her parents had gone shopping for a live Christmas tree. Her mom hated having a live tree because of the mess they made, but a twelve-year-old Lizzie had begged her for one until she finally gave in.

It had been an unusually cold December day as they walked among the aisles of Frasier firs trucked in from North Carolina and set up on a vacant lot in Winter Park. White Christmas lights were strung around the exterior of the lot and Christmas music came from the pickup truck by the entrance. Young Lizzie had studied each tree, finding some flaw with each one, until they came to the last row. There she found an eight-foot tree, perfectly round from trunk to tip. Her mother didn't see anything different about this tree from the fifty others they'd looked at, but Lizzie insisted this was the one. Her father had hoisted it onto his shoulder and carried it to their mini van while her mom paid. Lizzie clapped excitedly as her father tied it to the top of the van.

"Lizzie," Ian's voice brought her back to the present. "I'm sorry I got us into this mess," he said. The fire was now blazing again, warming the church. Lizzie set down the branch she'd been working on and looked deep into Ian's beautiful blue eyes.

"It's not your fault the horse got spooked," she replied softly.

"I just don't understand why the driver didn't come back for us after regaining control of the horses, or why he didn't at least return to the lodge and send someone else out to get us." Ian shook his head. "It doesn't make any sense."

"We don't know what happened to the driver. Maybe he was thrown from the sleigh or maybe there was an accident." Lizzie was suddenly struck by a terrible thought. "What if he's hurt, lying in the snow somewhere? We should have thought to look for him."

Ian's face fell. "I've been so focused on our rescue I didn't even think about that."

"Me either, not until now." Lizzie gazed past the fire into the darkness and shuddered at the sound of a coyote's howl.

"We have been operating under the assumption that he made it back to the resort. We didn't have any reason not to think that."

"Maybe for the first couple of hours, but after that we should have thought about the other possibilities. My dad would have thought of it and started a search hours ago." Lizzie fought back tears of anger and fear. Had she already forgotten so much of what she'd learned from her father?

Ian scooted closer to her and pulled her head onto his chest. He kissed her hair and searched for the words to sooth her. "Why don't you try to get some rest? I think it's warm enough now. We won't need to worry about hypothermia. I'll watch the fire."

Lizzie turned her face up to his and saw such a look of helplessness there she regretted looking up. When their eyes met, his expression quickly changed as he put on a brave face. She nodded slowly and took the scarf that dangled around her neck, folded it into a thick square, and lay down on the bed of pine, exhausted from all of the work and swarm of emotions.

Within ten minutes, Ian noticed her breathing had evened into sleep. He gazed down at her, lying on her side, curled in a fetal position. Her white blonde hair fell over her cheek and covered her eye. In sleep, her face relaxed into a peaceful picture of innocence and youth. Looking at her now, Ian's desire to protect her from all the hurt of the world grew. He fingered the small box in his coat pocket. Every day, Lizzie surprised him, but today most of all.

Her take-charge attitude had been one of the first things to attract him; her courage to tackle the task of renovating a house most men would have avoided, but today, the way she took command of their situation, when he still wasn't willing to accept the truth, made him realize she wasn't as fragile as he often let himself believe. An owl hooted in one of the trees, then there was a rustle of wings, and a triumphant screech. Ian added another log to the fire and stretched out his legs. It was going to be a long night.

# CHAPTER THIRTY

The sun had set and a thin crescent moon was rising as Michelle parked her car and climbed the stairs to her apartment. After dinner, she and Jeffrey had gone to a quiet little club in Winter Park. She was surprised when he ordered a Diet Coke and told her he didn't drink much anymore, only a glass of wine or champagne on special occasions. Michelle had felt uncomfortable with her tequila sunrise and nursed it for the next hour.

Any doubts she'd had about the possibility of Jeffrey changing were now gone. Michelle thought about their conversations today and realized that she'd done most of the talking and Jeffrey had been an attentive listener, showing real interest in everything she had to say. Not once had he made any advances or even given the slightest hint of flirtation. She had learned he wasn't currently dating anyone, which made his lack of action even more surprising. Didn't he find her attractive anymore?

Michelle went to the bathroom and studied her reflection. She wore a baggy t-shirt and jeans. Her eyes had faint circles under them and she realized she wasn't wearing any make-up. No wonder he hadn't hit on her. She looked like a middle-aged hag.

She reached up and rubbed the white scar above her eye. It was less than an inch long, but to Michelle it felt like it ran the length of her face. Why had she insisted on leaving it there? Did she really need yet another reminder of her terrible choice in men? Didn't her heart carry enough scars to remind her?

She looked at her watch and returned to the living room, where she picked up the phone and lowered herself onto the couch. Her boss had called during dinner, but she let it go to voicemail, unwilling to interrupt the conversation she and Jeffrey were having. She listened to the voicemail now.

"Michelle, it's George. I've been thinking and I want you take a few days off. Friday was very traumatic and you should take some time to recover. If there is anything we can do for you, please let me know."

A feeling of relief washed over Michelle as she listened to the message a second time. Closing out of voicemail, she dialed a new number and waited. After ten rings, she was about to hang up when there was an answer.

"Dr. Tushton, it's Michelle. Do you have a few minutes?"

"Of course, Michelle. Just give me a minute to go into another room."

Michelle could hear the doctor cover the phone and whisper something, then the slap of sandals on hardwood, a door closing, and a chair squeaking.

"Okay, I'm all yours. What's on your mind?" Tushton asked.

"I hope I didn't interrupt anything," Michelle replied.

"Not at all. A few friends are over, but they understand my job. They can make do without me for thirty minutes or so."

"I'm so sorry." Michelle felt awful for interrupting. "I can talk to you tomorrow."

"Nonsense. If you called now, then you need to talk now. Are you feeling anxious about work tomorrow?"

"Actually, I hadn't thought about it in a few hours, and I just got a message from my boss that I should take some time off."

"Really? That's great."

Michelle twisted a lock of hair around her finger, trying to gather the courage to speak, to ask the question that had been in the back of her mind all day.

"Michelle?" Tushton asked with concern.

"I'm here," Michelle replied with a sigh. "I guess I was just wondering if you believe in God."

"Do I believe in God?" she reiterated the question. "I'm not sure what I believe is relevant," Tushton deflected.

"So, does that mean you don't believe?" Michelle asked.

"I didn't say that. How do you feel about it? Do you believe?"

"I don't know. I haven't really thought too much about God before today. I mean, I guess I always thought there was some supreme power, but as long as I was a good person, didn't commit any crimes, you know, then that was all that really mattered. Now I'm not so sure."

"What changed today?" Tushton asked and Michelle could hear the click of a pen and the rustle of paper.

"You told me to find someone I could talk to about everything that's happened, so I called a guy I know. We went out a couple of times last year, but we haven't talked in months." Michelle lay back on the couch, tucked a pillow under her head, and stretched out her legs.

"Why did you call him?"

"He sent me flowers when he heard about Amanda. He's different from when I first met him. He told me about how he came to know God and how his life changed." Michelle stopped, taking a moment to reflect on her conversation with Jeffrey. "He asked me if Amanda's murder made me question my own mortality."

"And what did you say?"

"I thought it was ridiculous when you asked me, but when Jeffrey did, I realized I am afraid of dying. I've lived with that fear for years without really knowing it."

"It's not uncommon for us to fear death. It is an experience very few people have a chance to tell us about, and when we are told of near-death experiences we often find ways to discount them."

"But Jeffrey doesn't fear it. He worries about his family and friends should he die before them, but he said he isn't afraid of death anymore, because he believes in God and believes in heaven. To hear him talk about God is surreal to me. I mean, he was so, well, he wasn't anything like the people I expect to believe in God."

"Did he tell you what made him believe in God?"

"He actually said I was partly responsible. The last time we went out, he got drunk and became really possessive of me. We were invited to hang out with this band we'd gone to see and I really wanted to go. It was a great opportunity for me to network and maybe get the name of my own band out. Jeffrey and I fought and I left him there in the street.

A few weeks later, he came to apologize, but I told him to stay away from me. He said later that night he found himself at a friend's house asking her to tell him about God. I guess she'd tried to talk to him before, but he hadn't been ready to listen.

"I had my doubts about him really changing, but after spending several hours with him today, I know he's different. He is kinder and more reserved and he seems at peace. When we were talking about our lives, catching up on the past few months, I completely forgot about Amanda."

"That's good," Tushton replied cheerfully. "You will move on with your life and thoughts of Amanda won't fill your every thought. I'm glad you found a friend you can be yourself with."

"But I'm not sure I was myself," Michelle replied in frustration. "I was self-conscious when I ordered a drink and he just had a soda. I felt ashamed when I told him I didn't know if God was the answer to my problems, and yet he was still so accepting of me."

"So are you asking me if I believe in God to validate your lack of faith or to condemn it?" Tushton asked.

"I don't know," Michelle whispered. She rolled onto her side and pulled her knees to her chest. "I'm not sure what I want you to believe."

After Michelle hung up with Dr. Tushton, she wandered around the apartment, gathering up books and papers that were scattered on nearly every surface. She flipped through the neglected mail, discarding most of it as junk, but when she came across a postcard promoting a church in her neighborhood, she paused.

The front of the card was a glossy photo of the church, nothing special really. It was an older building that had been converted into a church. On the back was a message about the church and the times of services. At the bottom was the phone number, website, and an invitation to contact them for any prayer needs.

Michelle took the card to her desk and keyed in the web address. It was a simple site, with much of the same information as the postcard. She poured over the section on beliefs, comparing it to what Jeffrey had told her, then she clicked on the ministries tab. There were activities for children, teens, singles, couples, women, and men. She read about a women's group called God's Girls that not only had weekly Bible studies, but monthly social gatherings. Following the link to the calendar page, she saw they did scrapbooking, shopping, afternoon tea, clothing drives, holiday meal baskets, and there was even a group that went to the shooting range.

As she read more, she realized they seemed like normal people and wondered why she was surprised. What had she thought Christians were? Did she even know any Christians aside from Jeffrey? She ran through all the people she knew best; her band mates, Tiffani and Wendy from work, her family, some friends she kept in touch with from college, but she couldn't remember any of them ever talking about God. She considered all of them good people, but was that enough? Did any of them exude the peace she had seen in Jeffrey today?

She thought about Matt, how he never seemed to be bothered by things, his optimism each time the band had fallen apart and the two of them had to start over. She needed to talk to him, to find out what he believed, what made him so positive.

Stifling a yawn, she checked the time and found it was almost eleven. Where had the day gone? She shut down the computer, but left the postcard propped up against a cup full of pens.

# CHAPTER THIRTY-ONE

The fire burned low, a bed of hot embers on the wide stones of the church doorway. Ian lay with his back to Lizzie, one of her arms draped over his shoulder. He squinted at the fire and poked at it with a long stick. The unburned wood shifted and flames licked at it hungrily. Behind him, he heard Lizzie groan, then roll over, her hand sliding off his shoulder.

Slowly he sat up, careful not to disturb her. The pine needles under them had been warmer than he'd expected and he was grateful Lizzie had thought of spreading them on the floor. Careful not to make any noise, Ian rose and moved to one of the partially covered windows. The sky was painted a rosy pink even though he couldn't see the sun above the trees yet.

There was not a cloud in sight and the wind had died down during the night. Now it was perfectly still, the only sounds the crackling fire, a few lonely birdcalls, and Lizzie's deep, even breathing. He looked out on the cold expanse before him and wondered what his parents must be thinking. Why hadn't they sent someone out to look for him when they didn't return for dinner? Emma and Ron must be out of their minds with worry for Lizzie.

Ian turned back to watch Lizzie, sleeping so peacefully. He'd been awake most of the night, worried the fire would die. When Lizzie stirred again, he kneeled beside her, brushed several curls out of her eyes, and kissed her cheek.

"Wake up," he whispered, his lips brushing her nose as he spoke. Lizzie groaned again and rolled onto her back. Her eyelids fluttered, then opened. She looked at him, confusion filling her eyes, then recognition, and finally alarm. She sat up and looked around her.

"What time is it?" she asked, several moans of pain escaping her as she struggled to stand up.

Ian offered her a hand and pulled her to her feet. "A little after six. We should start walking if you are up to it."

Lizzie bent down to touch her toes several times, stretched her arms over her head, and leaned back as far as she could, then nodded. "How long do you think it will take?"

"A couple hours, but hopefully we'll encounter a rescue party on the way." He gave her an encouraging smile. The fire in the doorway had grown, blocking the exit, so Ian climbed out one of the windows, circled the church, and dropped several handfuls of snow onto the fire. When it was extinguished, Lizzie stepped over the smoldering branches and took Ian's hand. They turned toward the forest and the path they had come in on.

The morning was warmer than the past several days had been. As the sun appeared over the trees, the couple basked in the warmth of its rays on their faces. The path was wide and they could still see hoof prints from the horses that had rushed away the previous day. After half an hour, they came to a fork in the road. The hoof prints went one way, but there were tracks on the other path as well. Ian studied them both and decided to take the path on the left.

"The driver must not have been able to control the horses when they reached the fork and they went the other direction," Ian said.

"Should we go down there and look for them?" Lizzie asked. "What if he was thrown from the sleigh?"

Ian shook his head. "We get back to the lodge first, then we can check to see if the driver made it back. If not, we will notify the authorities. There may be another lodge or village in that direction where he spent the night."

Lizzie reluctantly agreed and they continued on. They slogged through the deep snow for another hour before Lizzie paused, out of breath.

"I need to take a break," she gasped.

Ian led her to an outcropping of rocks, brushed off the snow, and helped her sit down. He remained standing as Lizzie tried to catch her breath, his eyes flitting around them, taking in all of their surroundings.

"Listen, do you hear that?" Ian asked. He turned his gaze back to the path, but the road sloped upward. He pulled himself up on the rocks, but didn't see anything above the rise.

"I don't hear anything," Lizzie replied. "What is it?"

"I think it's a snowmobile." Ian closed his eyes and focused on the sound, a low whine in the distance, but he couldn't tell which direction it was coming from.

"Do you think you can walk again?" Ian asked. Lizzie nodded and slid off the rock. Ian carefully climbed back down to join her and took her hand as they started off again. Gradually the noise grew louder.

"I can hear it now," Lizzie exclaimed.

They tried to push forward faster, but this seemed to make them sink deeper into the soft snow. The sun was directly overhead when they reached the top of the ridge and stopped to search the road ahead of them. The road widened and the forest thinned on either side, dwindling down to a sparse scattering of trees a mile ahead of them. In the distance, they could see three snowmobiles headed toward them. Lizzie began to wave wildly at them.

Relief washed over Ian at the sight. Lizzie stopped waving and leaned against Ian, who circled her with his arms. He could feel her body trembling, from cold, exhaustion, or relief he didn't know, but he pulled her closer, his arms tight around her. They stood this way until the snowmobiles pulled up beside them.

"You folks need some help?" one of the men called above the noise of the engines.

"Yes, we are trying to get back to Bear Mountain Lodge," Ian replied.

"Sure. Hop on." The man slapped the seat behind him. Ian helped Lizzie straddle the seat behind the man before jumping on behind one of the other riders.

The snowmobiles made a wide turn and sped down the road one after the other. The lodge came into view less than ten minutes later. When they pulled to a stop in front of the lodge, Lizzie slid off the seat and hugged her rescuer. Ian appeared by her side and thanked the man as well. The three drivers waved and zoomed off.


Ian and Lizzie entered the warm lodge, their steps slow. Lizzie pulled off her gloves and unwound the scarf around her head and neck. Ian stuffed his own gloves into his jacket pocket and pushed the button for the elevator. Lizzie looked up at him and saw the exhaustion in his eyes. She reached up and caressed his face, then pulled him toward her and kissed him, a long lingering kiss, only letting go when the elevator doors opened.

They stepped inside the elevator, and when the doors closed, Ian kissed her again. He held her head in both his hands and she could feel the heat rising in her body. She ran her hands down his back and pressed her stomach against his. Longing ached within her, then she stepped back abruptly, pulling herself free of Ian's grasp. Cautiously, she lifted her eyes to his, expecting to see anger or frustration. Instead, she found relief. He gave her a weak smile and took a step back to lean on the wall of the elevator.

When they reached the fourth floor, Lizzie stepped out first, with Ian close behind. They walked in silence to Lizzie's door. She slipped the key into the lock and entered, surprised to find the suite dark.

"Maybe they are with my parents," Ian said after they had checked to make sure Ron and Emma weren't there. They found Ian's room dark and empty as well. Ian went to the phone and called the front desk to see if they had left a message for him.

"Mr. Cavanaugh? No, we don't have any messages, but I do believe I saw your parents leaving with another couple when I first came in this morning, around eight," the agent told him. "They seemed a bit upset, now that I think about it."

"Thank you." Ian hung up and pulled out his cell phone, only to find the battery had died. Lizzie checked hers and found it dead as well.

"Let me get my charger out of the bedroom."

Lizzie watched him disappear into the next room, acutely aware of how alone they were, and the longing rose within her again. When Ian returned, he no longer wore the jacket or sweatshirt, only a tight white t-shirt that showed the rippling muscles of his chest and stomach. She dropped her gaze to the carpet and listened as Ian plugged the phone into a nearby outlet.

When the phone came back on Ian pressed the speed dial for his father and waited impatiently. It went to voicemail and he hung up, immediately punching the button for his mother. After three rings, she answered.

"Ian! Where are you? We've been worried sick." Cassandra's words rushed out in a panic.

"We're okay. We just got back to the hotel. Where are you?" Ian spoke calmly.

"We finally found someone to take us out looking for you," Cassandra replied, calmer now.

"We'll tell you everything when you get back," Ian said through a yawn. When he hung up, Lizzie hazarded a look at him.

"Why don't you go lie down?" she said, taking a step toward the door. "I am going to crawl into a long hot bath until my bones don't ache from the cold."

Ian reached for her hand. They looked in each other's eyes and saw the desire burning inside. Ian lifted her fingers to his lips and dropped a soft kiss on them, then he let her go.

Lizzie hurried from the room, her hands shaking as she tried to unlock her own door. When she finally got inside, she ran into her bathroom, shut the door behind her, and started to fill the large bathtub with hot water. When the tub was half-full, she slipped in under the water and lavender-scented bubbles.

When the door closed behind Lizzie, Ian dropped to his knees and rested his head on the edge of the sofa. He'd felt physical attraction to women before, but the desire that burned within him now was like nothing he'd ever known. The attraction with Lizzie had always been strong, but surviving their night in the woods seemed to have magnified the longing and he knew she felt it too. In the past, she had been very guarded with him and made sure they weren't often alone and he respected her for that. Had she not chosen to leave just now he didn't know if he could have controlled his desire.

"Lord, I am weak and need your strength," Ian called out. "Help me to be an honorable man and respect Lizzie." Ian remained on his knees, struggling to hear God speaking to him. Gradually his racing heart slowed, his body relaxed, and peace filled his spirit.

# CHAPTER THIRTY-TWO

Detective Emerson sat at his desk, sipping a cup of coffee from Dunkin Donuts as he reviewed Amanda's case file. It had been three days since her body was discovered. If he didn't get a name for their suspect today, he was going to have to take the photo to the media.

"Someone here to see you, sir," a young cop said. Emerson looked up and saw a man in his early thirties with floppy brown hair, three days of stubble on his face, and wide brown eyes.

"How can I help you?" Emerson asked wearily.

"I'm Marty, you left me a couple of messages," the man replied.

Emerson perked up and offered the man a seat. "I appreciate you coming in. I've been told you might be able to ID a suspect we have in the murder of Amanda Barnes."

Marty looked alarmed. "Me? I didn't even know the woman."

Emerson pulled the photo out of the file and passed it to Marty. "Do you recognize this man?"

Marty studied the photo. "Yeah that's Randy. He's been at a few of *Tangled Web's* shows. I haven't seen him in a month or so, though."

"Do you know Randy's last name?" Emerson asked, his excitement growing.

Marty's brow wrinkled in concentration. "Little, I think. He's a mechanic at A to Z Garage. He did some work on my car."

"Do you know where he lives or where he might hang out?"

Marty shook his head. "We never talked about stuff like that."

"What did you talk about? Any little thing could help us out."

Marty scratched his head. "Mostly we talked about the band and cars. When he heard I had a '66 Mustang that needed some work, he was more than happy to help out."

"Did he mention having a girlfriend?"

"Nah," Marty shrugged. "I wish I could be more help."

Emerson stood and shook Marty's hand. "You have been helpful. I'll walk you out." On the way out, Emerson saw McDonald and waved for her to follow him. Outside Emerson thanked Marty again and waited for McDonald to catch up.

"What's up?" McDonald asked as she approached.

"We have a name and place of employment for our suspect," Emerson said, barely controlling his excitement.

"What are we waiting for?" McDonald asked and they took off at a jog for Emerson's car.

A wreck had several blocks closed and the detoured traffic moved at a snail's pace. Emerson drummed his fingers on the steering wheel, anxious to get to the garage. When they finally arrived, he advised McDonald to follow his lead.

"Mornin'," a scruffy man in his late forties wearing a dirty baseball cap, stained jeans, and a navy button-down shirt with a name patch sewn on that read "Eddie" greeted them. "What can I do ya for?"

Emerson noticed the man was missing three of his teeth and his words had a whistling quality to them. "I think the brakes need to be repaired. Would you mind taking a look?"

"Sure thing." The man turned back toward the garage. "Randy! Customer!"

Emerson tensed and shot a look at McDonald, who was easing her hand back to her holster. He gave her a slight shake of his head and she dropped her hand. Randy strolled out of the garage, a cigarette dangling from his mouth. Emerson studied the man as he approached, comparing him to the photo he knew so well by now.

Randy paused when he caught sight of Emerson. His eyes flicked from the detective to the Crown Vic several times, then he turned and ran, toppling two large garbage cans behind him.

"Call for back up," Emerson screamed as he took off after Randy. He heard McDonald call in their location and slam the car door as she threw the vehicle into reverse.

Randy turned down a narrow alley between the garage and another building, then made a quick left. Emerson pounded behind him, his suit coat flapping in the breeze. When he reached the corner, he paused, pulled his gun from the holster, and peeked around the corner. Randy was still running full speed. Emerson stepped out.

"Stop right there," Emerson shouted, raising his gun, but Randy continued to run until he reached another opening where he turned right. Emerson ran after him and rounded the corner in time to see Randy run into the street where McDonald was waiting, gun drawn. Randy paused a second, looked from McDonald back to Emerson, then turned and ran up the street.

Emerson came out on the sidewalk and looked in the direction Randy had fled, but he had disappeared in a crowd of tourists disembarking a large red tour bus. Emerson's shoulders slumped and he doubled over, trying to catch his breath.

"You okay?" McDonald asked. Emerson nodded and moved toward the car. He slipped into the passenger seat.

"Let's go back to the garage. See if we can get his home address," Emerson panted.

As McDonald drove, Emerson reached for the radio. "I need to put out an all points bulletin for Randy Little. Last seen fleeing on foot, north on..." Emerson craned his neck to see the street sign they were passing, "...north on White Oak Drive. Suspect is wearing jeans, and a navy shirt with a name patch."

When they arrived back at the garage, a police cruiser was parked in front. Emerson nodded at the officers standing menacingly on each side of the garage owner.

"I guess your brakes are okay after all," the owner nervously tried to joke.

"Seems that they are," Emerson replied. "I need Randy's home address and any other information you can give me about him; where he likes to hang out, who his friends are, anything that will help us find him."

"I have his address in the office, but I don't know much about him. He's only been working here a few months. Keeps to himself mostly." The owner led them into a cramped office that smelled of tobacco and grease. He pulled open a file cabinet drawer with a loud creak and retrieved a thin manila folder.

"This is all the information I have on him," he said, handing the folder to Emerson, who flipped it open and searched the few pages for a home address.

"Only a post office box," Emerson said in disgust, closing the file. He turned to one of the officers. "You two sit on this place in case he comes back." The officers nodded.

"What's our next move?" McDonald asked as they returned to the car.

"We try to get a warrant for the post office box and we set up surveillance on it." Emerson slipped into the driver's seat and slammed the door. He didn't wait for McDonald to buckle her seat belt before pulling out of the parking lot.

"How do we find out where the post office box is?" McDonald asked. "There must be hundreds of possibilities."

"The zip code," Emerson's response was curt. He was already thinking of other ways to track down Randy Little. They rode the rest of the way in silence. At the station, Emerson's long strides made McDonald run to keep up. He went straight to the tech team, stopping in front of the desk of a skinny man with thick black glasses and hair cut close to his head.

"Ernie, I need a records search on a Randy Little." Emerson tossed the file from the garage on the desk. "Social security number is in here. I need to know where he lives, if he owns a car, who he owes money to. I want to know everything there is to know about this guy!"

"Sure detective. I'll get to it as soon as I finish what I'm doing," Ernie replied, pushing his glasses up on his nose, only to have them slide down again.

Emerson slammed his palm on the desk, causing a can of soda to tip over and spill on a pile of papers. Ernie jumped up before the liquid ran into his lap and grabbed a bunch of napkins from a drawer.

"I don't care what you're working on now," Emerson growled, getting right in Ernie's face. "I need this information pronto."

"I...I...but," Ernie stammered.

"No excuses. Just get to work." Emerson glared at the man then turned and made his way to the captain's office.

# CHAPTER THIRTY-THREE

Renee Therriault found Stephen in the lobby at eleven sharp. She knew she looked stunning in a simple, yet elegant, sheath dress in a deep blue that brought out the color of her eyes, but the subtle look of appreciation she saw on Stephen's face still gave her a jolt of adrenaline. She willed her hands to remain at her sides, rather than fussing with the diamond studs adorning her ears.

"Your car is ready," Stephen said in greeting, escorting her to the porte cochere where a black Cadillac waited. Renee slid into the car with out acknowledging Stephen or the driver.

In the car, Renee opened a small compact and checked her make-up, puckering her lips to refresh her lipstick. She snapped the compact shut and looked out the window towards Lake Eola. In minutes, the car was pulling into a parallel parking spot in front of the Lakeview Inn.

Renee waited for the driver to open her door, watching a couple stroll down the sidewalk hand in hand, bundled in sweaters and scarves. She thought the idea of such warm clothing on this beautiful day, when it couldn't have been below fifty degrees, was laughable. Her friends in New York would kill for a February day this warm.

The driver opened the door and Renee stepped out onto the sidewalk. A brisk wind shook the bare trees along the street, their limbs making a loud scratching noise. The large windows of the restaurant reflected her image and she smiled at what she saw. It would be hard to guess that she was fifty-eight-years-old by looking at her.

Her stilettos echoed on the sidewalk as she crossed to the entrance. Inside, a handsome young man with a smile that would make any orthodontist proud greeted her. He escorted her to a table in a small alcove obscured by a large fern. Darren Kingsley stood to greet her, surprise registering on his face when their eyes made contact.

Renee embraced the man loosely and allowed him to kiss both of her cheeks. She was enjoying his speechlessness and decided to allow the shock to hang in the air a few more moments before speaking. She took a seat and crossed her legs, her back ramrod straight.

"I'm happy to see you remember me," Renee finally said. Darren, who was still standing, sat down and placed one palm on the table.

"I do. How long has it been?" Darren asked.

"Twenty three years, next week, if I remember right. How've you been Darren?"

"I've been well. Business is good. Family is great. I have a wife and three kids, one boy and two girls."

"Yes, I heard about your marriage. Your oldest is twenty now, isn't she?" Renee enjoyed the renewed surprise this comment elicited.

"How did you know?"

"I keep myself well informed." Renee smiled.

"Well, you're correct. Emma will be twenty in the spring." Darren took a sip of water.

"I must say. I'm quite surprised you wanted to meet with me." Darren set his water glass down.

"Why's that?"

Darren studied Renee before answering. The last time he'd seen her had been at a benefit for some museum she was on the board of. They'd been dating four years. Renee was the only daughter of a wealthy businessman who owned several resorts in Las Vegas, Vail, and Boston. Darren started out in the hotel business working for Renee's father. When Darren bought his first hotel, a small establishment in St. Augustine, Florida, Rene's father had been his advisor.

At the museum dinner, Renee had flown into a rage when she found Darren in the arms of another woman. He'd tried to explain he was trying to help the woman, who was very intoxicated, but she'd been resistant to his help and they had fallen into a tangle. Renee wouldn't listen and ended things with him then and there. Darren had tried for days to get her to listen to reason, but she wouldn't take his calls and after three days, she blocked his number.

"I believe your last words to me were, 'I don't ever want to see your cheating face again.'" Darren couldn't help smiling at the memory of her angry tirade.

"Yes, I may owe you an apology for that. I found out the next day you were telling me the truth, but it was for the best that we ended things. Our relationship wasn't going anywhere anyway." Renee waved her hand dismissively as if the past was an annoying fly.

"So you put my concierge through all the trouble of contacting me so you could apologize? I don't know Renee, that doesn't sound like you."

"Of course not, I said I *may* owe you an apology, but you should know there is very little I apologize for. I wanted to talk business."

"I hear you are in the cosmetic business," Darren replied.

"I'm not here to talk about cosmetics. I'm here to talk to you about Daddy's business. He's over eighty now and he has decided to sell his company. He wants to know if you'd be interested in buying it."

Darren choked on the water he had been drinking as she spoke. He patted his face with a napkin and tried to catch his breath between coughing fits. Renee studied her perfectly manicured nails, waiting for him to regain his composure. When the coughing stopped, she looked up.

"Your father wants me to buy his company?" Darren asked in disbelief.

"You and he always did get along and he's followed your career. He's been impressed with the business decisions you've made and feels like you would be the best man to take over Ryland Resorts. Your resorts here in Florida are nice, but you do need to diversify."

Darren was speechless, trying to wrap his head around this sudden offer. A server came to take their order, but Darren dismissed her.

"I don't know if I could even afford to buy the company," Darren finally replied, but his mind was already working furiously to find a way to make the deal happen.

"Don't play hard to get with me," Renee replied. "I know you want this."

"You seem to think you know an awful lot about me these days," Darren said, annoyed at the way he was allowing Renee to run this meeting. "I happen to be quite happy with business the way it is. Why would I want to take on a whole new company?"

"Because you would have inherited the company if we'd gotten married and you were more upset about losing that prospect than you were about losing me."

Darren started to protest, but she stopped him. "Don't insult me by denying it. If you really wanted to be with me, you wouldn't have given up after a week. I've had stray dogs follow me for longer. Plus, I know you and Daddy have kept in touch. You may not be the best of friends, but you do check in on him several times a year."

"What are the terms of the sale," Darren asked.

A slight smile pulled at Renee's lips. "The company is worth five hundred million, but Daddy would give it to you for two hundred. He certainly doesn't need the money and I'm doing quite well for myself. He would want you to retain as many employees as possible from the corporate office, but understands some may need to be let go due to redundancy with your own employees."

Darren swallowed hard at the numbers. "What about the location of the corporate office? I don't know if I would want to keep it in New York. I would probably want to combine the two companies in one location, here in Florida. That would certainly make a difference in which employees stayed. I can't imagine they would all be willing to move."

Renee nodded. "If you wish to do that, then Daddy asks you give them a year so those who don't wish to move can find other jobs. You might be surprised how many would take the move, though."

Darren ran calculations, shifted funds in his mind, and considered the pros and cons of this expansion. "I appreciate the offer, Renee, and I will seriously consider it, but I need a few days."

"Of course. We wouldn't want you to make this kind of decision lightly." She reached into her purse and pulled out a business card. "My personal numbers are on the back. I leave town tomorrow, but you can call me anytime. I'm sure Daddy would be happy to talk to you as well if you have any questions." Renee unrolled a napkin and set it on her lap with a flourish. "Why don't we have something to eat now?'

Darren and Renee caught up on the past twenty years of their lives over salads and grilled fish. Stephen had told Darren that Renee had been married at least twice, but he was surprised to learn it was actually four times.

"They just don't seem to stick," Renee said casually when he asked about it. "Men seem to find it hard to be with a woman who is more successful than they are."

"What about your current husband?"

Renee smiled sadly. "Stanley died eight months ago. He was the best, though."

"I'm so sorry," Darren replied, seeing a side of Renee he hadn't seen since they'd first met.


When Renee returned to the hotel, Stephen was waiting in the lobby. He spotted the car as soon as it arrived and hurried to the front door. She brushed past him without comment and he considered letting her go without speaking with her, but he caught sight of Ellen Cartwright entering the dining room and his resolve was stiffened.

"Mrs. Therriault?" Stephen said as he sped to catch up with her.

She turned and looked at him somewhat surprised. "What?" she snapped at him.

"I was wondering if you might have a moment. There was an incident I'd like to discuss with you." Stephen hoped he sounded more confident then he felt.

Renee stared at him waiting for him to continue.

"In private," Stephen said.

"Must it be now? I have a spa appointment."

"I know, and I already told the therapist you may be a few minutes late." Stephen shrank under the withering glare Renee gave him at these words. "I promise it will only take a moment, but I think you should know."

"All right," Renee sighed and followed Stephen into the office.

Stephen waited while Renee settled herself in a stiff chair. When she shot him a look of annoyance, he took a deep breath.

"Mrs. Therriault, yesterday, two of your employees were having a very loud argument in the lobby. I was able to get them to calm down and tried to help them discuss their concerns privately, but they wouldn't speak once I had them in the office."

"What business is it of yours?" Renee bit out.

"Protecting the reputation of this hotel as well as that of our guests is part of my job. It certainly doesn't look good if we allow scenes like that nor does it reflect well on your company. However, that isn't the real reason I wanted to speak to you." Stephen paused, drawing on every ounce of courage he possessed. "I believe Ellen Cartwright may be trying to do something behind your back and I think she is trying to use your assistant, Donna."

Renee's face was an unreadable mask. Her gaze burned into Stephen like a focused laser. Stephen waited for some reaction, hesitant to continue with his theory, but she remained silent. He opened his mouth to speak again, but she raised a hand.

"Young man, I don't know what kind of game you are playing, but that is a serious accusation. How do you know they were not arguing about a personal matter?"

"Well, I did hear Donna telling Ellen she works for you and no one else, and Ellen told Donna she is an employee of the company overall and should do what she is told. When I sat them down and inquired if I should contact you to help sort things out they both refused. It seemed like Ellen wanted Donna to do something that made her uncomfortable."

Renee gave a small laugh. "Ellen probably wanted Donna to pack for her or run to the store for something. She's always taking advantage of the assistants at the office."

"Maybe," Stephen admitted, beginning to feel like he hadn't really thought this through. "But I did some research on Ellen and found she has a history of trying to, how do I say this?" Stephen searched for a delicate term, but came up empty. "Well, stab her employers in the back."

"I know about Ellen's past," Renee replied curtly and stood to leave. "If that's all you have, I'll be going."

"Yes, ma'am." Stephen rose as well. "I just thought you should know."

"I would appreciate you minding your own business from now on," Renee replied hotly. She swung the door open and her heels clicked on the marble floors all the way to the elevator, a rapid *click, click, click* that Stephen would hear in his dreams.

# CHAPTER THIRTY-FOUR

The elevator doors slid closed and Renee allowed her rigid body to sag. If Stephen had been able to uncover solid information about Ellen, it certainly didn't reflect well on the hiring process for her company, but she was more concerned about the argument between Donna and Ellen.

She had spent years trying to find an assistant she could trust, and Donna had been a godsend. She knew when to leave a room and when to provide interference; she didn't mind traveling or working late; and most of all she had never violated Renee's confidence. Until now, Renee thought.

When the elevator chimed for the sixth floor, Renee straightened her shoulders and held her head high, just in case she encountered one of her employees on the way to her room. She entered the suite, tossed her handbag onto the sofa, and made a beeline for the wet bar. She poured a glass of white wine and swirled it around before taking a sip. Her massage appointment was in less than fifteen minutes, but she needed something to help her relax now.

Her mind raced, reviewing the past few weeks, searching for any memories of Donna acting differently. Could she have been upset with her Christmas bonus? It had been a little less than the previous years, but she'd received more stock options as well. Renee shook her head, set the empty wine glass on the bar, and left for the spa. She would have a talk with Donna this evening and clear things up.

Stephen sank into a chair and dropped his head into his hands. He'd made a fool of himself and he may have jeopardized any future business with Renee Therriault. What had made him think he could play detective? That he had any right to tell the woman how to run her company? His face throbbed, making him sit up and rummage in a desk drawer for a bottle of Tylenol. He couldn't remember how long it had been since his last dose, but he popped two pills anyway, twisting the cap off a bottle of warm water.

He flipped through the pages of his notebook, separating those with notes about Renee and Ellen. He grasped them in his hand, ready to yank them out and toss them in the trash, when the phone rang. He was surprised to see Renee's room number on the display.

"Hello, Mrs. Therriault, this is Stephen. How can I help you?" he answered in a shaky voice.

"I just realized I didn't get Darren Kingsley's phone number during lunch. Would you give it to me, please?" she asked as if their previous conversation had never happened.

Stephen hesitated. Mr. Kingsley had agreed to meet her, but shouldn't he have given her his number if he wanted her to keep in touch?

"Sometime today, please." Renee added the please, but it wasn't a request, it was a command.

"I'm sorry, Mrs. Therriault. I will have to check with him first," Stephen replied, knowing he was risking everything by refusing her.

Renee let out an irate sigh, and then there was silence; a silence that seemed to stretch on for hours. "Fine, but I need that number before I check out." Renee slammed down the phone.

Stephen replaced the receiver and laid his head on the desk, carefully cradling his throbbing face and nose. For the first time in more years than he could remember, he just wanted to give up. Between the pain of his broken nose and the fear of angering one of the hotel's most prestigious clients, he wanted nothing more than to leave, to go home, and hide until Lizzie returned.

The office door opened slowly, Ben cautiously peeking his head around before entering. He'd been doing that ever since hitting Stephen, and while it had been funny at first, it was beginning to annoy Stephen now.

"Just open the door," Stephen yelled in a tired voice.

Ben looked sheepish as he sat down across from Stephen. "Sorry, I don't want to hurt anyone else. Maybe we need to put a window in so we can see if someone is coming."

"Forget about it, accidents happen. I'm not mad at you." Stephen tried to smile at his coworker, but grimaced at the pain that shot through his swollen face.

"All the women are in the spa for the rest of the afternoon and it looks like it will be a quiet night. Why don't you go home early?" Ben offered.

"I need to make a couple of phone calls, but I would appreciate it if you could make sure the baggage collection for tomorrow morning is all set up and the letters telling the executives when they need to be ready to leave are delivered to their rooms tonight." Stephen pushed a carton of letters across the desk.

Ben stood and gave Stephen a salute before scooping up the box.

# CHAPTER THIRTY-FIVE

Emerson slammed down the phone, picked it up, and slammed it down three more times. Work continued around him without a single person stopping to look in his direction. All of the detectives were used to his bursts of anger and frustration by now.

"Lousy red tape," he growled to no one in particular. He leaned back in his chair until it groaned under his weight and threatened to split in half, then he stood and shuffled through some papers. He wasn't looking for anything in particular, but he couldn't sit still. He was so close to catching Amanda's killer and yet here he was sitting in the office, waiting for a warrant for the post office box. Anyone who believed justice was swift had never worked in law enforcement.

McDonald nimbly crossed the room, carrying two cups of steaming coffee. She handed one to Emerson without speaking. He accepted it and dropped back down into his chair.

"Thanks," he muttered as he tipped the cup back. When the liquid hit his tongue, his face screwed up and he nearly gagged. "What is that crap?" he yelled, tossing the full cup into the garbage.

Several guys nearby stifled their amusement, but McDonald gave a laugh. "It *was* a peppermint mocha. Thought you might want to try something new."

Emerson stuck his tongue out, scrunched up his eyes, yanked open a desk drawer, and rooted around until he found an old pack of gum. The stick was stiff when he popped it in his mouth and he had work to chew it into a little ball. It didn't taste much better than the coffee. More ripples of quiet laughter rolled around the room. Spitting out the gum, Emerson rose and stalked toward the break room. Three minutes later, he returned with a half-empty can of soda.

"When do you think we'll get the warrant?" McDonald asked.

"Not until late this afternoon. I'm hoping he will turn up at one of the places we have uniforms sitting on and save us the trouble, but I doubt he will."

"Have you talked to Michelle again? Maybe her band can get a gig somewhere to draw him out." McDonald took a sip of her own coffee, closing her eyes; an unashamed smile turned up her thin lips as she reveled in the sweet beverage.

Emerson polished off his soda and crushed the can. "I can't decide if Randy is such a pro he's never been caught before and therefore might be cocky enough to attend a show or if this is his first offense and now that we are on to him he is so scared he's holed up somewhere trying to plan a way out of town."

"I'd vote for the latter," McDonald replied thoughtfully.

"Why?" Emerson was interested in the young detective's reasoning.

"The way he ran when we showed up. A pro who doesn't think he can be caught would have stuck around, chatted with us to find out what we already knew and maybe even try to point us in a different direction."

"You think so?" Emerson asked in an unconvinced tone.

McDonald nodded. "Most serial killers don't think they *can* be caught. This guy was scared out of his mind."

Emerson considered this and nodded. "If that's the case, finding him isn't going to be easy."

"Maybe, but being scared, he is more likely to go someplace he feels safe, where he has some kind of support system. A bar where he's a regular, a good friend's house. Heck with a guy like this, if his mother is in town I'd check there first. If we were up north, I'd say he probably lives in her basement. What's the equivalent of that here in the flat land?"

Emerson chuckled. "Garage apartment." He was impressed. McDonald hadn't said much up to this point, remaining in the background, but she made some good points now. Obviously, she'd been paying attention to the evidence and formulating her theory. Emerson picked up the phone and dialed.

"Ernie, what have you got for me?" Emerson asked. "What do you mean you haven't started yet? I told you this was a priority." Emerson tapped a pen on the desk as he listened. "If you can't do it, then find another one of your nerds who can." He slammed down the phone, rocketed out of his seat, and barged into the captain's office. Captain Raley's withering gaze didn't slow Emerson down. He pushed past the officer who'd been giving Raley a report on a drug bust the night before.

"How am I supposed to solve a murder when the guys in tech are doing scut work that robbery is too lazy to do themselves?" Emerson roared.

"Detective," Raley said, her tone cool. "I am in the middle of a conversation. You are welcome to wait outside while I finish up."

The officer shuffled nervously behind Emerson. "I can come back ma'am," he said timidly.

"Why don't you do that?" Emerson said without taking his eyes off the captain.

"No, Detective Emerson is leaving," Raley replied, steel in her voice. "What were you saying about the boys that were rounded up in the bust?" Raley's gaze slipped around Emerson to the unsettled officer, who flipped back and forth in his small notebook.

"Um, I think that, oh yes, here it is." The officer skimmed the page before looking up again. "Two of the suspects we caught are willing to name their boss if we cut them a deal. The DA is working on those details now."

"Good." Raley smiled. "Anything else?"

"No, ma'am. That's about it." The officer slipped the notebook into his shirt pocket.

"All right then. Keep me posted." Raley nodded in dismissal and Emerson could hear the officer scurrying down the hall.

Emerson was seething. Raley must have seen the fire in his eyes, but she didn't address him right away. Instead, she turned to her computer and started typing. Emerson rolled back and forth on the balls of his feet until she finished typing and faced him.

"I should write you up for insubordination," Raley said.

"I'm just trying to do my job, but I can't do it alone." Emerson restrained himself, trying to keep his voice calm.

"There is no reason for you to barge into my office and interrupt a meeting. I've told you before and I won't tell you again. This is your last warning." Raley locked eyes with Emerson, making sure he understood she meant it. Emerson looked away first.

"Yes ma'am," Emerson replied with the slightest trace of remorse.

"Now, tell me what you need."

"I need a complete profile of Randy Little. I gave Ernie all the information I had four hours ago and he hasn't even started working on it." Emerson hated that he sounded like a whining child and cleared his throat. How did Raley do that to him, he mused. "I know he has other things going on as well, but if he couldn't do it, then he should have delegated it to one of the other guys. My suspect could be fleeing town right now."

"You're sure this is your guy?" Raley asked.

"Unless he had some legitimate reason to be in the building at the exact time of the murder, yeah, I'm sure." Emerson shoved his hands in his pockets, watching as Raley doodled on her blotter.

"I'll give Ernie a call and see if he can get you some information before the end of the day," Raley finally replied. With a dismissive wave, she picked up the phone. Emerson lingered a moment, but a look at the captain's pursed lips sent him back to his desk. More waiting. There had to be something he could do instead of just sitting around here.

McDonald was leaning on his desk looking at the crime scene photos when he returned. "Did you notice the logo on the sweatshirt?" she said, pointing to the picture of Randy Little.

Emerson picked up the photo and held it closer, squinting as he tried to make out the logo. "No, what is that?"

"Hard to tell. Maybe we can get it blown up."

"Maybe." Emerson dialed the number for the audio-visual room. "It's Emerson. Any chance we can get an image enhanced on the security camera photo of Randy Little." Emerson nodded at McDonald. "I'm looking at a logo in the upper left corner of the sweatshirt." The tech advised Emerson he'd see what he could do to enlarge the image.

"Good eye, McDonald," Emerson said after hanging up.

"I was also wondering, did you show his picture around at the Loaded Hog? Isn't that the bar where *Tangled Web* played most of their shows before the night of the murder?"

"Some uniforms showed his picture around, but no one seemed to remember him." Emerson considered this. If Randy had attended enough performances for the band members to recognize him, how had the bartenders and servers not?

"It might be worth a second visit, though. We can check out a few of the other establishments down there too."

Pocketing the photo and holstering his 9 mm, Emerson headed out to the street. In the parking lot, he tossed the keys to McDonald. Caught off guard, they bounced out of her hands and she bent over to pick them up.

"You want me to drive?" she asked, the corners of her lips twitching upwards.

"Sure, you earned it." Emerson settled into the passenger seat and strapped on his seat belt while McDonald fiddled with the seat adjustment.

"Just don't get too comfortable over there," Emerson said with a nudge.

The club was empty when the detectives walked in. Emerson wandered toward a door behind the bar. "Anyone here?" he called.

A young man, wearing a black t-shirt stretched tight across his bulging muscles and black jeans, black hair cropped close to his head, came out carrying four cases of beer. He settled the cases on the counter before addressing them.

"We don't open for a couple more hours."

Emerson flashed his badge. "We're here on business."

"Sure, I'm Jimmy. How can I help you?"

Emerson pulled out the photo of Randy Little and handed it to the bartender. "Do you recognize this man?"

The bartender took the photo and studied for a minute. "I don't think so. Should I?"

"He's been in here a few times," McDonald replied, surprising Emerson.

The bartender laughed. "You know how many people have been in here a few times?"

"This guy would have been in here on nights that *Tangled Web* played. Sat with Marty and Elliot at the front table the last few shows." Emerson said.

The bartender studied the photo again. "I don't get out from behind the bar much during the night. You'd probably have better luck with one of the waitresses. Sally is working tonight and she should be here in an hour or so."

Emerson nodded. "Thanks. We'll stop back by then."

Out on the sidewalk, Emerson looked up and down Orange Avenue. A line of cars idled before him at a traffic light. The stench of burning oil and a cloud of gray smoke puffed from an old SUV half a block away. He turned his back on the light and sauntered down the sidewalk to the next bar.

After forty-five minutes, Emerson and McDonald had visited all of the clubs on Orange Avenue. While a few people had recognized Randy Little, no one knew much about him. Emerson was tired and irritated when they returned to the Loaded Hog. Sally was a tall, broad woman, with hair the color of fresh, loamy soil, eyes like chestnuts, and an air of confidence that said, "Don't mess with me."

"I hear you are asking around about Randy," Sally said as she wiped down a table with a damp cloth. Emerson was relieved she was bending over so that he didn't have to look up to her.

"Yeah, we're trying to get in touch with him," Emerson replied casually.

Sally straightened to her full six-foot, two-inch height, and flipped the rag over her shoulder. Emerson could feel her sizing him up. "Is he in trouble?" she asked.

"We have some questions for him." Emerson didn't want to get into the details without knowing Sally's connection to Little.

"He's a suspect in a murder investigation," McDonald blurted out.

"Murder? Randy?" Sally laughed. "You have the wrong guy. Randy doesn't have it in him to kill nobody. He's been beat up a few times, usually for hitting on some other guy's girl, but he's harmless."

Emerson positioned himself in front of McDonald in an attempt to block her from the rest of the conversation. "He's usually out alone, looking to pick up women?"

"Yeah, he usually comes in alone, but he meets up with a few guys, depending on what night of the week it is. I'm telling ya, though. Randy didn't kill anyone. It just isn't possible."

"Do you happen to know where he lives?" Emerson asked.

"Nah, he's never mentioned it." Sally took the rag from her shoulder and moved to another table.

Emerson was beginning to think this was just another dead end. "Has he used a credit card to pay his tab?"

Sally paused. "Yeah, he has a few times."

"Do you think we can get copies of those receipts?" Emerson asked hopefully.

"I don't know. He hasn't been in for over a week. You'll need to talk to Jimmy to see if we still have those." Sally bent down to wipe the table and Emerson thanked her for her time. Jimmy was already heading towards the cramped office behind the bar and Emerson followed him. Five narrow filing cabinets crammed full of papers lined the walls.

Jimmy pointed at one wedged into a corner farthest from the door. "That's where we have all of the receipts for the past month. Feel free to go through them."

Emerson looked at McDonald and smirked. "You better get busy detective," Emerson said.

McDonald's eyes grew wide and she opened her mouth to speak, but no words came out. Emerson contained his laughter and left her alone in the office.

# CHAPTER THIRTY-SIX

After two hours in the spa, Renee Therriault returned to her room, but she didn't feel very relaxed. Throughout her treatments, she'd been unable to stop thinking about Stephen's findings. She still thought him an impudent whelp for investigating her employees, but the more she thought about it, the more she worried he may have stumbled upon a serious threat to the company she'd worked so hard to build. Silken Pleasures was the child she'd never taken the time to have. She was as protective of it as any mother was.

She strode to the desk, turned on her laptop, and moved to the wet bar for a bottle of water. She unscrewed the top on the large bottle of Evian and took a long drink before sitting down in front of the computer. She entered her password, then navigated to the personnel files she had on a secure server, accessible from wherever she was. Of course, she'd known about Ellen Cartwright's release from former employers, but the information Ellen had provided about these firings had been quite different from what Stephen had implied. She'd been naïve not to do her own research at the time, but she and Ellen had hit it off right away during the interview. She wondered now if Ellen had done her own research on Renee before the interview to make sure they clicked. The idea sickened her.

Renee clicked on Ellen's file, pulling a notepad from the desk drawer as the information loaded. Ellen's resume and cover letter were the first documents to open. Renee read them more carefully this time, noticing key words and phrases in the cover letter, which had attracted her attention to begin with. Most of them were common in the industry and were even used on the corporate website; words like "personalized beauty," "anticipating future consequences," "prestige," "commitment to protect values," "building relationships," "comfort," and "well-being." Then there were more subtle mentions of charities she supported, all of which Renee was either on the board of or actively involved with.

She combed through the resume, giving special attention to Ellen's description of her duties at the two companies, from which Renee knew she'd been let go. Looking at it now, Renee could see the glaring omissions under these headings.

Next, she looked at the notes she'd made after their first interview. Most of her comments were about how pleasant Ellen was and how surprising it was to find someone with whom she seemed to have so much in common. Her notes brought back memories of the interview and Renee realized how masterfully Ellen had controlled the conversation, subtly redirecting Renee when a question was asked about the gaps in her resume.

While the gaps were small, no more than three months, they had been something Renee wanted more information on, but Ellen had never answered those questions. Instead, she mentioned working on a fundraiser for the Make Children Smile Foundation, where Rene was a board member. The conversation had turned to how the event had almost been cancelled just days in advance when a water pipe burst in the Museum of Modern Art.

The more she read, the more Renee felt like she'd been duped. Ellen's powers of manipulation becoming clear. Renee read several performance reviews and noticed very little had changed on the last three evaluations, yet Ellen had received sizable pay increases each year. Renee closed the files and typed Ellen's name in to a web search engine. If a concierge could find dirt on her online then I shouldn't have any trouble, Renee thought.

The first several links she clicked were stories from the society pages of Ellen's appearance at benefits, concerts, and awards dinners. Farther down the page, Renee began to see stories speculating about Ellen's involvement with a batch of make-up recalled by a competing distributor less than six months prior to Ellen joining Silken Pleasures and only weeks after she'd been fired from the distributor.

An hour and several hurriedly written pages later, Renee pushed her chair back from the desk and stood up. Her eyes burned from reading countless news articles and blogs. The amount of information available about Ellen Cartwright was overwhelming.

Renee eyed the telephone and considered calling Stephen to find out what he'd found that had aroused his concern, but she decided against it, fearing it would somehow make her look weak in his eyes, and she never looked weak to those inferior to her.

She pulled another cold bottle of water from the mini-fridge and circled the room as she thought about all she'd learned, ending up by the large window overlooking Lake Eola. She watched a pair of joggers on the broad lake path. The phone rang, interrupting her thoughts and pulling her from the window. She reached for the extension on an end table by the sofa.

"Hello?" she answered distractedly.

"I hear you are already trying to get in touch with me again. Sorry I didn't give you my number at lunch."

"Oh, Darren, thanks for calling. You know, I don't remember now why I wanted to get in touch with you." Renee shifted her focus from her concerns about Ellen.

"Well, why don't I give you my number and you can call me if your remember. You have a pen?" Darren rattled off his number. "While I have you, I meant to ask, do you have a current prospectus on your father's company?"

"Sure, I can email it or courier it to your office if you'd like."

"Actually, I'm still in the area. Mind if I stop by the hotel?"

Renee's thoughts snapped into focus. "That would be fine. I'm in the Lake Trasimeno suite." She hung up the phone and tidied up the desk area, then went into the bedroom to change and put on make up. She was walking out of the bathroom ten minutes later, fastening the backs of a pair of diamond earrings when Darren knocked on her door.

"Come in," Renee greeted Darren with a brilliant smile. Darren stepped inside and looked around the spacious suite.

"It's been a while since I've been in here," he admitted. "I'm glad to see they seem to be keeping it up well. I really should do more surprise inspections."

"That used to be one of the highlights for Daddy," Renee warmed at the memory and gave a quiet chuckle. "I just remembered a trip we took when I was ten. We arrived under a fake name and stayed in the least expensive room. I asked him why no one recognized us and why our room was so small. He told me it was important to make sure housekeeping was giving these rooms the same treatment they would give our suites."

Darren nodded. "He was always talking about how much harder people in the lower rooms often had to work to afford even that." His gaze dropped to the floor. "I'm afraid I haven't been as blunt with my own staff."

Renee offered him a drink, which Darren declined. "I have a copy of the prospectus in my briefcase, if you don't mind it being a bit rumpled." Renee lifted a hand tooled, brown leather briefcase from the floor beside the desk and pulled out a stack of papers.

"Is this a copy I can keep?" Darren asked, accepting the spiral bound pages.

Renee hesitated. "Actually, I'd rather send you a fresh copy. I have a few notes on this one I might need."

Darren arched an eyebrow. "Anything I might find interesting?" He fanned through the pages.

"I doubt it, unless you are interested in the chemical properties of women's make-up," Renee smiled. "I had an unexpected conference call a couple of nights ago and had to grab the closest thing to take notes on."

"Hmm, while I probably should be more interested in the things my wife puts on her face, I think I'll pass." Darren scanned the first couple of pages of the document, an overview of Ryland Resorts' enhancements over the past year.

Renee took a seat on the sofa and crossed her long legs, watching Darren read. She gave him several minutes of quiet before leaning forward and touching his leg.

"Darren, I need to ask you something," she said in a quiet voice. Darren lowered the papers and turned his attention to her. Renee met his eyes and felt her heart quicken. How did he still have this effect on her after so many years?

"I think I may have a problem with one of my executives," Renee spoke slowly. "As much as I hate to admit it, I think I have hired someone who may have malicious intentions, and I'm afraid she may already be setting plans into motion to damage my company."

"What do you mean?" Darren asked.

Renee quickly shared the information she'd learned in the previous hours and her suspicions of Ellen's intentions.

"The worst part is, I had to find all of this out from your concierge," Renee concluded with an air of annoyance.

"Excuse me?" Darren nearly rose from his chair, but Renee patted his leg and shook her head.

"Don't be mad. As much as I want to be angry with Stephen, his concern and instincts may have saved my company. Not that I would ever let him know," she hastened to add. "I'm embarrassed he was able to figure out in less than a day, what I have been oblivious to for years."

"He shouldn't have been digging around in your business, though," Darren replied, his words harsh, his eyes blazing.

Renee considered this, remembering her own first reaction to Stephen's concern. "Perhaps not, but I do give him credit for having the nerve to approach me about it and not to go straight to the press. There are certainly those less scrupulous who wouldn't have hesitated to make a quick buck selling a story like this. I know what you're thinking," Renee broke into his thoughts. "I'd appreciate it if you didn't mention any of this to Stephen. Even if he may have saved my company, I don't want him to think I owe him anything."

Darren chuckled at Renee's rapid return to the haughty princess. "I can't say I won't have a talk with his manager about his impertinence, but I won't mention you specifically. I expect all of my employees to respect our guests and their privacy. This is a blatant disregard for privacy." Darren paused. "Although, now that I think about it I shouldn't be surprised. He did violate my privacy by tracking me down for you. He's definitely resourceful. Maybe I need to see about having him moved to a department where his talents would be better suited."

"Forget about Stephen." Renee was growing impatient. "What am I going to do about Ellen? I can't fire her. Her work has been impeccable. But if I keep her on, she will have more time to put whatever plan she has into place."

Darren stood and walked to the window. "You have two choices. Hire a private investigator to dig into Ellen's past, find evidence of her involvement with sabotage of her former employers, and find out what her end game is with you."

"That could take months. If she's talking to my personal assistant already, I may not have that much time." Did Darren really think she hadn't already considered this option?

Darren turned to face her again. "The other option is to confront her. Tell Ellen you know about the argument with Donna and her history of leaving companies right as bad things happen, and you want to know what her intentions are."

Renee rose from the sofa and circled the living room. She stopped in front of the desk and dragged her fingers across the keyboard of her open laptop. "Did you not listen when I told you how she manipulated her entire interview?" Renee said bitterly. "She won't tell me her game plan. She will act offended and hurt, then turn the conversation back on me."

"She will probably try, but you know what to expect, so you will have the upper hand. Even if you had a reason to fire her, you don't know she doesn't already have something in place that can hurt the company. Your only choice for a quick resolution is to confront her." Darren gave Renee a hard look.

"Unless you've gone soft and don't have the nerve. The Renee I knew wouldn't even be asking this question. She would have stormed into Ellen's room the moment she found out there was any question about the woman's loyalty."

Renee lifted her head, her back straightening. "How dare you call me soft?" she bit out between clenched teeth.

Darren shrugged. "Just calling it like I see it. You are in here wringing your hands about an employee and applauding the service staff. That's not the woman I knew."

Renee turned on her heel and stormed out of the suite, allowing the door to slam closed behind her. She pounded on the door to Ellen Cartwright's suite. When there was no answer, she beat on it again. "Ellen, open the door," she demanded.

A housekeeper emerged from a room on the opposite side of the hall and timidly approached Renee. "Ms. Cartwright is no there," she said in a thick Spanish accent.

That ingrate must still be in the spa, Renee thought. I hope she's enjoying her last pampering on my dime. She considered storming into the spa, but didn't want Stephen to learn there was substance to his suspicions. Instead, she went to Donna's room.

Donna opened the door almost immediately. "I hope you had a nice massage," she said, stepping back to allow her boss into the room.

"Donna, I heard you and Ellen had an argument in the lobby the other day. You know I expect more decorum from my employees," Renee replied coldly.

Donna froze, fear filling her eyes as she looked at Renee. "I'm sorry. I should have..."

Renee held up a hand to stop the woman. "Don't. Just tell me what Ellen wants you to do."

Donna hesitated and sank onto the edge of an overstuffed chair. "I told her I wouldn't do it, Mrs. Therriault. You have to believe me. I would never betray you. This is the best job I've ever had." Her words trailed off into sobs.

"Oh stop it," Renee said impatiently. "What does she want you to do?"

Donna reached for a tissue and blew her nose. "She wants me to copy her on your emails to certain clients, record phone calls, send her copies of reports on the new products we have in development. She wants to steal your clients and ideas to start her own company. She tried to offer me money, then she threatened to tell you I was stealing from the company."

Renee walked to the window, hands clasped at the small of her back, trying to stretch the muscles between her shoulders where she could feel the tension building. So much for the seventy-five minute massage she'd just had. Ellen wasn't just trying to sabotage her company; she was trying to destroy it.

"I'm not stealing from you," Donna said quietly. "I would never do that."

Renee turned around and studied Donna then offered a sympathetic smile. "I know." She moved toward the woman and sat down across from her. "Did Ellen tell you which clients she was interested in?"

Donna shook her head. "She only approached me about this a couple weeks ago. At first, she started being nice to me, talking to me more than usual. Then she started asking questions. They seemed fairly innocent, but then, I don't know, I got a bad feeling and I tried to avoid her as much as possible. The other day she cornered me and demanded I do what she told me to."

"Why didn't you come to me when you first questioned her motives?" Renee asked.

"I thought about it, but you've been so busy getting ready for this meeting and preparing for the launch of the new fragrance line. I thought I would talk to you after the launch if I still had concerns. I also wasn't sure you would believe me. It would have been my word against hers, and you two seem so friendly."

Her last words struck Renee to the core. Her assistant, who had worked for her for five years, wasn't sure she could trust her. Hadn't she been good to Donna? Hadn't she shown her more respect than any of her other assistants? Did Renee and Ellen appear to be such good friends to others?

She thought back over the past year and how many parties she and Ellen had attended together, how Ellen had been at her side when her husband died. They had been good friends, or so Renee had thought.

Renee patted Donna's knee. "You and I have worked together a long time. I know you would never bring anything to me if you didn't think it was important. I don't want you to ever doubt my faith in you."

"I'm sorry," Donna whispered, eyes downcast.

"Now we need to figure out what we are going to do about this." Renee stood again and started pacing back and forth. She always thought better when she was moving.

"I want you to meet with Ellen this evening after dinner. Tell her you and I had an argument and you have decided to help her. Find out which clients and products she wants you to feed her information on." Renee paused. "Do you have the tape recorder you use for our meetings with you?"

Donna nodded.

"Good. Take it with you and record the conversation. Then I can use it to confront her."

"She won't believe I had a change of heart so soon," Donna said.

"Maybe we need to have the argument in public then." Renee inwardly cringed at the thought, but knew Donna was right. Ellen would be cautious of any advances Donna made unless she thought that there was a rift between them after Donna's recent adamant display of loyalty.

"When we meet for dinner tonight, you come in a few minutes late. Is your nephew still over in Iraq?" Donna nodded. "I hate to ask you this, but it may be the only thing she will believe." Renee laid out her plan and Donna reluctantly agreed.

When Renee returned to her suite, she was surprised to find Darren waiting for her.

"How did it go?" Darren asked.

"She wasn't in her room, but I think I have a plan now." Renee noticed his empty wine glass. "Would you like some more?" she asked.

"Only if you're drinking with me," Darren replied with a wink.

"Heaven knows I need it," Renee replied. She poured them each a glass of wine and sat down on the sofa next to Darren. "When did running a company get so complicated?"

Darren laughed. "This isn't the first complication you've encountered."

Renee took a long sip of the wine, savoring the sweet taste of citrus, tarragon, and fresh cream. "I've never been blindsided like this before. Maybe I am getting soft." She sighed and set the glass on the table then leaned back on the couch, her head resting against the wall.

"It's bound to happen to us all sooner or later," Darren replied. "I looked over the prospectus and can tell you I'm definitely interested."

Renee closed her eyes. "Daddy will be happy to hear that."

Darren stood. "I'll get going and let you rest. What time is your flight?"

"It's scheduled for one, but I may move it up. Depends on how things go tonight."

"Okay. If I don't talk to you before you leave, have a good trip. I'll be in touch in a couple of days about the purchase." Darren leaned down, kissed Renee on the cheek, and let himself out of the suite. Renee didn't bother moving from the couch. Within minutes of Darren's departure, she was asleep.

# CHAPTER THIRTY-SEVEN

McDonald tugged on the top drawer of the filing cabinet, paper exploding from it as it popped open. She shook her head in disbelief and kneeled down to gather the receipts. Taking the pile to the desk, she began to sort through them.

McDonald was a stickler for organization, so sitting in this cluttered office made her skin crawl. It took all of her restraint not make order of the chaos before focusing on the receipts. Instead, she contented herself with clearing the desk and making neat piles of the receipts, placing them in order by date and time. When Emerson returned half an hour later with a large soda from a nearby convenience store, she had only gone through a third of the first drawer.

Emerson looked at the desk with more than twenty neat piles before addressing her. "What are you doing?"

"Trying to make sense of this mess," McDonald replied.

"You aren't their accountant; you're supposed to be looking for one receipt."

"I know, but I'd just be spinning my wheels digging through these drawers. It's like to trying to find the proverbial needle in a haystack. This way at least I know what I have already gone through." McDonald continued placing receipts in their respective piles, undeterred by Emerson's frustration.

Emerson sighed. "What can I do to help?"

"Start on the second drawer. It seems like they fill one drawer before starting on the next and I would guess there are about a week's worth in each drawer," McDonald replied without looking up.

Emerson closed the top drawer and opened the next one, the explosion of papers more substantial this time.

"Oh, I should have warned you," she said as several pieces of paper fluttered to the ground. "Looks like business was better that week,"

Emerson scooped up the receipts and looked around for a place to divide them up. Not seeing another clear area in the office, he shuffled out to the bar and dropped his armload on the scratched surface.

McDonald could hear the bartender asking how long this was going to take. "We are supposed to open in a couple of hours."

"It will take as long as it takes," Emerson replied gruffly. McDonald chuckled and stood to get more receipts.

McDonald quickly found her rhythm again and tuned out all of Emerson's disgruntled comments. She worked silently, her eyes automatically zooming from date, to time, to signature, marveling at how poorly most people wrote.

"I've got something," McDonald called out an hour later. Emerson rushed into the office and swiped the paper from McDonald's hand.

"That's a hefty tab," Emerson said.

McDonald gathered her neatly stapled stacks and started to return them to the filing cabinet.

"What are you doing?" Emerson asked.

"Cleaning up," she replied matter-of-factly.

Emerson was shaking his head. "No you're not, we have to go. Clean up is their problem."

"But…" McDonald started to protest, but a look from Emerson her cut her off. With a resigned shrug, she closed the drawer and left the office. There was no offer for her to drive back to the station and they made the short ride in silence.

# CHAPTER THIRTY-EIGHT

Emma and Ron returned to the suite and found Lizzie curled up in her bed under a mountain of blankets. Emma crept close to the bed and looked down on the young woman. Ron came up behind her and wrapped his arms around her, preventing Emma from leaning down and waking Lizzie. The couple stood, looking down at their adopted daughter, then Ron gently pulled Emma from the room.

"Don't you want to know what happened?" Emma asked when they were back in the living room.

"Of course I do, but obviously she needs rest. There will be plenty of time for details later." Ron gazed at his wife lovingly. "All that matters is she is back safe."

Emma nodded and buried her head in Ron's chest. "I don't know what I would have done if she had been harmed," she mumbled against his soft flannel shirt.

Ron held her head with one hand, his other looped around her full waist. "I know, sweetheart."

A knock on the door broke the couple apart. Emma sank onto the couch while Ron went to answer it. Ian stood on the other side, hands stuffed in the pockets of his jeans, chin resting on his chest. He looked up when the door opened and Ron could see weariness in his eyes.

"Come in," Ron invited softly, placing a hand on his shoulder. Ian followed Ron to the couch and took a seat across from Emma. Ron joined his wife on the sofa and took her hand.

"I am so sorry," Ian said, looking them each in the eye, then he looked around the large room. "Is Lizzie here?"

"She's sleeping," Ron replied.

Ian nodded. "I just finished explaining what happened to my parents. I understand the sleigh driver didn't return to the hotel yesterday. We called the police so a search can be conducted in case he was injured." Ian quickly filled them in on the details of the previous day.

Ron noted the pride Ian displayed as he told them about Lizzie's resourcefulness in making their shelter warmer.

"I'm not sure if we would have made it through the night if she hadn't taken charge the way she did," Ian concluded.

"I had no idea she knew so much about wilderness survival," Emma commented, turning wide eyes to her husband.

"She told me about camping trips her dad took her on and how he'd teach her different survival tricks," Ian replied.

Emma shook her head. "Your parents knew you must be in trouble when you didn't make it back for dinner. I just thought you lost track of time. By the time I realized there was a problem, it was already dark. The lodge manager told us the police wouldn't begin a search until you'd been missing twenty-four hours."

"We insisted you must be in trouble," Ron said, "but the manager insinuated you had gone off to another hotel to have some time alone." Ron chuckled. "You should have seen your mom's face when he said that. She was furious."

The bedroom door opened and a groggy Lizzie shuffled into the room, wearing a sweatshirt, sweatpants, and thick wool socks. Ian rose and was at her side in seconds. When he released her, she went to the couch where Ron and Emma stood and wrapped her in their arms.

"Did you tell them what happened?" Lizzie asked, turning to Ian.

"I did and my parents have called the police to look for the sleigh driver. You may have been right about him being hurt."

"Oh no," Lizzie cried.

"There is no way we could have known," he assured her. "If we had gone out looking for him, we may have gotten lost in the woods and that wouldn't have helped anyone."

Ian looked at his watch. "My parents made dinner reservations at Chops Grill for six o'clock to celebrate our homecoming. Do you think you are up for that?"

"Sure," was Lizzie's less than enthusiastic reply.

"I can tell them that you need to rest," Ian interjected.

"No, really, I'm fine." Lizzie mustered a bit more excitement.

Ian turned to Ron and Emma. "Is that okay with you guys? I know you probably didn't get much sleep last night."

"As long as we are back by ten I think it would be nice to get out," Emma said after a long pause.

"We'll meet you in the lobby at five-thirty then." Ian stood and Ron walked him to the door. Emma scooted closer to Lizzie.

"Why don't you want to see his parents?" Emma asked.

"I don't know what you mean," she stammered.

"Did you go to sleep as soon as you returned?"

"Well, not right away. I had to sit in the tub for half an hour to get the chill out of my bones."

"Still, you slept nearly five hours. Any more and you won't sleep tonight. So, I ask you again, why don't you want to see his parents?" Emma's tone had turned to that of a mother interrogating her child.

Lizzie slid her hands up into the sleeves of the sweatshirt, opening and closing her fingers, stretching the fabric. "What are they going to think? I spent the night alone with their son."

Emma burst out laughing. "Honey, didn't you hear what Ron said about Cassandra getting angry when the manager insinuated that? The thought of you and Ian having sex never crossed her mind."

Lizzie pushed her hands out of the sleeves again and ran her fingers through her hair. "But she thought we might be hurt then. Now she knows we were never in any real danger. What if…"

"Lizzie, Cassandra and Colin wouldn't be inviting us to dinner at a nice restaurant if they were angry at you. They may not have known you long, but it doesn't take long for people to see the light of God shining in you." Emma cupped Lizzie's cheek with her hand and smiled.

Lizzie reached up and took her friend's hand, giving it a soft squeeze. "Thank you, Emma."

"Are you ladies going to get dressed or what?" Ron asked in a loud, jovial voice.

Lizzie stood. "I don't know what I will wear. It sounds like a really nice place."

"Glad I brought a sport coat," Ron agreed.

"I better go check my suitcase," Lizzie replied.

When the bedroom door closed behind her, Emma stood as well. "You don't think anything happened between them last night do you?" she asked as she slipped an arm around her husband.

"Woman, you just told her that Ian's parents didn't suspect it and here you are questioning." Ron shook his head and pulled her into the bedroom. "Let's get dressed."

Lizzie stood in front of her open suitcase, gazing blankly at the mound of clothes. While Emma's words had been reassuring, Lizzie was still nervous about seeing Ian's parents again. What if he'd told them about her tainted past? Wouldn't they assume she might have tried to seduce Ian? Generating extra body heat was a good way to prevent freezing to death. But if they already knew about her past, why had they welcomed her so eagerly and been so loving toward her?

She exhaled loudly, blowing curls out of her face. She was being ridiculous. Hadn't she just resolved to allow her past to remain in the past? She had freedom through Christ, yet here she was holding on to it, like a security blanket. The only thing it was keeping her safe from was moving on with her life and finding happiness.

Right then she made a new promise to herself; this was the last time she would second-guess herself in matters of the heart; the last time she would allow Satan to hold her mistakes in her face, driving a wedge between her and God.

With renewed energy, Lizzie sifted through the clothes until she found a simple black dress. Made of spandex and polyester, it could be crumpled in a ball and not wrinkle, so she'd taken to packing it everywhere she went.

The lobby was bustling with activity, skiers returning from the slopes, families gathering to share their adventures, and couples ready to hit the town. Ian and his parents were waiting when Emma, Ron, and Lizzie stepped out of the elevator. Ian felt his heart stop for a moment when Lizzie emerged from behind Emma. She wore a black dress that skimmed her knees, brushing her curves, still loose enough to leave room for his imagination. Her legs shimmered in silky stockings that accentuated firm calves. Her loose curls bounced with tendrils hugging her face, setting off her blue eyes. She smiled when she saw him. He felt his heart quiver inside his chest as if he'd received an electric shock.

"Oh, Lizzie, I'm so happy you are okay," Cassandra gushed as she took the young woman in her arms. When Cassandra released her, Colin stepped forward and embraced her as well.

"You two sure gave us a scare, but I hear you are quite the wilderness woman. I'm glad you were there to protect Ian." Colin smiled down at her.

Lizzie giggled. "Yeah, I'm not sure he would have made it without me. He was absolutely hopeless out there." They all laughed and Lizzie looped her arm through Ian's as they walked out in the cold night air.

# CHAPTER THIRTY-NINE

Stephen wandered down the service corridor toward the kitchen, his thoughts still filled with his conversation with Renee Therriault and her dismissal of his concerns. Maybe she was right. Maybe he was digging into things that weren't any of his business and reading more into the situation than was really there. It wasn't unusual for employees to have arguments. It didn't happen often within his team, but he knew there was some resentment from Ben about him being left in charge this weekend. He'd be glad when Lizzie returned and he could go back to being just one of the team members. He certainly had a renewed respect for all Lizzie had to deal with.

Upon entering the kitchen, Stephen quickly made his way to Chef Gustave's office, but the chef wasn't there. Except for the sounds of fire from the grill, pots being shifted on burners, and whisks in glass bowls, the kitchen was eerily quiet. The cooks were not talking amongst themselves, laughing at some joke, or being yelled at by Chef Gustave.

"Why's it so quiet?" Stephen asked one of the cooks.

The cook's eyes darted around the kitchen, then he leaned close and whispered, "Chef is in a foul mood. Worst I have seen in months."

"But where is he?"

The cook nodded toward the large walk-in cooler and continued beating a bowl full of egg whites. Stephen considered his options, then cautiously approached the cooler as if a wild beast might pop out of it at any moment. When he reached the large steel door, he hesitated, then turned the handle.

He stepped inside and found rows of shelves containing plump, red tomatoes, crisp, green heads of lettuce, large wheels of cheese, red, green, and yellow peppers, vats of salad dressing, and links of sausage. He took a few tentative steps.

"Chef Gustave?" he quietly called. The big man appeared from behind a rack of meat.

"What do you want?" the chef bellowed.

"I just wanted to make sure everything was okay. I know how much you have enjoyed cooking for Silken Pleasures and this is their last dinner." Stephen took another step toward the man.

"So what if it is their last dinner? I have many other guests to cook for as well. Phillipe can manage their dinner," he replied sullenly.

"It's okay to be sad they are leaving. Mrs. Therriault has been very appreciative of your food and I know that isn't always the case," Stephen consoled him. "It is nice to be appreciated."

"Hmph," was all Chef Gustave stated before turning to inspect several chicken breasts.

"Okay, well, if you need anything, I'll be around until they are seated." Stephen waited a moment, but when he received no response, he backed out of the cooler. He slipped between the quiet cooks and found Phillipe, the assistant chef, the polar opposite of Chef Gustave. Tall, thin, and always smiling, Phillipe was the one willing to mingle with the guests and share cooking secrets. He was the face of the Hotel Lago kitchens.

"I hear you are in charge of the Silken Pleasures dinner tonight," Stephen said.

"This is true," Phillipe replied and Stephen detected sadness in his tone.

"What's wrong? You seem disappointed."

"Chef should be doing this dinner. He works hard and doesn't often receive the respect or appreciation he deserves. Mrs. Therriault has been good for him. That he refuses to see her before she leaves is wrong, but what can I do?" Phillipe shrugged and gave Stephen a forlorn look.

"I'm surprised he isn't soaking up every bit of her attention. Maybe it's his French pride."

"Maybe." Phillipe lifted a spoon and gingerly tasted the soup he had been stirring. "Mmm, that is nice."

"I need this dinner to go off without a hitch," Stephen said. "Things have gone well this weekend. I think as long as we end on a high note there is a good chance we can get them to come back next year."

Phillipe smiled. "Lizzie would be proud of how you have handled things."

Stephen felt his cheeks redden and he thanked the man for the compliment then made his way back to the office. He wanted to check in with Mrs. Therriault before the dinner and apologize for his actions earlier. He dialed the room and waited.

"Hello?" Renee answered in a groggy tone.

"Mrs. Therriault, I'm sorry if I woke you." Stephen beat his fist against his forehead. He just couldn't catch a break today.

"Stephen? What time is it?"

"A quarter to six," Stephen replied, realizing she was supposed to be at her dinner in fifteen minutes and wondering why she had been asleep.

"I have to get dressed," Renee cried and hung up the phone.

Stephen listened to the dial tone a moment then hung up.


Renee leaped from the sofa and ran into the bedroom, where she tore a sleek black dress from a hanger. Tugging the dress over her head as she walked, she entered the bathroom and gave her face a critical look in the mirror. Her right cheek was red, but nothing she couldn't cover up. She quickly brushed her teeth and, with skilled hands, applied her make-up.

Three minutes before six, she exited the elevator and strode across the lobby toward the conference room. When she reached the room, she found most of the executives already there, milling around in groups of two or three, talking and laughing. When Renee entered the groups slowly broke up and drifted to their seats around the long table.

Renee took her seat at the head of the table and glanced around to see who was missing. Only Donna and Ellen were late. She felt a flutter of fear when she noticed Ellen's empty seat, but relaxed a moment later when the woman came rushing through the door.

"Blasted dry cleaner didn't return my dress on time," Ellen said in a loud voice as she took her seat.

Renee did her best to offer an understanding smile, then nodded to the banquet captain to begin serving. Bowls of a rich, creamy, roasted tomato soup were set before each of the executives. The aroma of fresh basil filled the air. Renee took three careful spoonfuls of the soup before turning her attention to her employees.

"I want to thank you all for a wonderfully productive weekend. I believe we accomplished some great planning and had a chance to get to know each other better. I may not tell you often enough how much your hard work is truly appreciated." Renee reached for her glass of white wine and raised it. "I propose a toast. To Silken Pleasures and those who have made it such a success."

The others clinked their glasses together and offered her their own thanks, each trying to sound more ingratiating than the others. Conversation drifted to the activities of the afternoon as the women compared their spa treatments and the men told of their golf outing. Apparently, they had encountered an alligator sunning himself on the course and after much debate, the men had decided to skip that hole.

As the soup bowls were being cleared away, the conference room door opened and Donna came stumbling in, her nose red, pressing a tissue to her eyes. Renee rose and approached the woman.

"Donna, whatever is the matter?" Renee asked.

"My brother called," Donna said, gasping for breath. Renee put an arm around her shoulder to steady the woman. She could feel all eyes on them.

"What did your brother tell you that has you so upset?"

"My nephew..." Donna bent over with a fresh wave of sobs. Renee's arm rested limply on Donna's back. "My nephew is missing," Donna finally continued. She straightened and made her way to the closest chair, which one of the men gladly gave up for her.

"What do you mean missing? He's a grown man isn't he?" Renee asked.

"He's in Iraq, in the army. He was out on patrol two days ago, and…" Donna dropped her head into her hands as she tried to control her tears. When she looked up again Renee saw black tracks where her mascara had washed down her face. She obviously isn't using our products, Renee caught herself thinking as she looked into her assistant's swollen, red eyes.

"I need to go home to be with my brother. Johnny is all he has." Donna looked up at her boss with an imploring gaze, begging for kindness.

"We will be back in New York tomorrow afternoon. Once we get back and you help me catch up from being out of the office you can go see your brother. Friday at the latest," Renee told her coolly.

Donna sprang from her chair, toppling it behind her. "Johnny could be dead and you want me to help you catch up?" she screamed.

"Calm down Donna," Renee reached out to her assistant, but Donna batted her hand away. "Really, what can you do for your brother right now? I'm sure the army is doing all they can to locate your nephew."

"You really are a cold-hearted shrew" Donna yelled and ran out of the room. Renee watched her go, actually feeling a bit wounded by Donna's words. The room was silent and Renee turned back to the table where she found everyone deeply interested in the tablecloth in front of them. A few scraped at crumbs from their crispy baguettes. Renee noticed Ellen dared a fleeting glance at her, then returned her gaze to the table.

The banquet captain cleared his throat at the door to the kitchen. Renee spun around and shot him a withering look, returned to her seat, replaced the linen napkin on her lap, then nodded to the captain. Servers emerged from the kitchen carrying trays laden with Caesar salads. Everyone seemed relieved for the distraction. Renee kept her head high and made no apologies for the scene. The salad course was finished in silence.

When the main course—stuffed Cornish hen with asparagus and carrots in a butter sauce—arrived, Renee directed her attention to the woman seated on her right side.

"Carol, I hear you recently got engaged. Congratulations." Renee set her fork down, her gaze never leaving Carol's face.

Carol, the youngest of the executives, with thick brown hair, brown eyes, and a sprinkling of freckles across her cheeks, seemed stunned by this remark. Carol set down her own fork and looked up at Renee.

"Yes," she replied in a shaky voice. "Two weeks ago." Shyly, she lifted her hand and showed Renee the ring, a beautifully cut half-carat set in a white gold band.

"How sweet," Renee said with a forced smile. Carol dropped her hand back to the table. Renee looked at Ellen, sitting three chairs down to her left. She noticed Ellen seemed to be deep in conversation with Bill, the chief financial officer, her body turned away from Rene.

Lisa, seated to the left of Renee, spoke up. "Congratulations, Carol. I hadn't heard. How did he propose?"

Carol reddened slightly. "It wasn't anything special really. Ric and I have been together for five years. He asked me at dinner one night."

"That's still nice. Where did he take you?" Lisa asked.

The flush on Carol's cheeks brightened. "Actually we were at home. I made pot roast."

"Oh," Lisa said.

While the tension in the room eased some throughout the meal, Renee could still feel her employees' furtive glances in her direction. She heard a couple of them whispering as they left the conference room at the completion of the meal. Only Ellen lingered with Renee.

"Quite a scene," Ellen remarked, lifting her glass and draining the last drops of red wine.

"Yes, and Donna knows better than to behave like that," Renee replied, keeping her tone even.

"I was surprised you wouldn't let her go home early. We aren't meeting in the morning and I know for a fact that she's been keeping up with your emails and phone messages this weekend." Ellen set her glass on the table and rubbed a finger around the rim.

"I have two conference calls when we return and a meeting with a new buyer. Donna knows how busy we are right now."

Ellen scrutinized Renee for several minutes. "Still, it seems cold, even for you."

Renee calmly placed her palms on the table, pushed her chair back, and stood. She looked down on Ellen with distaste. "I'm sorry you feel that way, but I will manage my employees how I see fit. I don't have to explain myself to you or anyone else." Head held high, back rigidly straight, Renee marched out of the room.

# CHAPTER FORTY

Colin pulled up in front of the large chateau, which housed Chops Grill, and Lizzie, Ian, Emma, Ron, and Cassandra piled out of the car. Ian held the heavy oak door open as Lizzie led the women in, with Ron and Ian bringing up the rear. The sounds of laughter, sizzling grills, and jazz washed over her as she stepped inside.

The restaurant was dimly lit, but she could make out large beams along the ceiling. The walls were waxy yellow, reminding her of a Venetian plaster she'd seen on a home improvement show. The kitchen was open to the dining room, where a dozen cooks, oblivious to their audience, were flipping steaks and chicken on flaming grills. The smell of the steak made her mouth water.

When Colin arrived, the hostess led them to a large table with a clear view of the kitchen. Lizzie couldn't help thinking about Chef Gustave and how much he would hate working in the open with everyone watching him. It was the first time she'd thought about work in three days and she was swept with a wave of guilt. She felt Ian's hand on her back.

"What's wrong?" he whispered.

Lizzie pushed aside her thoughts of work and shook her head. "Nothing." She could tell Ian wasn't convinced, but he didn't ask anything more.

"I'm getting the porterhouse. Anyone want to share with me?" Ian asked, smiling an invitation to Lizzie.

"Yes, please," Lizzie said. The orders were quickly placed, then a server appeared with a bottle of champagne.

When the glasses were filled, Colin stood. "I'd like to propose a toast. To Lizzie and her family. It has been a pleasure getting to know you this weekend and we hope to have many more gatherings in the future."

Lizzie felt herself blushing as she took a sip of her champagne. Cassandra, who was sitting to Lizzie's left, smiled warmly.

"We haven't met many of Ian's girlfriends, but I have to say, you are our favorite," Cassandra said softly.

Lizzie felt tears stinging her eyes. The love and acceptance overwhelmed her. Except for Emma and Ron, it had been so long since she had felt part of a family.

"Excuse me," Lizzie said, pushing her chair back. She weaved through the tables toward the front of the restaurant, stopping only when a server with a large tray blocked her way.

"Where is the restroom?" she gasped.

"Right around this corner." The server pointed out a narrow hallway.

Lizzie fled into the quiet sanctuary and locked herself in one of the stalls. She struggled to catch her breath and fumbled to open her wallet. Pulling out the well-worn photo of her parents, she focused on each of their faces until her breathing slowly returned to normal.

She could taste her salty tears and unrolled the toilet paper, blotting her face and blowing her nose.

"Lizzie," Cassandra's voice called softly as the bathroom door opened. "Are you all right?"

Lizzie returned the photo to her wallet, drew in a deep breath, then straightened her dress, and brushed at her eyes one more time before opening the stall door.

Cassandra took a cautious step toward Lizzie. "I'm sorry if something Colin or I said upset you."

Lizzie was touched by the concern in Cassandra's eyes and summoned a reassuring smile. "I had forgotten what it's like to be part of a family. This trip has brought back so many memories." Lizzie felt a lump rising in her throat again. "I don't know if I deserve to be part of a family again."

Cassandra crossed the distance between them and slipped her arms around Lizzie, who swallowed hard, willing her tears away.

"You are a very special woman," Cassandra said.

"You don't know the things I've done," Lizzie replied.

Cassandra gently cupped Lizzie's chin and tipped her face up so that their eyes met. "We all have baggage, Lizzie. It's how we carry it that matters. When you completely give it to God to carry, you will stop feeling so undeserving."

Cassandra's words acted as a salve to Lizzie's soul, quieting the voices taunting her with her transgressions. In the quiet that followed, Lizzie closed her eyes and prayed for God's forgiveness, yet again.

"Thank you." Lizzie's voice was hoarse when she spoke.

"This weekend I have seen Ian happier than he has ever been and I know God wouldn't have brought you into his life if you weren't right for him," Cassandra said.

Lizzie couldn't find words to express the deep gratitude she felt. Cassandra understood the demons that dogged her.

"You ready to go back? I'm starving," Cassandra said

Lizzie turned and checked her reflection in the mirror, appalled to see the dark circles around her eyes. Cassandra stepped up behind her and handed a slim compact over Lizzie's shoulder. Lizzie giggled and accepted it before leaning forward and splashing her face with water.

"Remember, God is bigger than all of us and He can carry the load no matter how much we pile on Him," Cassandra said as she watched Lizzie dry her face and apply the powder. When she handed the compact back, Cassandra gave her hand a loving squeeze.

"Take another minute to catch your breath. I'll see you out there." As quietly as she had arrived, Cassandra disappeared back into the restaurant.

Lizzie took a last look in the mirror, tucked a wayward curl behind her ear, and followed a minute later.

At the table, Lizzie could feel Ian studying her, wanting answers to the questions he couldn't ask here. She leaned over and kissed him on the cheek.

"We'll talk later," she whispered.

# CHAPTER FORTY-ONE

Emerson's cell phone rang as they entered the building. "Emerson."

McDonald followed behind him like a punished puppy as he listened to the caller. When he stopped abruptly, she nearly ran into him. The detective didn't even look at her as he turned down a side hallway. Emerson stuffed the cell phone back into his pocket without a word and she followed him into Ernie's small office.

"'Bout time you got something for me," Emerson barked.

The research analyst's nervous gaze jumped from Emerson to McDonald. "Yes, well," Ernie stammered. "Once you gave me the social security number, it wasn't too hard."

"Then why did it take you so long?" Emerson stepped closer to tower over the seated man.

Ernie didn't answer; he just shrank back in his chair and handed a piece of paper to Emerson.

"You've got to be kidding me." Emerson read the information again, shaking his head.

"What is it?" McDonald asked, trying to peer around his shoulder.

Emerson turned to face her. "He lives in a garage apartment at his mother's house."

McDonald had to bite her lip to hold back her laughter. Emerson pushed past her and disappeared down the hallway. McDonald allowed herself a smirk and gave Ernie a grateful nod, then raced back to the squad room.

She found Emerson in the captain's office, briefing her on this new development. McDonald waited outside until he emerged.

"So do we go there now and take him down?" she asked, her excitement building.

"Yeah, we get some back up, head over there, and hope he's home." Emerson went to a storage closet, pulled out a couple of bulletproof vests, and handed one to McDonald.

McDonald dropped the vest over her head.

"Make sure it fits good and tight," Emerson advised.

The streetlights were flickering on one by one when they met a group of officers outside. The evening was crisp and clear, with a mild breeze. McDonald scanned each of their serious faces as Emerson outlined the mission and passed out photos of Randy Little.

"I want him alive, but if he runs again, take the shot," Emerson said before ducking into his car.

They flew through the streets, sirens blaring, flashing lights reflecting off the windows of dark offices and stores. McDonald had to brace herself with one hand on the dash, the other clutching her seat belt to keep from flying forward each time Emerson slammed on the brakes or whipped around a corner. Her heart was racing, adrenaline racing through her veins, and she couldn't stop grinning.

Emerson must have seen this out of the corner of his eye. "What are you smiling about?" he demanded. "We are heading into a potentially dangerous situation. There's nothing to smile about until this guy is taken down."

"I'm sorry," McDonald replied, trying to take sound serious and contrite, but she knew her excitement came through.

Several blocks from the house, Emerson cut his sirens and instructed the others to do the same. "I don't want to spook him if he is home," he said over the radio. Emerson edged his Crown Vic up to the house with the cruisers following, one blocking each end of the street.

McDonald studied the house, surprised by how large the lots were in this area. She estimated the closest neighbor on either side to be a quarter of an acre away. The Little house was a two-story affair of stucco and Spanish tile. Several lights were on in the main house, but the apartment above the garage was dark. She heard Emerson pull his gun from his holster and rack the weapon to load a round into the chamber. She reached for her own weapon and did the same.

"All right, I want two guys to go around back, quietly," Emerson directed. "Two more cover the stairway up to the apartment, and three of you make sure the garage is contained. McDonald and I will approach the front of the main house and speak with the mother, make sure he isn't in there having a nice dinner."

McDonald watched as the officers melted into the darkness at the edge of the yard and took up their places around the house. When everyone radioed in that they were in place, she followed Emerson up the driveway to the front door. She felt a bead of sweat run down her spine as Emerson raised his hand and knocked.

They waited and Emerson knocked again. McDonald saw a shadow moving behind the thin curtains and dropped her hand to her holster. Two minutes later, as Emerson was preparing to knock again, the door opened.

A thin old lady with hunched shoulders, thick glasses, and wispy gray hair stood before them. Her dress was wrinkled and hung from her body as if it was two sizes too large. She leaned on a sturdy black cane, and McDonald noticed her fingers were swollen and knotty.

"Yes?" she asked in a voice that reminded McDonald of creaking hinges.

"Mrs. Little, I'm Detective Emerson and this is Detective McDonald. We're looking for your son, Randy. Is he home?" Emerson spoke quickly and McDonald could tell the old woman hadn't understood him.

"What did you say?" Mrs. Little asked, cocking her head slightly.

"We are looking for your son," McDonald spoke loud and slow.

"You're looking for Randy?"

"Yes, ma'am," McDonald confirmed.

"I haven't seen him all day. Did you check his apartment?" Mrs. Little stepped through the doorway and pointed to the garage.

"I have some men checking there now," Emerson replied. "Do you mind if we come inside and take a look around for ourselves?"

Again, McDonald saw the look of confusion on Mrs. Little's face. She took the lady's arm and led her into the house. "Do you mind if Detective Emerson takes a look around while you and I talk?" McDonald asked.

Mrs. Little smiled. "That would be fine. Would you like some tea?"

"Oh, I don't want to be any bother," McDonald replied. She nodded to Emerson who peeled off from behind the women to search the house. McDonald helped Mrs. Little into the spacious kitchen.

"I have a kettle full of water that can be heated in just a couple of minutes," Mrs. Little pointed toward a red electric kettle on the countertop.

"A cup of tea would be nice, but I don't want to be any trouble. Why don't you let me get the tea things together?" asked McDonald, thinking this would be a good excuse to go through the cabinets.

McDonald settled Mrs. Little into a chair at the small table and went over to the kettle. She found the power switch and turned it on, then deftly rummaged through the cupboards, not finding anything significant, and brought out two cups and some tea bags. She was sitting down with the tea when Emerson entered the kitchen with a slight shake of his head.

"Do you know where Randy might be?" McDonald asked as she poured hot water over the tea bags.

"Let's see, is today Monday?" Mrs. Little asked, looking to McDonald for confirmation. When McDonald nodded, Mrs. Little removed her glasses and rubbed at the bridge of her nose. "He usually comes straight home after work."

"What time is that?" McDonald asked

"Six, sometimes seven."

"Does he ever go anywhere instead of coming straight home? Any restaurants he likes to go to?" McDonald continued to speak slowly and she could see Emerson growing impatient.

"Sometimes he goes to the dog track. I keep telling him he needs to stop going there. He gets in nothing but trouble when he starts betting on the dogs."

"Would you mind if I stayed here with you until Randy comes home tonight?" McDonald asked.

Mrs. Little's face lit up and she gave McDonald a warm smile. "That would be very nice. Do you watch the *Wheel of Fortune*?"

McDonald laughed. "Every chance I get."

Mrs. Little beamed and struggled to stand up. Emerson stepped forward and helped the woman, holding onto her until she was steady on her feet.

"It will be on in a few minutes," Mrs. Little said, shuffling off toward the living room. McDonald hung back to speak with Emerson.

"Why don't I stay here with a few of the guys and you head out to the track. I'll radio if he shows up," McDonald said.

Emerson seemed to consider the options before agreeing. "You be careful though. Don't let your guard down just because she seems like a nice old lady, and don't try to take on Randy alone if he shows up."

"I'll talk to her some more and let you know if I find out any other places he might be hiding." McDonald slipped out of the kitchen in the direction Mrs. Little had gone and found the woman in a dark blue recliner.

# CHAPTER FORTY-TWO

Ellen watched Renee leave the conference room and leaned back in her chair, pondering the events of the evening. The outburst was certainly surprising and could be to her advantage, if it was real. Ellen reached for the half-full bottle of wine in the middle of the table and retreated to her room.

The room was dark and hot when she entered. Setting the bottle on the coffee table, she moved to the thermostat and lowered the temperature, then she sat down to finish the wine. She tried to remember if she'd ever heard Donna mention a brother or a nephew in the military before. She had a faint memory of asking Donna what she had done for Christmas three years ago and hearing about visiting family in Virginia, but really hadn't paid much attention.

For the first time she realized how sloppy she'd been in courting Donna, not taking the time to get to know more about her, and her weak spots. Ellen chastised herself for this failure. She was getting complacent and that was a sure way to get caught.

Draining the last of the wine, Ellen decided to check on Donna, see if she was still as upset as she'd been at dinner. When she reached Donna's room, she placed her ear to the door, but only heard a popular, prime time soap on the television. She knocked and waited nearly two minutes before Donna opened the door, eyes red, still sniffling.

"What do *you* want?" Donna asked, her body blocking the doorway.

"I just wanted to see if you are okay," Ellen replied innocently.

"I'm just great," was Donna's sarcastic answer.

"I am sorry about your nephew. How old is he?" Ellen asked, trying to build a rapport.

"Twenty-three." Donna slumped against the door. "Do you want to come in?"

"I don't want to intrude," Ellen responded, "but if you need to talk I'd be happy to listen."

Donna opened the door wider and turned back toward the bed. The room was much smaller than Ellen's. She tried not think about the tiny space and noticed a half-full suitcase open on the bed.

"Do you mind if I continue packing?" Donna asked, reaching for a shirt hanging in the open closet.

"Of course not. Are you leaving early after all?" Ellen asked in surprise.

"Of course I'm leaving," Donna's face flushed. "No job is worth abandoning my family." Donna balled up the shirt and shoved it into the suitcase.

"Does Renee know you are leaving?" Ellen asked.

"She'll know when I don't show up for breakfast in the morning." Donna stuffed a pair of pants into the suitcase and pulled the last dress off its hanger. With the clothes packed, she moved to the bathroom, and Ellen could hear her throwing toiletries into a bag.

Maybe there really is a crack in the armor, Ellen thought, her mind whirling at the possibilities. Again, she wished she had paid more attention so she would know the best way to handle Donna now. Did she need comforting or would a comrade-in-arms against Renee's cold-heartedness be the best approach? Donna emerged from the bathroom with her toiletry bag, dropped it into the suitcase, and struggled to zip it closed.

"You're leaving tonight, then?" Ellen asked.

"You better believe it. I was able to book the last flight out," Donna replied.

"I won't keep you then. Is there anything I can do for you?" Ellen asked.

Donna scanned the room, then rested her gaze on Ellen. "Do you still want me to get you information on the new products being developed?"

Ellen considered this. Was Donna angry enough to turn on Renee now? "We can talk about it when you know if Johnny is okay," she replied cautiously.

Donna shrugged. "Whatever you want, but if you are interested, the new buyer she is meeting with this week is our biggest client yet. If Renee loses them, it will be a big blow to Silken Pleasures."

Ellen narrowed her gaze. "Really? Why's that?"

"Our numbers might look good right now, but several of our partners are considering other options. If we don't get this distributor, those partners might pull out altogether." Donna set the suitcase on its wheels and pulled it toward the door. Ellen followed her into the hall.

"Why are you telling me this?" Ellen asked.

Donna stopped and the look in her eyes made Ellen take a step back. "Because NO ONE messes with my family." Donna's words were like ice and Ellen knew this was for real. She watched as Donna marched down the hall and punched the elevator button. Even after she disappeared behind the elevator doors, Ellen didn't move. Taking down Silken Pleasures would be her biggest coup yet and she'd just been handed the keys to the kingdom.

Outside, Donna ducked into a waiting taxi and shut the door. As they pulled away from the hotel, she reached into her pocket, retrieved her digital recorder, and turned it off. The ride to the airport took half an hour, but felt longer. The cab deposited her at the curbside check-in where Renee waited. Donna handed her the recorder.

"She bought every word," Donna said.

Renee hugged her assistant. "I'll see you back in the office Wednesday."

"What are you going to do about Ellen?" Donna asked.

"If I know her, and I think now I finally do, she is calling Jean Luc as we speak and spinning a story he can't help but believe. He will thank her for bringing whatever it is she is telling him to his attention, and he certainly can't be involved with Silken Pleasures after learning this. Then he will assure her I won't ever find out she told him. Meanwhile he is recording the call." Renee smiled. "Jean Luc likes being played for a fool about as much as I do. He was only too happy to help when I told him the situation."

"So this will all be over by the morning?" Donna asked hopefully.

"Maybe not by morning, but by this time tomorrow, most definitely." Renee dropped the recorder into her purse and slipped in the waiting cab.

# CHAPTER FORTY-THREE

Emerson parked in front of the Sanford-Orlando Kennel Club and waited for the six other officers to join him near the entrance. The temperature had dropped rapidly and now he wished he had a coat. That was the problem with Florida; you never knew what the weather would be like. At least back in Indiana, he'd known February would be brutally cold and he'd always have a heavy coat with him. Now he stamped his feet and shoved his hands into the pockets of his thin cotton pants.

"You all know what Randy Little looks like, so fan out and see if he's here. If you find him, don't approach him alone. Call it in and wait for the rest of us to arrive." Emerson spoke rapidly, making eye contact with each man to make sure they all understood. "Now, let's get in out of the cold."

The officers entered and spread out in every direction, with Emerson bringing up the rear. Emerson went directly to the security office, where he flashed his badge and took a seat in front of a bank of television screens.

"Have you seen this guy tonight?" Emerson asked, handing the photo to the guard next to him.

The guard studied the photo. "Can't say I've seen him tonight, but he does come in pretty regular."

Emerson scanned the monitors for Randy Little. The crowd was thin, making it easy for Emerson to track the movement of the officers he'd brought with him. He watched them slip from one screen to the next, occasionally stopping to speak to an employee, probably asking if they'd seen Randy. It didn't take long for everyone to report in that Randy wasn't there. Emerson pounded a fist on the desk and stood up so quickly, he hit his head on a nearby shelf.

Rubbing his head, Emerson left the office and met with the rest of the team by the front door. "Bobby, I want you to stay here, keep an eye on things. Call it in if he shows up."

"Will do," Bobby replied.

Emerson dialed McDonald's number. "He's not at the track. Has his mom given you any more information?" When McDonald told him she hadn't learned anything new, Emerson hung up without responding.

"You guys head back to the station. Looks like Little is in the wind." Emerson dismissed the remaining officers and returned to his own car. With the heat running full blast, he sat, trying to get inside Randy's head. Where would a guy like that go when he was in trouble? Based on the limited information he'd gathered thus far, Emerson kept coming back to one thing, home. Maybe McDonald was right, this was his first offense, and he would hole himself up with his mother like a scared little kid. Then why wasn't he there when they showed up?

The question nagged at Emerson, making him feel like he'd missed something. A sense of unease was growing in the pit of his stomach. He shifted into drive and headed back to the Little house.

The closing credits for *Wheel of Fortune* were playing when McDonald heard a noise in the backyard. She went to a window, peering out into the darkness. The wind was picking up and she could see a small box blowing across the yard.

"Would you like some more tea, Mrs. Little?" McDonald asked, returning from the window.

"No, thank you. I have to watch what I drink in the evenings or I am up all night going to the bathroom," Mrs. Little replied.

McDonald settled back into a worn armchair. "You were telling me about Randy as a teenager. Sounds like he was a good kid."

Mrs. Little smiled. "Yes, he was." Her smiled faded and she seemed to retreat into a dark place. McDonald waited, respecting the woman's memories.

"Something changed after high school, though," Mrs. Little said, her voice trembling. "He didn't want to go to college. One day, he left home and didn't come back for two years. He never told me where he went."

McDonald wished there was something she could say to comfort the old lady, but she knew Mrs. Little was only in for more heartache when the police tracked Randy down. Again, she heard the noise, but dismissed it as something else the wind had knocked over.

"How long has Randy been working as a mechanic?" McDonald asked.

"He was always good with his hands. He's been at the garage for, oh, I don't know, six or seven years now."

McDonald remembered the owner of A to Z telling them Randy had only worked for him for a few months. "What's the name of the garage again?" she asked.

Mrs. Little's brow wrinkled. "It's a catchy name, something like The Three R's. 'Repair, repaint, and replace,' I think they stood for."

McDonald's pulse quickened. She knew the place, or at least their jingle. She could hear the commercial in her head and she knew it was their logo on Randy's sweatshirt. She jumped up. "Would you excuse me a minute, Mrs. Little? I just need to use the restroom."

McDonald left the room as fast as she could without alarming her hostess, pulling her cell phone from a pocket as she moved. As she entered the kitchen, she dialed Emerson's number.

"Don't move," she heard a man say behind her. Slowly she turned and found Randy Little less than five feet away with a gun pointed at her head.

"Put the phone down," Randy instructed her. McDonald complied, setting the phone on the counter. Randy waved the gun towards the table and McDonald backed toward it.

"Now take a seat," he said. McDonald was surprised by how calm Randy seemed, making her question her initial assessment of him.

"Randy, I'm not alone here," McDonald said, trying to make her voice sound calm, but she could hear the tremor.

Randy smiled, displaying crooked teeth stained by tobacco. "You weren't alone. Those guys won't be helping you now."

McDonald felt as though her Kevlar vest had just been pulled tighter around her chest. "What did you do, Randy? Killing a police officer is serious."

"Only if I get caught," Randy replied, "and I don't plan on getting caught."

Randy came closer, the gun now just inches from her forehead. With his free hand, he reached down and slipped her gun from its holster, shoving it into the waistband of his pants.

"What about your mother?" McDonald asked.

"That old bag? She's on her last leg, but I wouldn't kill her. She doesn't know where I will disappear to anyway." Randy stepped back.

"Why'd you kill Amanda Barnes?" McDonald wanted to keep him talking as long as she could.

"Was that her name?" Randy asked.

"You didn't even know her name?" McDonald couldn't hide her shock.

Randy shrugged. "She was a hot chick. I tried to buy her a drink, but I guess she thought she was too good for me. They all think they're too good for me."

"Who else has thought that?" McDonald's whole world seemed to be turning upside down.

"Hot chicks, I don't know their names," Randy replied. McDonald heard the TV in the living room turn off. "Why don't you say good night to my ma and we'll go someplace more private." Randy grabbed McDonald's arm and pulled her from the chair. She was surprised by his strength.

He pushed her out in front of him, the gun pressed into her back, and marched her down the hall. At the entrance to the living room, he pushed her forward and she felt the gun leave her back. Could she make a run for it? Then she felt his breath on her neck.

"Don't try anything funny or I will have to kill her too. Wish her a good night and go to the front door," Randy whispered.

McDonald entered the living room. "I'm going to get back to the station," she said. "It was very nice meeting you."

Mrs. Little struggled to get out of her recliner. "I'll walk you to the door."

"No need, I can let myself out."

Mrs. Little slumped back in the chair with a look of gratitude. "It was nice meeting you too. Come back any time."

McDonald moved down the hallway to the front door where she found Randy waiting and wondered how he had gotten there without her or his mother noticing.

"Good job," Randy sneered. "Now let's go to my place."

He shoved her out the door. On the porch, he wrapped one arm around her neck, holding the gun to her head with the other. He smelled of alcohol, tobacco, and grease, and with his thin body pressed against hers, she could tell he was more muscular than he appeared. He guided her down the porch, past the garage door, and up the stairs to his apartment.

"Open it," he hissed in her ear when they reached the door. McDonald gripped the cold handle and turned. When the door opened, she was assailed by the smells of rotting food. Before pushing her deep into the dark room, Randy pulled the handcuffs from her belt and clamped them on one of her wrists.

"Now lock up your other hand," Randy ordered.

Inside, she stumbled over a pile of clothes, struggling to make out shapes in the dim light from a window overlooking the street. With her hands cuffed, she couldn't push herself off the floor. Randy looked down at her and laughed.

"You ain't as pretty as most of my girls, but I never had a cop before." Randy came closer, leaned down, putting his face close to hers, then he slapped her. McDonald's vision blurred and she could taste blood in her mouth.

Randy stood up and tossed his gun onto a couch across the room, then he pulled her gun from his pants and tossed that one too. Before she knew what was happening, Randy lifted her off the floor and threw her onto his bed. Everything she'd learned in training was gone. Her mind was blank except for the intense fear taking control of her body.

She began to wriggle and kick, which seemed to amuse Randy. She screamed as loud as she could, but knew there was no way the police would get there in time to save her.

Randy slapped her again, and shoved a t-shirt in her mouth. It tasted of dirt and motor oil, and she felt her stomach beginning to roil. She pulled her knees up to her chest and used them to punch at Randy, but he ducked aside, laughing.

"The fight is half the fun," Randy said, peeling off his shirt.

McDonald's gaze darted around the room, searching for anything she could use as a weapon, then she remembered the guns he'd tossed aside. She gauged the distance from the bed to the couch, tightened her stomach muscles, and pulled herself to a sitting position. Randy seemed to understand her mission and crossed the room in a flash, grabbing one of the guns.

"I don't like using guns. They are so impersonal, but if that's the way you want it, I can make an exception." Randy raised the weapon and took aim.

The door burst open and McDonald could see Emerson barreling into the room. He came to a halt when Randy swiveled toward him.

"Drop the gun" Emerson shouted.

"You first officer," Randy replied in such a cold tone, McDonald knew she'd been completely wrong about Little. He was a career criminal who'd just been too good to get caught. Slowly, Randy inched back toward the bed.

"Stop right there," Emerson commanded.

A shot rang out and McDonald instinctively ducked. When she looked up she didn't see Emerson at first, then she was able to pick out his prone figure near the pile of dirty clothes. Randy laughed.

"That was too easy." Now Randy was only steps away from McDonald. She scooted to the end of the bed, but as she pushed to stand up, Randy was on top of her. He pushed her onto her back the cold steel of the gun against her cheek. There was another shot and hot blood sprayed her face. McDonald's throat opened to scream as Randy's body fell forward onto hers.

# CHAPTER FORTY-FOUR

Ian and Lizzie remained in the lobby when Emma, Ron, Cassandra, and Colin disappeared into an elevator. They found a quiet corner and sat down with mugs of hot chocolate. Lizzie held the warm cup in both of her hands, allowing the heat to seep into her body. The meal had been exceptional and she really wanted to go to her room and crawl into bed, but she knew she owed Ian an explanation.

Lizzie looked around the spacious lobby, memorizing every detail: the chandeliers made from antlers, the hunter green of the throw pillows, and the detailed metalwork of the fireplace screens. Ian sipped his drink in silence, and Lizzie knew his gaze never left her face.

She lowered her cup to her lap and looked into his blue eyes, the blue of a deep Caribbean sea. "This weekend has been perfect," she said.

"Even with our little misadventure in the woods, and my Valentine's surprise?" Ian asked.

Lizzie could hear the uncertainty in his voice and she ached knowing her actions had put it there. She took Ian's hand and held it tightly.

"Even with those things," she assured him. "I never thought I could find a man who could accept me for who I am, blemishes and all, much less a family that would do so. I've never really forgiven myself for my relationship with Kevin, and I haven't allowed myself to be in a relationship again, fearing I couldn't overcome the temptation to go down that path again."

"You don't have to..." Ian started to say, but Lizzie squeezed his hand.

"Everything changed when I met you. For the first time, I wanted to let someone in. When Jeffrey told me how he felt about me, I thought maybe he was the one I was supposed to be with. We shared so much of the same baggage, but I couldn't stop thinking about you. About how you hadn't judged me when I told you about Kevin and how ashamed I was. You were right, you and I can't move on until I forgive myself, and I am working on it.

"I was so nervous about seeing your parents tonight. I was convinced they would think I had engineered us being stranded in the woods so that I could seduce you." Lizzie had to stop, her voice was shaking, and tears threatened to pour forth again.

"Lizzie," Ian sat his cocoa down and cupped her face with his hand. It was warm and she leaned into it.

"I'm okay, but I have to tell you everything." Lizzie closed her eyes, took several deep breaths, and continued. "When your father gave that toast, I lost it. Everything you have given me along with your parents' acceptance and love was too much.

"I am broken and dirty and unworthy. These are the bags I've been carrying which I've refused to give over to God, to protect me from getting close to anyone.

"But your mom, she said what I have known all along, deep down inside." Lizzie saw Ian open his mouth to speak, so she hurried on. " I want complete honesty between all of us, and your parents' acceptance is precious to me."

"Mom and Dad love you Lizzie. Who could *not* love you?" Ian said.

"I know I'm not going to stop feeling unworthy overnight. I will have to lay that burden at God's feet on a daily basis until I am able to completely give it over to him, but this weekend has given me a reason to do so. I know in order to have a future with you I have to learn to love myself at least half as much as you love me, and I want a future with you more than I have ever wanted anything."

The joy that lit up Ian's face almost made up for the hurt Lizzie knew she had caused him. He drew her into his arms and she inhaled his scent, remembering the first time she had smelled it in the church vestibule.

Ian could feel the velvet box in his pocket pressing against his ribs as Lizzie nestled into his arms, her head resting on his heart. He was glad he had waited to give it to her. He hadn't realized how harshly she judged herself for her past until this trip and he knew now they needed time for her to heal. Knowing she wanted to do so in order to be with him washed away any fears he may have had for their future. There would be plenty of time to give her the box in the months to come.

He stroked her hair. Going home tomorrow, back to their busy lives and leaving this fairy tale behind would be difficult, but he felt they were closer now than they had been before and hoped that would carry over into their daily lives. Maybe she wouldn't bury herself in her work so much. She had managed to go the whole weekend without worrying about work despite the important group he knew was in-house. Ian made a mental note to thank Stephen for not calling in a panic about anything.

All too soon, Lizzie was pulling away, his arms sliding across her shoulders. She looked up at him and he saw hope in her eyes.

"I will always love you, Elizabeth Marie Reynolds," Ian said. When she leaned forward to kiss him, he ran a hand up through her hair and held her lips against his for a long time. This was the moment he knew she had given her whole heart to him.

# CHAPTER FORTY-FIVE

Emerson found a light switch before moving to the bed to roll Randy's body off McDonald. He helped the detective sit up, and unlocked her handcuffs. McDonald pulled the t-shirt from her mouth and vomited.

Emerson stood by, happy she'd missed his shoes, but unsure what he should do. McDonald was still doubled over as if expecting another wave of sickness. Emerson took a step closer and awkwardly rubbed her back.

McDonald stood up a minute later, struggling to find words. "Thank you," she said in a hoarse whisper.

Emerson shrugged, not wanting to make a big deal out of the situation. He'd just done his job. The pounding of shoes on the stairs alerted the detectives to the arrival of back up. Emerson looked to the door where six uniformed officers were streaming in, guns at the ready.

"It's okay, suspect is down," Emerson said, pointing to the body.

"The officers on perimeter watch," McDonald croaked. "Did he kill them?"

"No, ma'am. Just knocked them out and tied them up. Paramedics are checking on them now," one of the officers replied before leading the men back down the stairs.

"You should get checked out too," Emerson said.

"I'm fine," McDonald replied shakily. Emerson eyed the blood on her face and shook his head.

"You've got his blood all over you. No telling what diseases he might've been carrying. You're going to the hospital. That's an order." Emerson held out his hand to McDonald. Paramedics met them at the bottom of the stairs and Emerson handed McDonald off to them.

"I need to get a statement from her before you take her to the hospital," Emerson said. The paramedics nodded and led McDonald away. Emerson looked around at the mass of cars and flashing lights.

He noticed a couple of neighbors across the street standing on their porch.

Emerson made his way to the front door of the Little house and knocked several times before Mrs. Little answered. He couldn't believe the woman hadn't heard the gunshots or sirens. She stood there in a flannel nightgown and fuzzy red slippers.

"Detective Emerson?" A look of confusion crossed her face.

"Mrs. Little, I'm afraid I have some bad news." Emerson didn't need to remember to speak slowly. Giving news like this always made him slow down. "May I come in?"

"Is everything all right?" Mrs. Little asked as she opened the door wider to allow the detective inside.

"I'm afraid not. You should sit down." Emerson followed Mrs. Little into the living room and waited for her to sit in the recliner. She looked up at him, her eyes full of uncertainty.

Emerson tried to break the news gently, but there really wasn't an easy way to tell her. "Mrs. Little, Randy is dead."

"What?"

"He tried to assault Detective McDonald and I had to shoot him." Emerson watched as her eyes filled with tears, but she didn't cry out.

"Why would he try to hurt such a nice woman?" Mrs. Little asked.

"We have reason to believe Randy killed a young woman several days ago. That's why we were looking for him. He must have come home when Detective McDonald was leaving. I don't have all the details yet." Emerson couldn't bring himself to tell Mrs. Little that her son was attempting to rape McDonald. She didn't need to know that detail.

Tears spilled down Mrs. Little's face and she dropped her head into her hands. Emerson gave her several minutes to grieve, knowing things would only get worse for her when the whole story came out.

"I need to get back outside and wrap things up. Is there anyone we can call for you?" Emerson asked, growing anxious to get McDonald's story while it was still fresh.

"No, thank you, though." Mrs. Little brushed at her tears.

"Are you sure?" Emerson hesitated, but when the woman nodded, he slipped out of the room. He found McDonald sitting on the bumper of an ambulance. Her face had been cleaned off, and he could see large bruises forming across her cheekbones.

"She's shaken up, but appears to be physically fine," one of the paramedics advised Emerson. "At the hospital, we will run some blood tests and let you guys know if there is anything to worry about."

"Can you tell me what happened?" Emerson asked.

"He came out of nowhere," McDonald said.

"Start at the beginning. What did you do after I left?" Emerson asked.

McDonald gave him an account of her conversation with Mrs. Little. "When she told me he'd been working at the same garage for six or seven years I knew that didn't match up with what we learned from the owner of A to Z and thought this other place might be where he'd go to hide out. I went to call and tell you, but Randy had gotten in the house."

"Good thinking to keep the phone line open when he told you to put it down. I heard everything until you left the kitchen," Emerson said. "Did he tell you anything more once you got outside?"

"I'm pretty sure Amanda wasn't his first kill." McDonald's face grew even paler than it already was, making the bruises appear darker. "He told me I wasn't as pretty as most of his girls, but he'd never had a cop before. He's a serial rapist, at least, if not killer." McDonald grew quiet and the paramedics gave Emerson a look that told him to stop asking questions. Emerson tried to place a reassuring hand on McDonald's shoulder, but she flinched, shrinking away from him.

"You need to get some rest." Emerson looked around and caught the attention of one of the officers milling on the lawn. "This officer is going to pick you up from the hospital and take you home. You want me to call anyone for you?"

"No, I'll call my folks when I get home."

Emerson nodded. "We'll talk more tomorrow."

The paramedics helped McDonald into the back of the ambulance and slammed the doors shut. A police cruiser followed as the ambulance did a three-point turn and headed to the hospital. The forensics team and medical examiner arrived a few minutes later and Emerson walked them through what had happened.

"Are we sure this is the guy who killed Amanda Barnes?" Dr. Robinson asked as she studied the exit wound on Randy's chest.

"He as much as admitted it to Detective McDonald. I guess if we can match his DNA to the skin found under her nails, we have a closed case," Emerson replied.

# CHAPTER FORTY-SIX

Michelle cut off the television and collected her empty ice cream bowl from the coffee table. It had been strange not going to work, but at the same time she was grateful her boss had given her the time off. She loved her job, but had no idea if she could face returning to the office. The thought of it made her chest tighten.

As she stood at the sink, running hot water over the bowl, she replayed Friday morning, surprised at how blurred the images had already become. She tried to remember exactly what position Amanda's body had been lying in when the light from the hallway spilled into the bathroom.

The ringing of her cell phone jarred her from her thoughts and caused her to drop the bowl. It hit the stainless steel sink with a loud thud. She hurried to wipe her hands on a dishtowel and returned to the living room.

"Hello?" she answered.

"Ms. Burton, it's Detective Emerson."

Michelle swallowed hard. He sounded tired and she wondered why he would be calling her so late.

"I know it's late," Emerson continued before she could respond, "but I have news about Amanda's killer."

"You found him?" Michelle's mouth felt dry as she spoke.

"We did." Emerson sighed. "You don't need to worry about him anymore."

"Did he confess? Was it the guy you showed me the picture of?" Michelle's mind was racing, already jumping ahead to the trial.

Emerson cleared his throat. "He didn't confess, exactly."

"Are you going to need me to testify? I'm not sure I can do that. My memories are already getting mixed up."

"There won't be a need for you to testify." Emerson let out a long breath. "Randy Little, that was his name, is dead. He attacked my partner and I had to shoot him."

Michelle dropped onto the couch, Emerson's words ringing in her ears. "He's dead?"

"I know these past few days have been difficult for you. I hope this news will give you some closure."

Michelle didn't know what to say. She was relieved, but there were still so many unanswered questions.

"Ms. Burton, are you still there?"

"Yes, I just..." Michelle stopped. Where did she start?

"I know you probably have questions, and I wish I could give you answers, but we didn't have much opportunity to question him. From what we do know, Randy Little was a disturbed man. It doesn't appear he and Ms. Barnes had any previous connections. We don't think she was his first victim either."

"Thank you for calling, detective." Michelle hung up before Emerson could respond. Setting the phone on the table, she leaned back on the couch and pulled a blanket up around her shoulders.

It was over. Amanda's killer was now dead and there was no good reason for any of it. How could there be such evil in the world?

# CHAPTER FORTY-SEVEN

Stephen entered the office feeling relaxed for the first time in a week. Silken Pleasures was leaving today and aside from telling Renee Therriault he thought one of her employees had malicious intentions, things had gone extraordinarily well.

"Good morning," he called out to the handful of people in the office.

"Stephen, would you come here for a moment?" Jonathan called from his office.

Stephen stepped inside the front office manager's office, expecting to receive some kind of praise for his performance over the weekend.

"Sit down," Jonathan instructed.

Stephen's high spirits sank.

"I understand you called Mr. Kingsley not once, but twice over the past few days. Is this true?"

How had Jonathan found out? Stephen nodded, too nervous to speak.

"I don't even want to know how you got his personal phone number. It is highly inappropriate for you to have called him." Jonathan's face was grim and Stephen feared he was about to be fired.

"Mrs. Therriault asked me to get in touch with him. I was trying to keep her happy so she will—" Stephen hurried to explain himself, but Jonathan cut him off.

"It was still inappropriate. You should have come to me and I would have taken the request to the general manager. Lucky for you, Mr. Kingsley was impressed by your initiative and resourcefulness. He wants to meet with you next time he is in town."

Stephen didn't know if he should be relieved or worried. Surely, Mr. Kingsley didn't want to meet simply to fire him personally.

"On a related note," Jonathan continued, "I spoke with Mrs. Therriault this morning and she was very pleased with how smoothly things went this weekend and she is already planning another retreat here next year."

"That's great." Stephen felt his chest puff with pride.

"It doesn't change the facts. You should have come to me."

Stephen nodded.

"Now get back to work." Jonathan dismissed him. Stephen returned to his desk with more assurance in his step.

"Morning, boss." Ben sat with his feet up on Stephen's desk, a large cup of coffee in one hand, a bagel in the other.

"Isn't it a beautiful day?" Stephen replied, unbothered by Ben's attempt to rile him.

Ben dropped his feet to the ground. "You're in a good mood."

"Why not? Silken Pleasures is checking out, Mrs. Therriault was happy with our work, and Lizzie will be back in town this evening. What more could I ask for?"

"Didn't you hear about what happened at dinner last night?" Ben asked, eyes wide with surprise.

Stephen gave him a sharp look. "What do you mean?"

Ben leaned forward, speaking in a hushed tone. "Renee and her assistant had a huge fight. I heard the assistant packed her bags and took off in a cab."

Stephen felt like he'd been kicked in the gut. "Are you serious?"

Ben nodded. "Kitchen staff says the assistant called Renee a heartless shrew. Not sure I can disagree with her there."

"But Jonathan said he talked with her this morning."

Ben shrugged. "I don't know, sounded like the fight was personal. Something about letting the assistant leave early."

Stephen's heart was racing. Why would Donna want to leave early and why would she make a scene about it?

Stephen raced out of the office, across the lobby, to the kitchen. The clatter of breakfast prep was deafening when he pushed through the doors. Finding two of the cooks who'd been working the previous night, Stephen made his way to their workstation, careful to stay out of Chef Gustave's line of sight.

"I heard there was some excitement with the Silken Pleasures dinner last night," Stephen tried to keep his tone casual. "Do you know what happened?"

One of the cooks gave a nervous look around the kitchen before giving Stephen a run down of the argument. Stephen listened intently, shocked by what he heard.

When the cook finished telling the story, Stephen walked off without replying. Renee had been difficult to please, but he thought there was a closer bond between her and Donna than just boss and assistant. He wondered if the information he'd given Renee about Donna's argument with Ellen had influenced her decision to deny Donna the chance to be with her family now.

"Oh, good, there you are," Stephen heard as he crossed the lobby. He looked up to see Renee Therriault coming toward him.

"There's been a slight change of plans. I need to have the car service here at ten instead of eleven thirty."

It took Stephen a minute to process her request. "Sure, not a problem," he replied.

"I also wanted to give you this." Renee handed him a small envelope, which he immediately slipped into his jacket pocket. "I hope to see you again when we return next year."

"Thank you. I hope to see you as well." Regaining his composure, Stephen offered her his hand. "It has been a pleasure working with you.

"I doubt that," Renee said with the hint of a smile. "I must finish packing."

The *click, clack* of her shoes filled the quiet lobby. Stephen waited for the sound to disappear before returning to the office and calling the car service.

# CHAPTER FORTY-EIGHT

The first two floors of the parking garage were full when Michelle arrived. She found a spot on the third level and cut the engine. Several other cars had followed her up the ramp and she now heard car doors slamming shut as the occupants hurried to their offices. A knock on the window startled her and she looked to see Wendy waving at her. Slowly she gathered her purse and opened the door.

"Morning," Wendy greeted her in a chipper voice that wasn't natural.

Michelle eyed her friend suspiciously. "Don't you and Tiffani usually ride to work together?"

"Yeah, but she's on vacation this week." Again, she spoke in a high-pitched voice meant to sound happy and Michelle cringed.

"Why are you being so..." Michelle struggled to find a polite word, "...so, fake?"

Wendy's face fell and Michelle wished she hadn't said anything.

"I was trying to make things feel more normal for you," Wendy said, her voice back to its normal level.

Michelle found herself laughing. "You don't normally meet me in the parking garage or talk like a woman without a brain in her head, but I appreciate it. I don't know if I would have gotten out of the car if you hadn't come by."

Wendy looked a bit happier and the women fell into step together. On the way to their office, Wendy caught Michelle up on what she'd done over the weekend, keeping up a steady stream of chatter all the way to the sixth floor. They turned down the hallway toward their department and Michelle stopped.

From where she stood, she could see the bathroom. There was no crime scene tape, no police, no body, but Michelle couldn't move. Wendy slipped her arm through Michelle's and led her down a different hall.

"We don't have to go past there," Wendy said gently. The women walked around the opposite side of the building until they had circled almost the entire perimeter to reach their desks.

Wendy made sure Michelle was settled in at her desk before moving two cubicles over to her own office. Michelle turned on her computer and hung her coat on the back of her chair. There was a knock on the cubicle wall and she turned to see George Appleton, her manager, standing there. His glasses were perched precariously at the end of his nose leaving his gray eyes unobstructed and she could see his concern.

"I'm fine, Mr. Appleton," Michelle assured him before he even spoke.

"Are you sure you are ready to be here? I expected you would take the whole week off."

"I have to face it sooner or later, but I might have to go to another floor to use the restroom." Michelle tried to joke, but she knew it came out just as seriously as if she meant it. There was no way she was going back in there today, maybe not this month.

"You feel free to let me know if you need to leave early. I can even make arrangements for you to work from home if it gets to be too much being back here."

"I appreciate it. I think what will help me most is if everyone can act as normal as possible." Michelle sat down and opened her phone message pad to write down her voice messages.

"I'll let everyone know that's the way you feel," George replied.

Michelle squared her shoulders, dialed into her voicemail, and took down the dozen messages she'd received over the weekend. Most of them were from clients who'd heard about the murder on the news. The few business-related messages she made asterisks next to so she would remember to call them first.

# CHAPTER FORTY-NINE

Renee checked the room one last time for anything she may have forgotten before turning off the light and closing the door. A bellman had collected her luggage already so she carried only her briefcase and a small handbag. She arrived in the lobby with ten minutes to spare. Outside, she could see the cars were already waiting. The weight of Donna's digital recorder in her pocket was reassuring. So far, everything was going as planned.

When her team began to appear, she hurried them into the waiting cars. "I need to take care of the bills and I will be right behind you," Renee told them and waved as they pulled away. She had instructed the pilot to begin preparations for take off as soon as the executives arrived so they could leave when she finished up.

"Would you please call Ellen Cartwright's room for me?" Renee asked one of the front desk agents. When she was handed the phone, Renee waited for her adversary to answer.

"Hello?" Ellen answered.

"Ellen, why aren't you down here? Everyone else has already left for the airport," Renee tried to imagine the woman's frantic expression.

"You said we weren't leaving until eleven thirty."

"Oh, did I forget to tell you we moved that up? So sorry." Renee bit back her simmering anger.

"I'll be down in ten minutes."

"Do hurry." Renee hung up before Ellen could say more and took a seat on a sofa in the exact middle of the lobby. Her distaste for public scenes would have to be forgone today.

Eight minutes later, Ellen raced into the lobby. Renee stood, but waited for Ellen to come to her.

"Why the change in time?" a breathless Ellen asked.

"I wanted to have a private chat with you," Renee said. "I hear you have some ill intentions for my company."

"What? Where did you hear that?" Ellen's face flushed slightly.

"I have some very reliable sources."

"I would never try to hurt you or your company." Ellen had regained her composure and Renee knew the spin was about to begin. "You and I are friends. Why would I want to hurt you?"

"Friends? I thought so, until I found out you've been manipulating me since we first met. You didn't start working with Children Smile until two months before you interviewed with me, after you'd lost your previous job."

"What does that have to do with anything?"

"Everything. A large reason I hired you was because of the interests we shared, but you really don't care about those things." Renee's anger threatened to boil over, as her voice rose.

"I don't understand where this is coming from."

Renee pulled Donna's digital recorder from her pocket and pushed play. Ellen's eyes narrowed at the sound of her voice.

Ellen folded her arms across her chest. "I was shocked when Donna told me those things. I planned to tell you about it on the plane. She really shouldn't be trusted."

Renee fast-forwarded and pushed play again.

"Jean Luc, this is Ellen Cartwright with Silken Pleasures."

"Ms. Cartwright. This is a surprise."

"I don't want to alarm you, but I just learned some things you might want to consider before you sign any agreements with Renee."

"Really?"

"I feel like you and I have developed a strong relationship as we have reviewed the benefits of merging our companies, so when I found out Silken Pleasures isn't as financially sound as I thought, I knew I had to call you."

"What do you mean? How can you just be learning there is a problem with the financial stability?"

"It seems Renee hasn't been completely honest with anyone at Silken Pleasures and the relationships with several of our distributors are tenuous."

"I see. I appreciate you letting me know. It's definitely something to consider before my meeting with Renee."

By the time Renee stopped the recording, Ellen's face was pale. "You might want to see if the concierge can help you find a flight home, Ellen. The company jet is reserved for employees only."

Renee dropped the recorder into her pocket, turned, and walked away.

"To the airport," she said as the driver held the door of the black town car open for her.

The door from the front desk to the office flew open and Stephen looked up to see one of the front desk agents speeding toward him.

"Stephen, one of the ladies from Silken Pleasures is out front. She said she needs to book a flight and she seems pretty upset."

"What? They were supposed to have left half an hour ago."

"I don't know, but she's demanding to speak to you."

Stephen stood and followed the agent to the desk. When he saw Ellen Cartwright, he stumbled over feet that suddenly couldn't move. He entered one of the empty stations at the end of the long desk.

"Ms. Cartwright, what can I do for you?"

"It seems I need to book a flight. I don't suppose you know anything about why that is?"

Stephen was surprised by her bitter tone. "No, ma'am. I spoke with Mrs. Therriault this morning and she asked me to order the cars earlier than planned. She didn't mention anyone would be leaving on a separate flight."

"Don't just stare at me. When can I get a flight out of this hole?"

"Do you have a preference on which airport you return to in New York?"

"Just get me the earliest flight you can find."

"Why don't you go to the lounge and have a drink while I make the arrangements," Stephen offered. "Tell Howard I'll cover it."

Ellen gave a loud harrumph and stormed off. Stephen watched her plop down in a chair at the very edge of the lounge, then returned to his desk, trying to control his laughter.

It only took him twenty minutes to find a flight into JFK, print the confirmation, and call a cab. When he handed Ellen the paperwork, he could read her disapproval before she even spoke.

"Coach? You booked me in coach?"

"It's all I could get on the next flight out. If you want to wait until this evening or tomorrow, I might be able to get a first class seat." Stephen was never more grateful for the training Lizzie had given him on understanding basic personality traits than he was now.

Eight months ago, he would have been a shaking, terrified mess; a disgrace to the male species, in the face of the wrath he knew was about to befall him. Today he stood tall, confident, and in control. He knew Ellen was studying him, planning her attack, but he simply locked eyes with her.

"Just get me out of here," Ellen capitulated. She sucked down the last of her drink and slammed the glass on the table.

"Your cab will be here any minute. Do you need help with your bag?" Stephen reached for her Louis Vuitton suitcase, but she slapped his hand away.

"I'm sure you had something to do with this. You and your prying. You better hope I never see you again." Ellen yanked at the handle of her suitcase and toddled out the front doors.

# CHAPTER FIFTY

The morning went by quickly, catching up on emails and returning calls. By twelve thirty, Michelle was starving and walked over to see if Wendy wanted to go to lunch.

"I'd love to, but I'm swamped. Would you mind picking me up a salad?" Wendy pulled some bills from her wallet and handed them to Michelle. Michelle remembered the pizzeria where she'd had lunch with Jeffrey several months ago and decided to run over.

The restaurant was more crowded than the last time she'd been there. Every table was full, so she decided to get an order to go. She skimmed a menu, picked a salad for Wendy and a calzone for herself, and moved aside to wait for her food.

"Michelle?" she heard someone call. She scanned the faces until she saw Jeffrey. He was waving her over, so she threaded her way through the crowded tables.

"Why don't you join us?" Jeffrey asked.

"I just placed an order to go," Michelle replied, looking back toward the front of the restaurant, afraid she might lose her food.

"No problem. Gina," Jeffrey called and a waitress hurried over. "My friend here placed an order to go," Jeffrey looked to Michelle.

"A Greek salad and a mushroom and cheese calzone," Michelle provided.

"Would you mind bringing it over here when it's ready?" Jeffrey asked.

"Sure thing, Jeff. Would you like something to drink?" Gina asked Michelle.

"Water is fine, thanks." Michelle took the seat closest to Jeffrey.

"Michelle, this is Wally." Jeffrey introduced her to his companion.

"Nice to meet you," Michelle said. Wally nodded in agreement, his mouth full of pizza.

"Are you back to work already?" Jeffrey asked and Michelle took note of the tenderness in his voice.

"Yes, but it's not as bad as I feared. I can't walk down the hallway where, well, you know." Michelle felt self-conscious talking about it with Wally there.

"One day at a time," Jeffrey replied. "I'm glad I ran into you. I felt bad I wasn't able to answer more of your questions Sunday. Lizzie gave me a book, actually more of a pamphlet, after I gave my heart to God. I found it last night and thought you might find it helpful. It's in my truck. Would you mind if I dropped it by your office this afternoon?"

Michelle was surprised at Jeffrey's openness about his conversion, as he'd called it to her. "That would be fine," she replied. "I'll be there until five thirty."

"Great, I'll be by around four. I have a dinner meeting or I would have offered to take you to dinner."

Michelle felt the warm glow within her again. Even if they weren't going to dinner tonight, he had thought about it. Was he still interested in her? Gina returned with Michelle's calzone and Wendy's boxed salad.

"I'm going to head back to the site," Wally said, tossing ten dollars onto the table.

"What's the hurry?" Jeffrey asked.

"I need to make a few calls," Wally replied as he stood to leave.

"Okay," Jeffrey said.

"Sorry if I interrupted your meal," Michelle said, feeling like an intruder.

"Nah, Wally gets uncomfortable when I talk about God. He doesn't understand why I've changed my life," Jeffrey said, and Michelle thought she heard a touch of sadness.

"You have to admit you seem to have done a complete 180," Michelle replied. "It is pretty hard for someone who knew you before to wrap their head around."

Jeffrey smiled. "Does that mean you see I've changed?"

"I was skeptical at first, but now I'm a believer. I still don't quite understand it, but I want to." Michelle took a bite of her calzone.

"Have you heard if the police are any closer to catching the killer?"

"You didn't hear? The police caught up with him last night and had to shoot him."

Jeffrey shook his head. "Shame it had to come to that. How do you feel about it?"

Michelle shrugged. "It's good to know it's all over."

When Michelle finished her calzone, Jeffrey walked her to the end of the block where he turned left toward the Plaza construction site. Michelle strolled back to her office, thinking about Jeffrey's ease with his newfound faith. Could that be the answer for her too?

She rode the elevator to the sixth floor alone and entered the financial firm's office. Without thinking, she turned down the hallway and passed the bathroom, not stopping until she reached the break room, where she came to a screeching halt. She looked over her shoulder at the bathroom door ten feet away. With a new courage, she spun around and pushed open the door.

The lights were on and she could hear water running. She stepped in and found Wendy at the sink, washing her hands. Michelle looked from Wendy to the floor, where there wasn't a trace of blood, no reminders of the vicious attack that had taken place here.

"Michelle," Wendy cried in surprise.

"It's okay, Wendy, I'm okay." Michelle looked at her friend with the first true smile she'd had in days.

Promptly at four o'clock, Michelle received a call from the receptionist that Jeffrey was there to see her. She met him in the lobby, passing the bathroom without hesitation.

"I did it," Michelle said as she approached Jeffrey. "I went into the bathroom." She noticed a couple seated in a pair of chairs near the door gave her a funny look, but she didn't care. The look of admiration she received from Jeffrey was all that mattered.

"Congratulations. One step at a time, one day at a time. That's all you can do." Jeffrey pulled the pamphlet from his back pocket. "Sorry it's kind of beat up. I carried it with me everywhere for a month."

Michelle took the pamphlet and nearly laughed aloud when she read the title, *I'm Saved, Now What?* "You're kidding right?" she said.

"Nope. Feel free to laugh, I did," Jeffrey replied, "but it really does answer a lot of your questions in an easy to understand way. Give it a read and let me know what you think. Lizzie will be back in town today. If you still have questions I'm sure she'd be happy to talk to you."

"I'll read it, but I can't promise anything," Michelle said as she thumbed through the worn pages.

"I understand." Jeffrey punched the elevator button. "I hope we can talk again soon."

"Me too." Michelle waited until the elevator doors closed, then returned to her desk, already reading the first pages.

# ACKNOWLEDGEMENTS

I had a great deal of fun writing Winter's End and I am truly thankful for all those who provided encouragement and support throughout this process. The bulk of the first draft was written in November, 2011, particularly the week of Thanksgiving when I visited my parents in North Carolina. Each day mom sent me off to the bedroom to write for two hours in the morning and two hours in the evening. Without that time it would have taken a lot longer to put this story together.

I have to thank my beta readers, Jeanette Cornforth, Pam Gheen, and Sharon Twigg. The input you each provided was invaluable and I am grateful for you taking the time out of your busy lives.

Many thanks to my editor, Beth Lynne and my cover designer, Laura Wright LaRoche. You can find out more about the services Beth and Laura offer at http://www.bzhercules.com and http://www.llpix.com.

I would also like to thank Pam Gheen, Sharon Twigg, and Wanda Rogers for graciously hosting Afternoon Teas with the Author to promote my books.

The pamphlet Jeffrey gives Michelle at the end of the boom, *I'm Saved, Now What?* is not real as far as I know, but there are several similar pamphlets available through Lifeway Christian stores.

To learn more about my current and upcoming novels you can follow me on Twitter @RebekahLyn1, become a fan of my Facebook page at www.facebook.com/authorRebekahLyn or follow my blog, http://rebekahlynskitchen.wordpress.com.

Keep reading for a sample of *Spring Dawn*.

# Spring Dawn

## Seasons of Faith, Book 3

## April 2005
## CHAPTER ONE

Stephen fumbled the phone into its cradle and leaned back in his chair. What had he just agreed to? He'd had no idea stopping a corporate coup for one of the hotel's newest clients would draw so much attention to him.

A shadow fell over the desk and he felt a hand on his shoulder. He looked up, his brown eyes meeting the quizzical blue ones of his boss and friend, Lizzie Reynolds.

"Did you hear me?" She studied him, one eyebrow arched.

"What?" Stephen shook his head to clear his rushing thoughts.

Lizzie ran a hand through her rumpled blond curls in a failed attempt to calm them. "I asked if you were going to be at the Concierge Club dinner Tuesday."

"Oh. Yeah, I'll be there." He'd forgotten about it, but knew he didn't have any other plans. "Cafe Marie at six, right?"

Lizzie nodded. "I can't wait to hear what everyone is planning for Bacchus Bash."

"What is that again?"

"You've never been?" Lizzie cried.

"I don't think so."

"It's a charity event put on by the Central Florida Hotel and Lodging Association to raise funds for hospitality schools in the area. There are food booths sponsored by hotels and restaurants, entertainment, and a silent auction. You never know who you will run into. Last year I saw a singer from a popular boy band," Lizzie blushed, "not that I knew who he was, but Stephanie recognized him."

"Sounds like fun. When is it?"

"The second Friday of April."

"That's next week."

Lizzie glanced at the desk calendar. "I guess it is. Time has flown by since I returned from Vermont."

"Seems like you've been living here since your trip," Stephen said.

Lizzie shrugged and indulged herself in a slow neck roll. "There's been a lot to do between the Spring Break rush and the boom in our summer wedding reservations. Tammy needs to hire someone to help with groups and weddings."

"Maybe when Mr. Kingsley finalizes the deal to buy out Ryland Resorts," Stephen stopped when he saw the surprised look on Lizzie's face.

"What do you know about that?"

"Nothing," Stephen sputtered, "just the rumors."

"No, you know something else." Lizzie leaned over, placed her elbows on the desk and rested her chin on her hands. "Spill."

"I don't know much. Mr. Kingsley is running backgrounds on everyone working for Ryland and asked me to review a few people he had some concerns about."

Lizzie's elbows slipped, her chin having a near miss with the desk. "He asked you to what?"

"To, to…"

"I heard you, I just can't believe it."

"Me either," Stephen admitted. "He said he was impressed with my instincts and resourcefulness."

"When was this?"

Stephen pointed to the phone. "A few minutes ago, before you came over."

"That explains why you looked so preoccupied. Is this about that business in February with the Silken Pleasures corporate group?"

"I should have minded my own business."

"You saved Mrs. Therriault from losing her company and your actions secured her business here for the next three years."

"The signs were all there. Mrs. Therriault admitted to her assistant she would have seen them herself if Mrs. Cartwright hadn't cozied up to her and lulled her into a sense of camaraderie. It was dumb luck on my part. I don't know how I'm supposed to investigate these people for Mr. Kingsley. What if I screw up?"

"He was right, you do have good instincts and you have a way of seeing through the facades people put on. You'll do fine."

"I'm glad you're so sure. I don't want to lose this job. I'm kind of starting to enjoy it."

Lizzie laughed. "Well, we can't have you losing a job you kind of like. I'll help you out any way I can."

Stephen stood and brushed at some lint on his pants. "No reason worrying until I get more information from Mr. Kingsley. Right now I believe it's time to make my rounds in the concierge lounge."

"Anyone exciting staying with us? I haven't had a chance to review the guest manifest this morning."

"None of the regulars are in this week. The hotel is at sixty percent occupancy with only twenty percent in concierge. Kind of a nice lull." Stephen grinned.

"You can say that again. Memorial Day will be here before we know it and the summer crowds will descend. I'm going to catch up on some paperwork. Pop into my office after your rounds." Lizzie gave Stephen a pat on the shoulder before disappearing into a tiny office.